STAR WARS™
— ADVENTURES —
SMUGGLER'S RUN

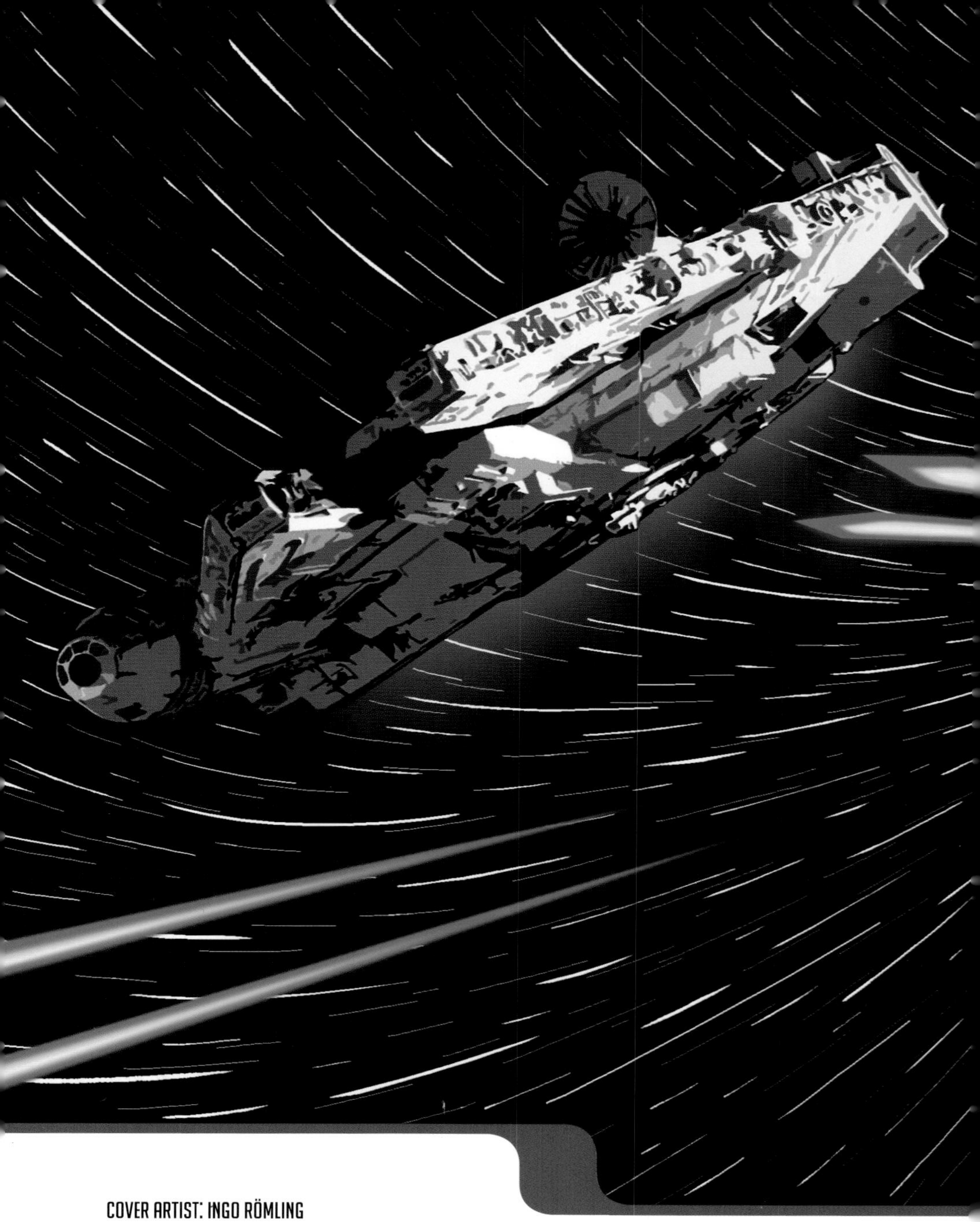

COVER ARTIST: INGO RÖMLING

SERIES EDITOR: ELIZABETH BREI

SERIES ASSISTANT EDITOR: RILEY FARMER

COLLECTION EDITORS: ALONZO SIMON & ZAC BOONE

COLLECTION DESIGNER: CLYDE GRAPA

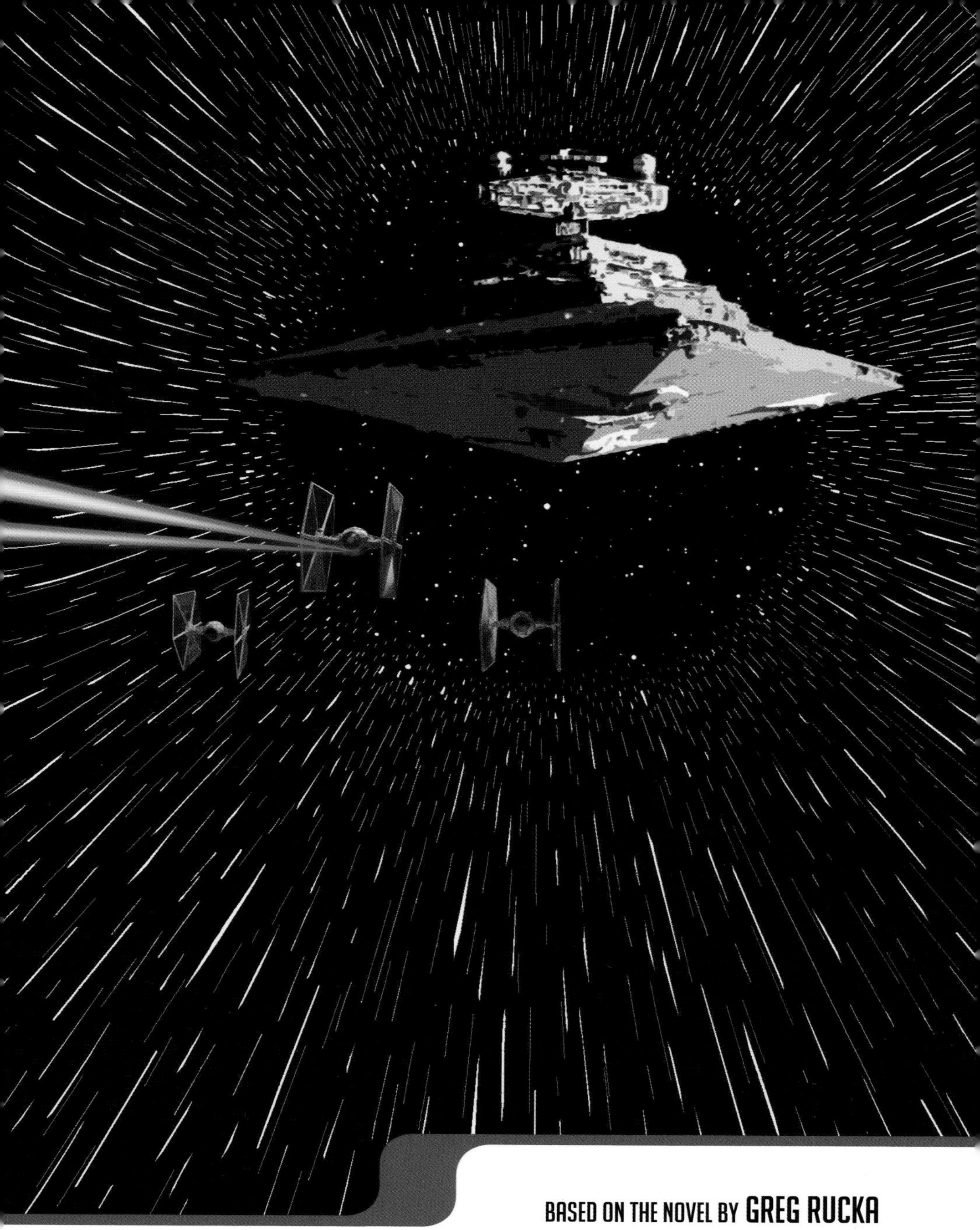

BASED ON THE NOVEL BY GREG RUCKA

ADAPTATION BY ALEC WORLEY

ART BY INGO RÖMLING

TRANSLATION BY EDWARD GAUVIN

LETTERS BY AMAURI OSORIO

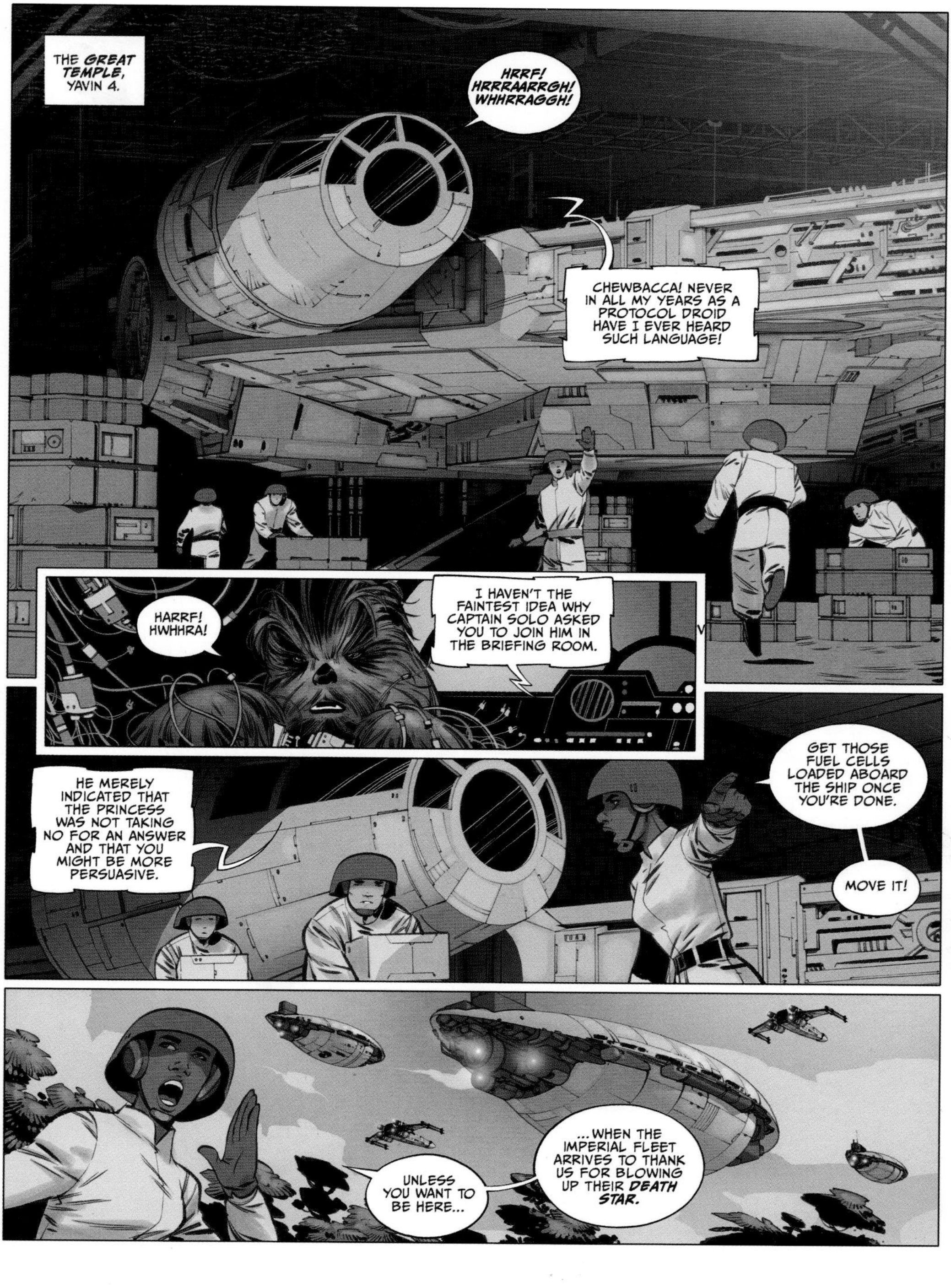
THE GREAT TEMPLE, YAVIN 4.
HRRF! HRRRAARRGH! WHHRRAGGH!
CHEWBACCA! NEVER IN ALL MY YEARS AS A PROTOCOL DROID HAVE I EVER HEARD SUCH LANGUAGE!
HARRF! HWHHRA!
I HAVEN'T THE FAINTEST IDEA WHY CAPTAIN SOLO ASKED YOU TO JOIN HIM IN THE BRIEFING ROOM.
HE MERELY INDICATED THAT THE PRINCESS WAS NOT TAKING NO FOR AN ANSWER AND THAT YOU MIGHT BE MORE PERSUASIVE.
GET THOSE FUEL CELLS LOADED ABOARD THE SHIP ONCE YOU'RE DONE.
MOVE IT!
UNLESS YOU WANT TO BE HERE...
...WHEN THE IMPERIAL FLEET ARRIVES TO THANK US FOR BLOWING UP THEIR DEATH STAR.

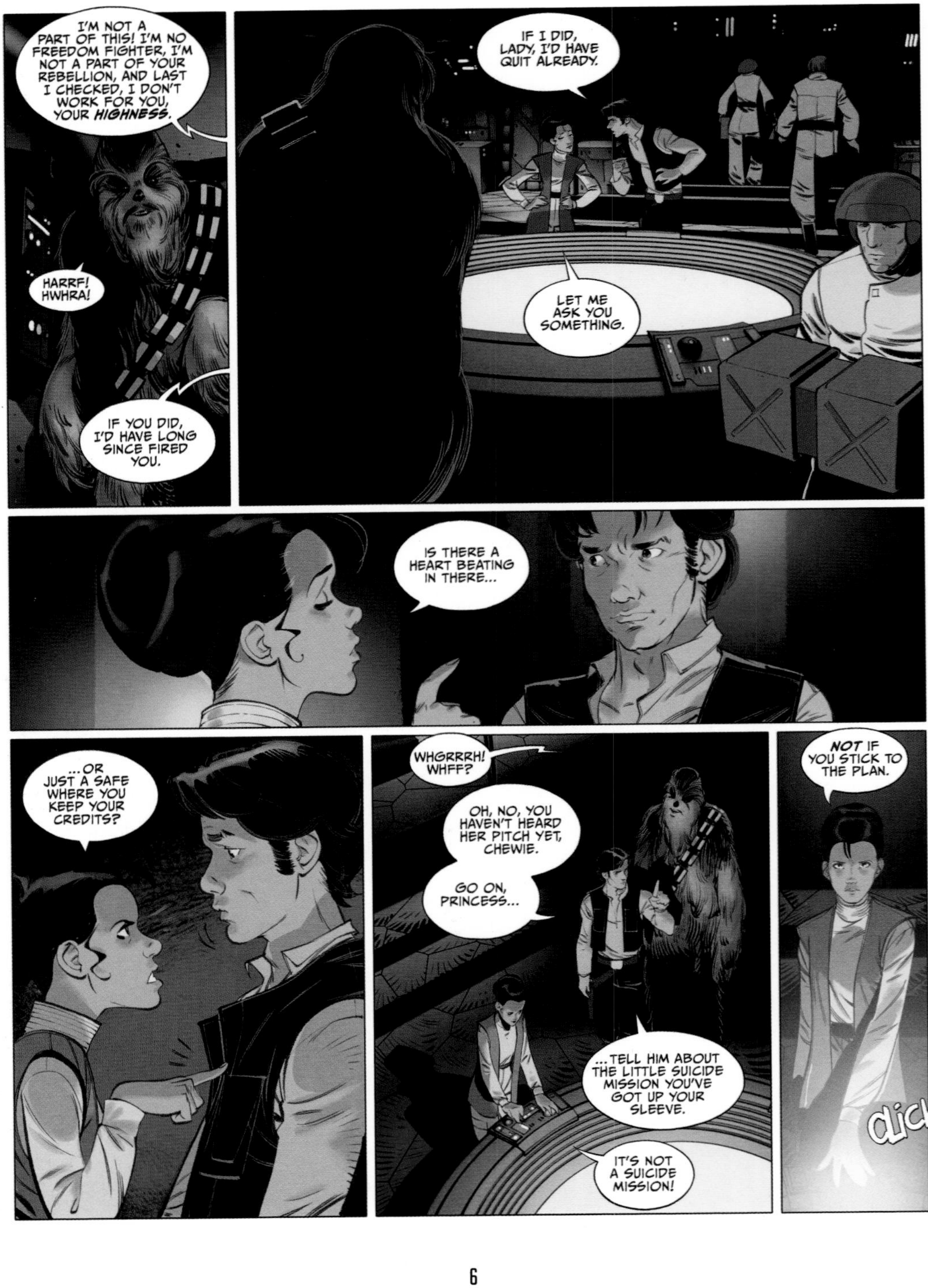

I'M NOT A PART OF THIS! I'M NO FREEDOM FIGHTER, I'M NOT A PART OF YOUR REBELLION, AND LAST I CHECKED, I DON'T WORK FOR YOU, YOUR ***HIGHNESS***.
HARRF! HWHRA!
IF YOU DID, I'D HAVE LONG SINCE FIRED YOU.
IF I DID, LADY, I'D HAVE QUIT ALREADY.
LET ME ASK YOU SOMETHING.
IS THERE A HEART BEATING IN THERE...
...OR JUST A SAFE WHERE YOU KEEP YOUR CREDITS?
WHGRRRH! WHFF?
OH, NO, YOU HAVEN'T HEARD HER PITCH YET, CHEWIE.
GO ON, PRINCESS...
...TELL HIM ABOUT THE LITTLE SUICIDE MISSION YOU'VE GOT UP YOUR SLEEVE.
IT'S NOT A SUICIDE MISSION!
NOT IF YOU STICK TO THE PLAN.
CLICK

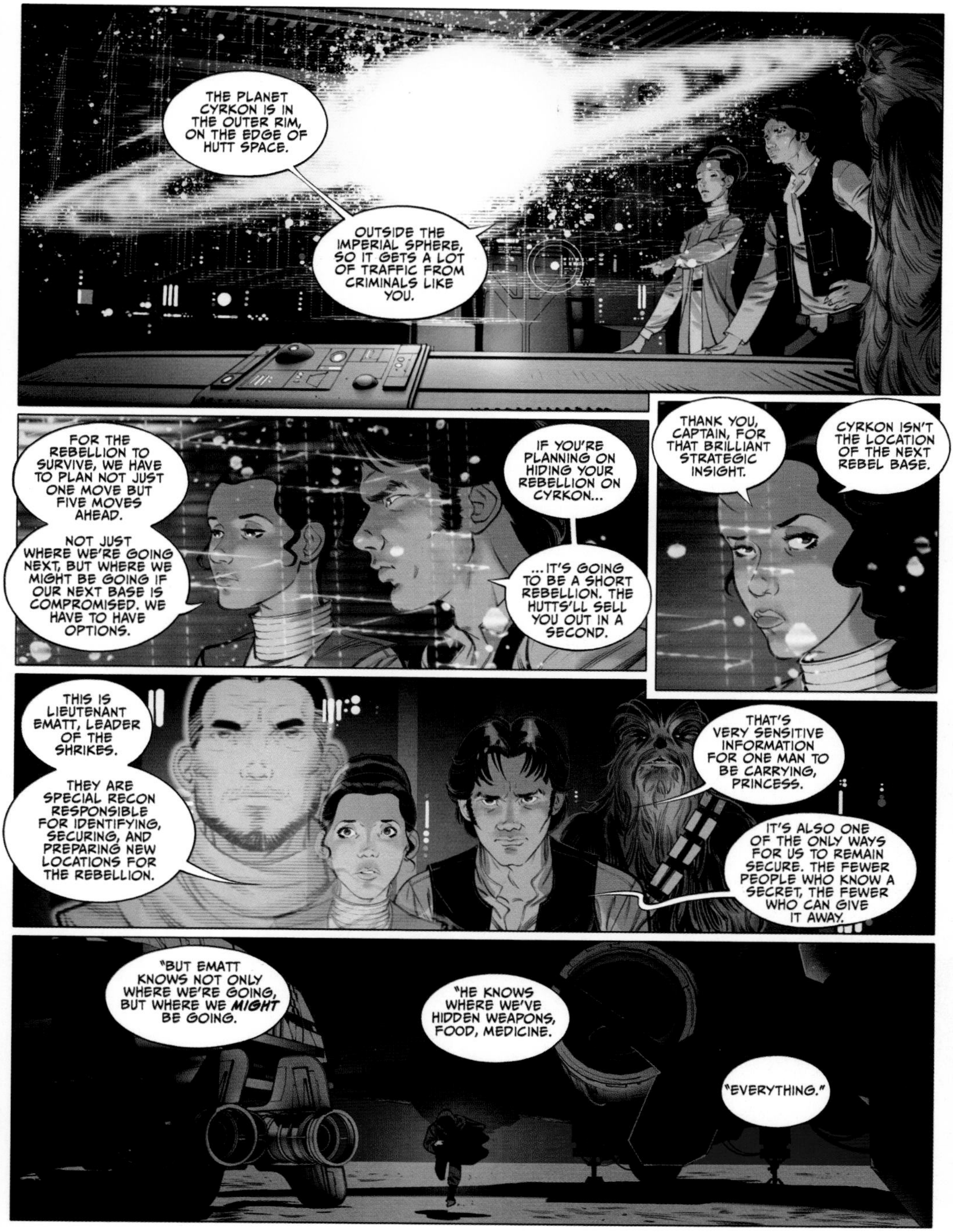
THE PLANET CYRKON IS IN THE OUTER RIM, ON THE EDGE OF HUTT SPACE.
OUTSIDE THE IMPERIAL SPHERE, SO IT GETS A LOT OF TRAFFIC FROM CRIMINALS LIKE YOU.
FOR THE REBELLION TO SURVIVE, WE HAVE TO PLAN NOT JUST ONE MOVE BUT FIVE MOVES AHEAD.
NOT JUST WHERE WE'RE GOING NEXT, BUT WHERE WE MIGHT BE GOING IF OUR NEXT BASE IS COMPROMISED. WE HAVE TO HAVE OPTIONS.
IF YOU'RE PLANNING ON HIDING YOUR REBELLION ON CYRKON...
...IT'S GOING TO BE A SHORT REBELLION. THE HUTTS'LL SELL YOU OUT IN A SECOND.
THANK YOU, CAPTAIN, FOR THAT BRILLIANT STRATEGIC INSIGHT.
CYRKON ISN'T THE LOCATION OF THE NEXT REBEL BASE.
THIS IS LIEUTENANT EMATT, LEADER OF THE SHRIKES.
THEY ARE SPECIAL RECON RESPONSIBLE FOR IDENTIFYING, SECURING, AND PREPARING NEW LOCATIONS FOR THE REBELLION.
THAT'S VERY SENSITIVE INFORMATION FOR ONE MAN TO BE CARRYING, PRINCESS.
IT'S ALSO ONE OF THE ONLY WAYS FOR US TO REMAIN SECURE. THE FEWER PEOPLE WHO KNOW A SECRET, THE FEWER WHO CAN GIVE IT AWAY.
"BUT EMATT KNOWS NOT ONLY WHERE WE'RE GOING, BUT WHERE WE ***MIGHT*** BE GOING.
"HE KNOWS WHERE WE'VE HIDDEN WEAPONS, FOOD, MEDICINE.
"EVERYTHING."

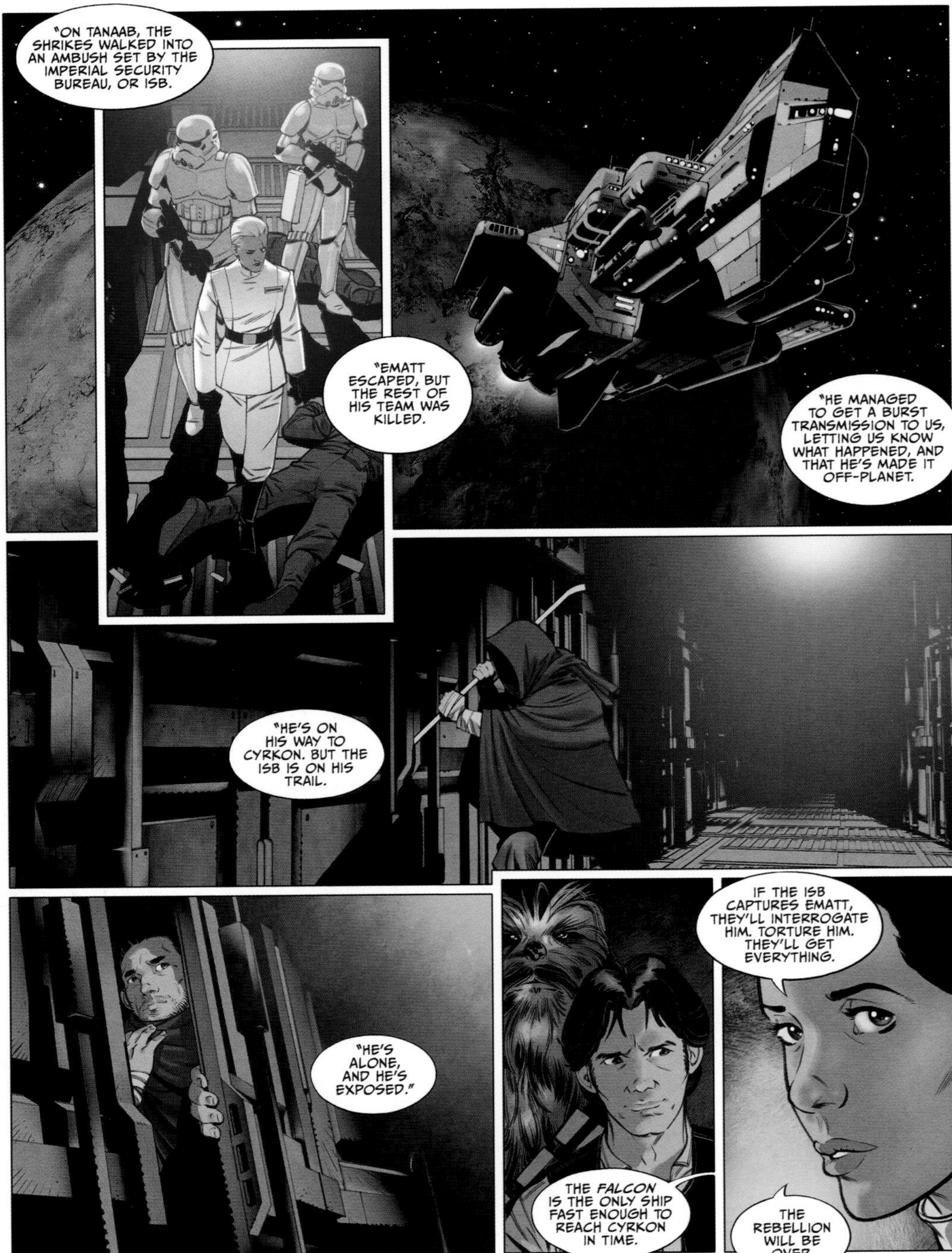
"ON TANAAB, THE SHRIKES WALKED INTO AN AMBUSH SET BY THE IMPERIAL SECURITY BUREAU, OR ISB.
"EMATT ESCAPED, BUT THE REST OF HIS TEAM WAS KILLED.
"HE MANAGED TO GET A BURST TRANSMISSION TO US, LETTING US KNOW WHAT HAPPENED, AND THAT HE'S MADE IT OFF-PLANET.
"HE'S ON HIS WAY TO CYRKON. BUT THE ISB IS ON HIS TRAIL.
"HE'S ALONE, AND HE'S EXPOSED."
IF THE ISB CAPTURES EMATT, THEY'LL INTERROGATE HIM. TORTURE HIM. THEY'LL GET EVERYTHING.
THE *FALCON* IS THE ONLY SHIP FAST ENOUGH TO REACH CYRKON IN TIME.
THE REBELLION WILL BE OVER.

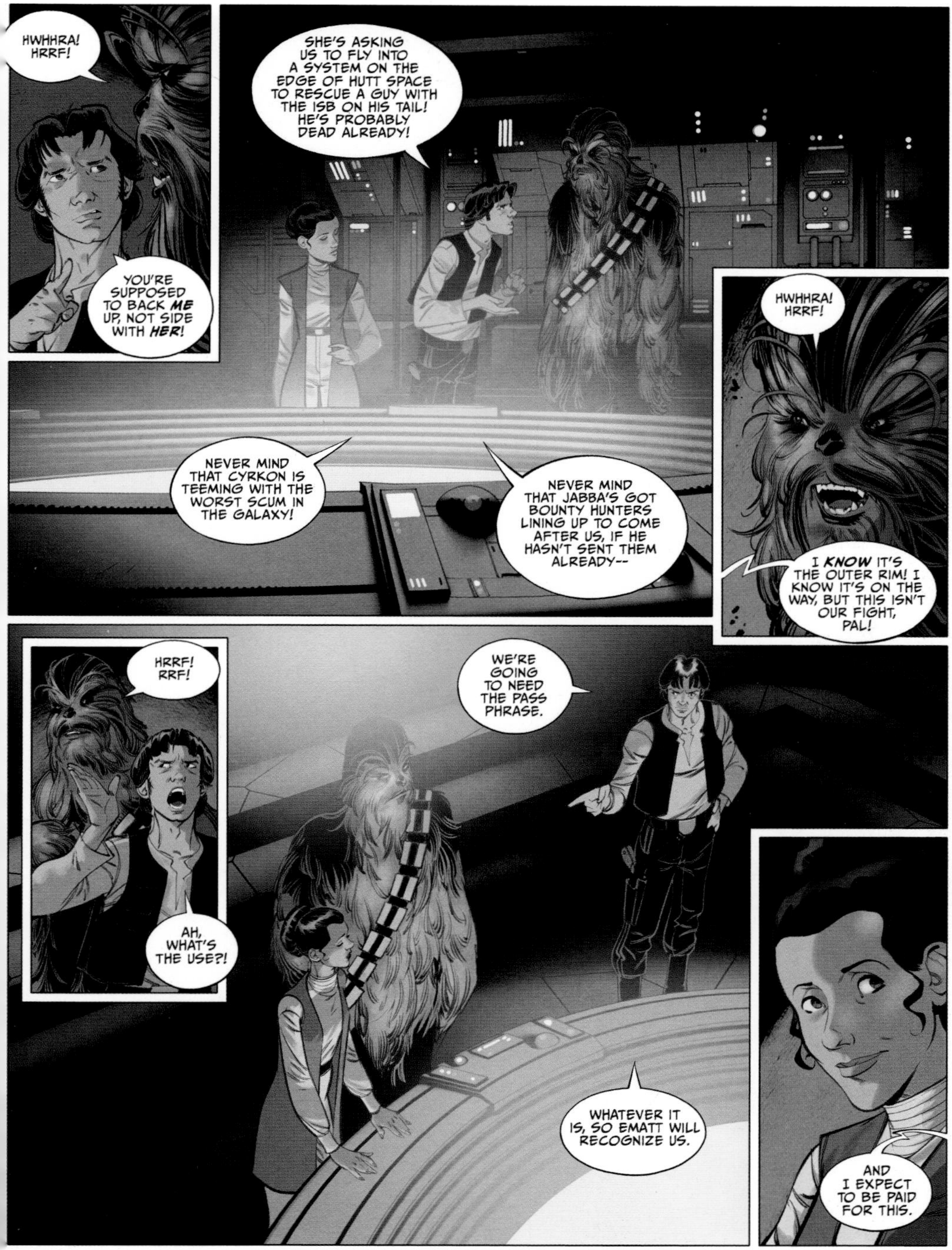
HWHHRA! HRRF!
YOU'RE SUPPOSED TO BACK **ME** UP, NOT SIDE WITH **HER**!
SHE'S ASKING US TO FLY INTO A SYSTEM ON THE EDGE OF HUTT SPACE TO RESCUE A GUY WITH THE ISB ON HIS TAIL! HE'S PROBABLY DEAD ALREADY!
NEVER MIND THAT CYRKON IS TEEMING WITH THE WORST SCUM IN THE GALAXY!
NEVER MIND THAT JABBA'S GOT BOUNTY HUNTERS LINING UP TO COME AFTER US, IF HE HASN'T SENT THEM ALREADY--
HWHHRA! HRRF!
I **KNOW** IT'S THE OUTER RIM! I KNOW IT'S ON THE WAY, BUT THIS ISN'T OUR FIGHT, PAL!
HRRF! RRF!
AH, WHAT'S THE USE?!
WE'RE GOING TO NEED THE PASS PHRASE.
WHATEVER IT IS, SO EMATT WILL RECOGNIZE US.
AND I EXPECT TO BE PAID FOR THIS.

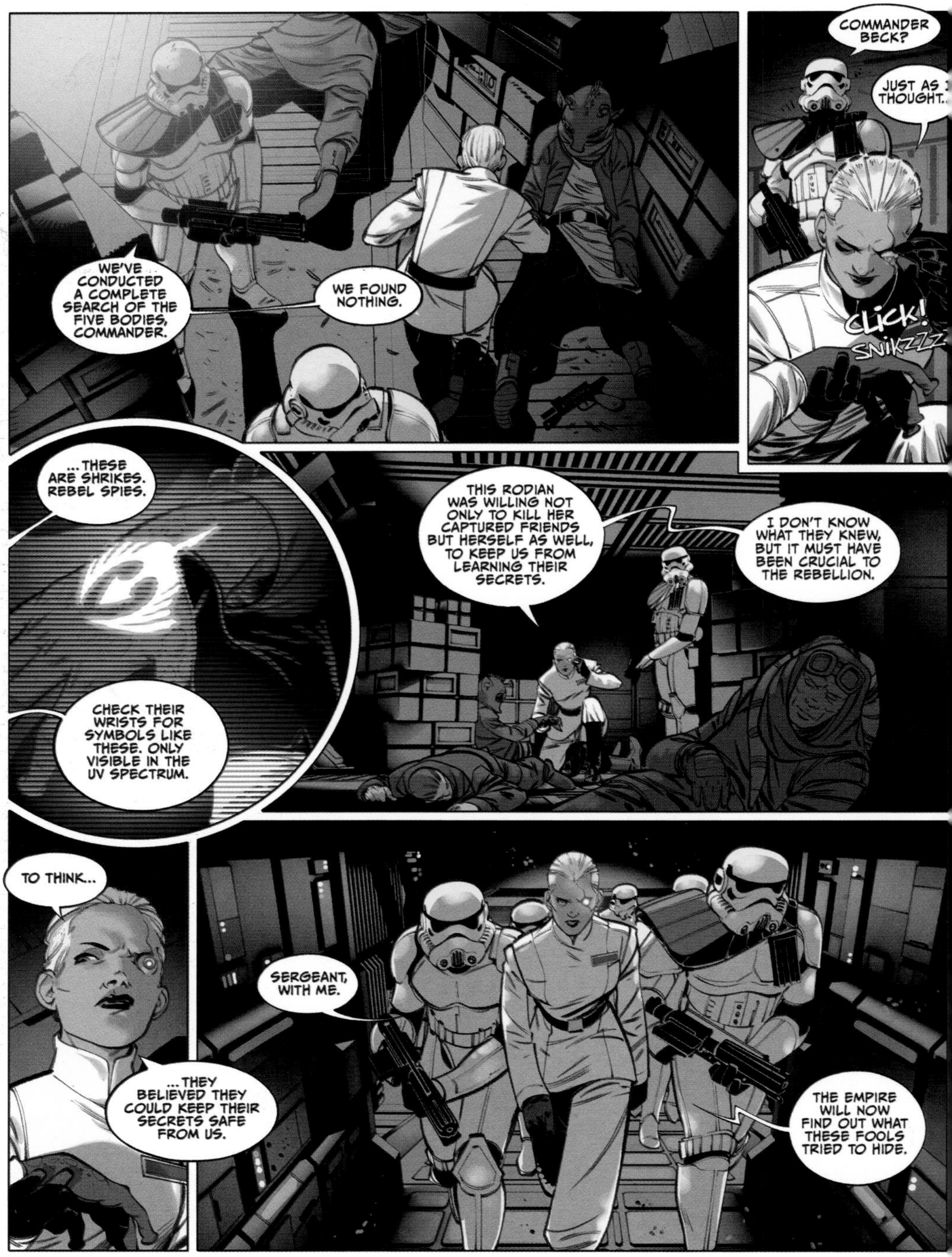
WE'VE CONDUCTED A COMPLETE SEARCH OF THE FIVE BODIES, COMMANDER.
WE FOUND NOTHING.
COMMANDER BECK?
JUST AS I THOUGHT...
CLICK!
SNIKZZZ
...THESE ARE SHRIKES. REBEL SPIES.
CHECK THEIR WRISTS FOR SYMBOLS LIKE THESE. ONLY VISIBLE IN THE UV SPECTRUM.
THIS RODIAN WAS WILLING NOT ONLY TO KILL HER CAPTURED FRIENDS BUT HERSELF AS WELL, TO KEEP US FROM LEARNING THEIR SECRETS.
I DON'T KNOW WHAT THEY KNEW, BUT IT MUST HAVE BEEN CRUCIAL TO THE REBELLION.
TO THINK...
...THEY BELIEVED THEY COULD KEEP THEIR SECRETS SAFE FROM US.
SERGEANT, WITH ME.
THE EMPIRE WILL NOW FIND OUT WHAT THESE FOOLS TRIED TO HIDE.

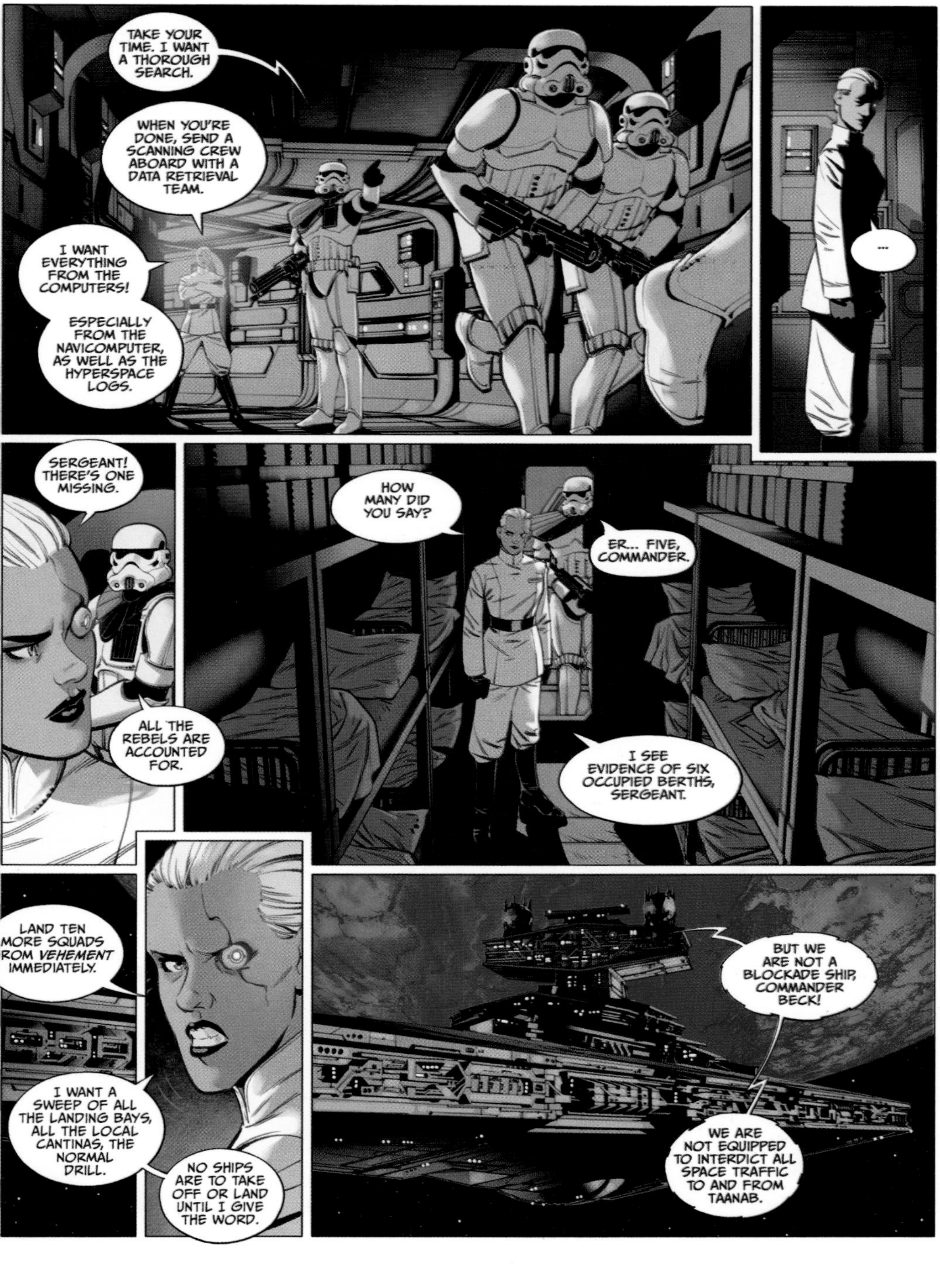
TAKE YOUR TIME. I WANT A THOROUGH SEARCH.
WHEN YOU'RE DONE, SEND A SCANNING CREW ABOARD WITH A DATA RETRIEVAL TEAM.
I WANT EVERYTHING FROM THE COMPUTERS!
ESPECIALLY FROM THE NAVICOMPUTER, AS WELL AS THE HYPERSPACE LOGS.
...
SERGEANT! THERE'S ONE MISSING.
ALL THE REBELS ARE ACCOUNTED FOR.
HOW MANY DID YOU SAY?
ER... FIVE, COMMANDER.
I SEE EVIDENCE OF SIX OCCUPIED BERTHS, SERGEANT.
LAND TEN MORE SQUADS ROM *VEHEMENT* IMMEDIATELY.
I WANT A SWEEP OF ALL THE LANDING BAYS, ALL THE LOCAL CANTINAS, THE NORMAL DRILL.
NO SHIPS ARE TO TAKE OFF OR LAND UNTIL I GIVE THE WORD.
BUT WE ARE NOT A BLOCKADE SHIP, COMMANDER BECK!
WE ARE NOT EQUIPPED TO INTERDICT ALL SPACE TRAFFIC TO AND FROM TAANAB.

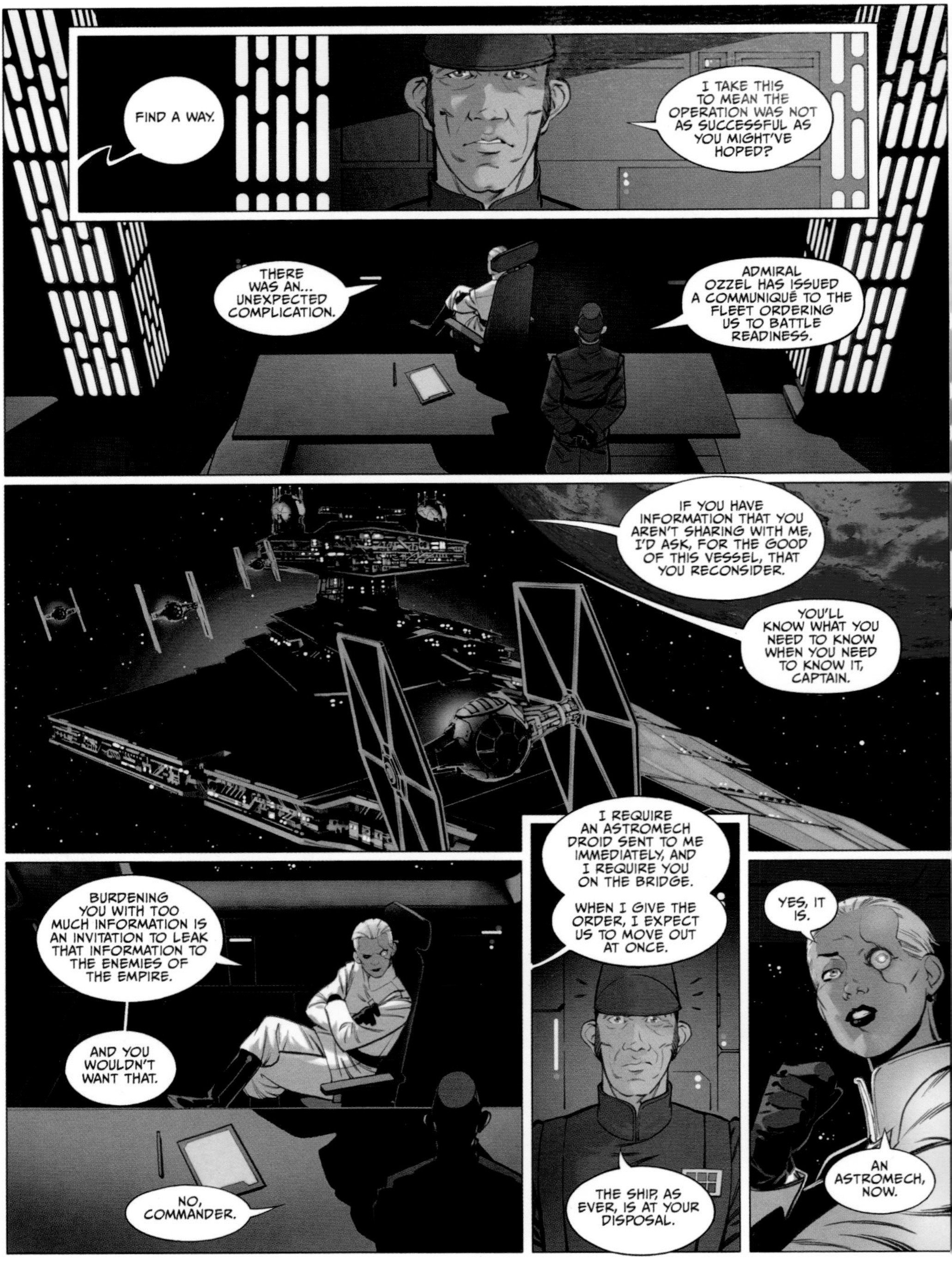
I TAKE THIS TO MEAN THE OPERATION WAS NOT AS SUCCESSFUL AS YOU MIGHT'VE HOPED?
FIND A WAY.
THERE WAS AN... UNEXPECTED COMPLICATION.
ADMIRAL OZZEL HAS ISSUED A COMMUNIQUÉ TO THE FLEET ORDERING US TO BATTLE READINESS.
IF YOU HAVE INFORMATION THAT YOU AREN'T SHARING WITH ME, I'D ASK, FOR THE GOOD OF THIS VESSEL, THAT YOU RECONSIDER.
YOU'LL KNOW WHAT YOU NEED TO KNOW WHEN YOU NEED TO KNOW IT, CAPTAIN.
BURDENING YOU WITH TOO MUCH INFORMATION IS AN INVITATION TO LEAK THAT INFORMATION TO THE ENEMIES OF THE EMPIRE.
AND YOU WOULDN'T WANT THAT.
NO, COMMANDER.
I REQUIRE AN ASTROMECH DROID SENT TO ME IMMEDIATELY, AND I REQUIRE YOU ON THE BRIDGE.
WHEN I GIVE THE ORDER, I EXPECT US TO MOVE OUT AT ONCE.
THE SHIP, AS EVER, IS AT YOUR DISPOSAL.
YES, IT IS.
AN ASTROMECH, NOW.

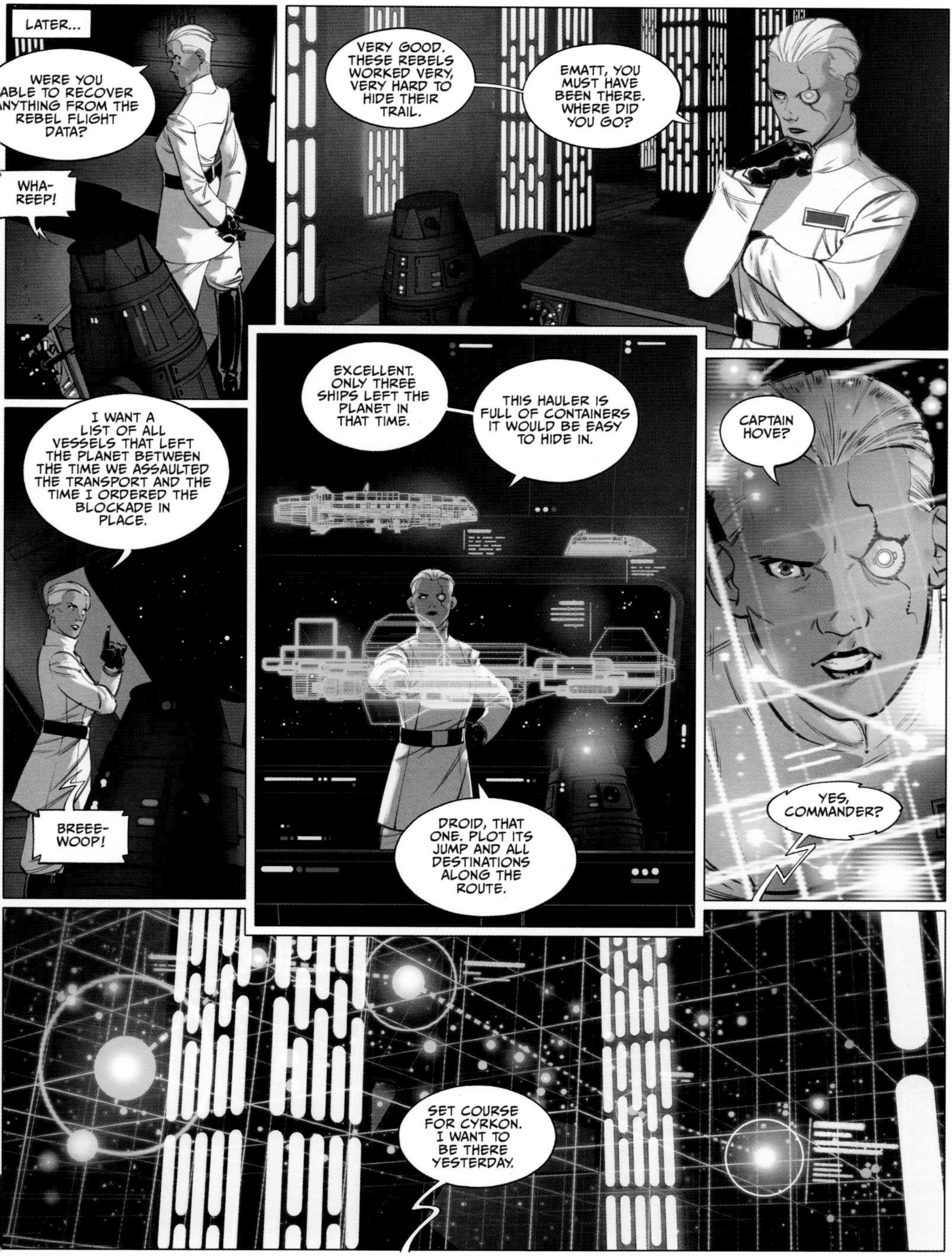

LATER...
WERE YOU ABLE TO RECOVER ANYTHING FROM THE REBEL FLIGHT DATA?
WHA-REEP!
VERY GOOD. THESE REBELS WORKED VERY, VERY HARD TO HIDE THEIR TRAIL.
EMATT, YOU MUST HAVE BEEN THERE. WHERE DID YOU GO?
I WANT A LIST OF ALL VESSELS THAT LEFT THE PLANET BETWEEN THE TIME WE ASSAULTED THE TRANSPORT AND THE TIME I ORDERED THE BLOCKADE IN PLACE.
BREEE-WOOP!
EXCELLENT. ONLY THREE SHIPS LEFT THE PLANET IN THAT TIME.
THIS HAULER IS FULL OF CONTAINERS IT WOULD BE EASY TO HIDE IN.
DROID, THAT ONE. PLOT ITS JUMP AND ALL DESTINATIONS ALONG THE ROUTE.
CAPTAIN HOVE?
YES, COMMANDER?
SET COURSE FOR CYRKON. I WANT TO BE THERE YESTERDAY.

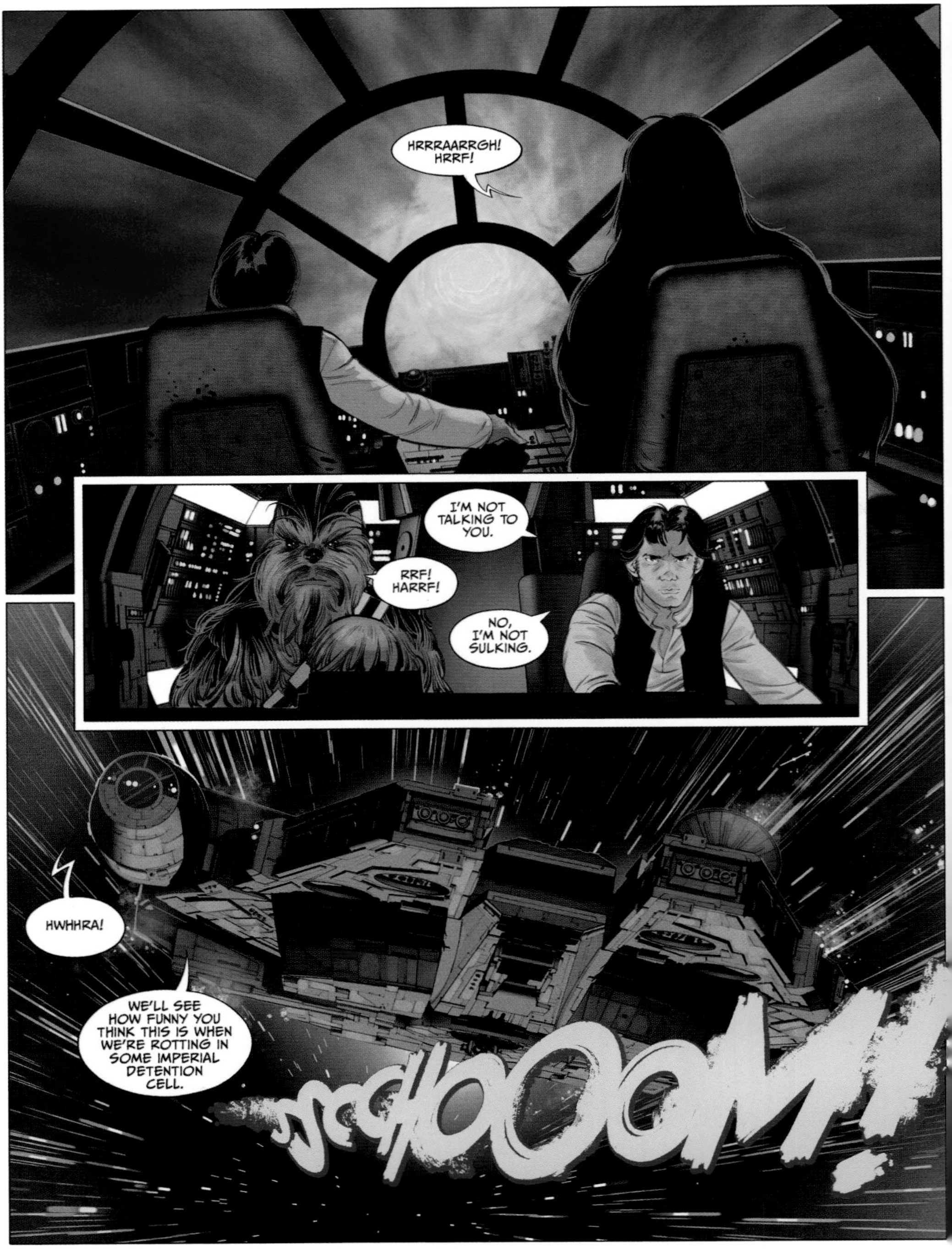
HRRRAARRGH! HRRF!
I'M NOT TALKING TO YOU.
RRF! HARRF!
NO, I'M NOT SULKING.
HWHHRA!
WE'LL SEE HOW FUNNY YOU THINK THIS IS WHEN WE'RE ROTTING IN SOME IMPERIAL DETENTION CELL.
SSCHOOOM!

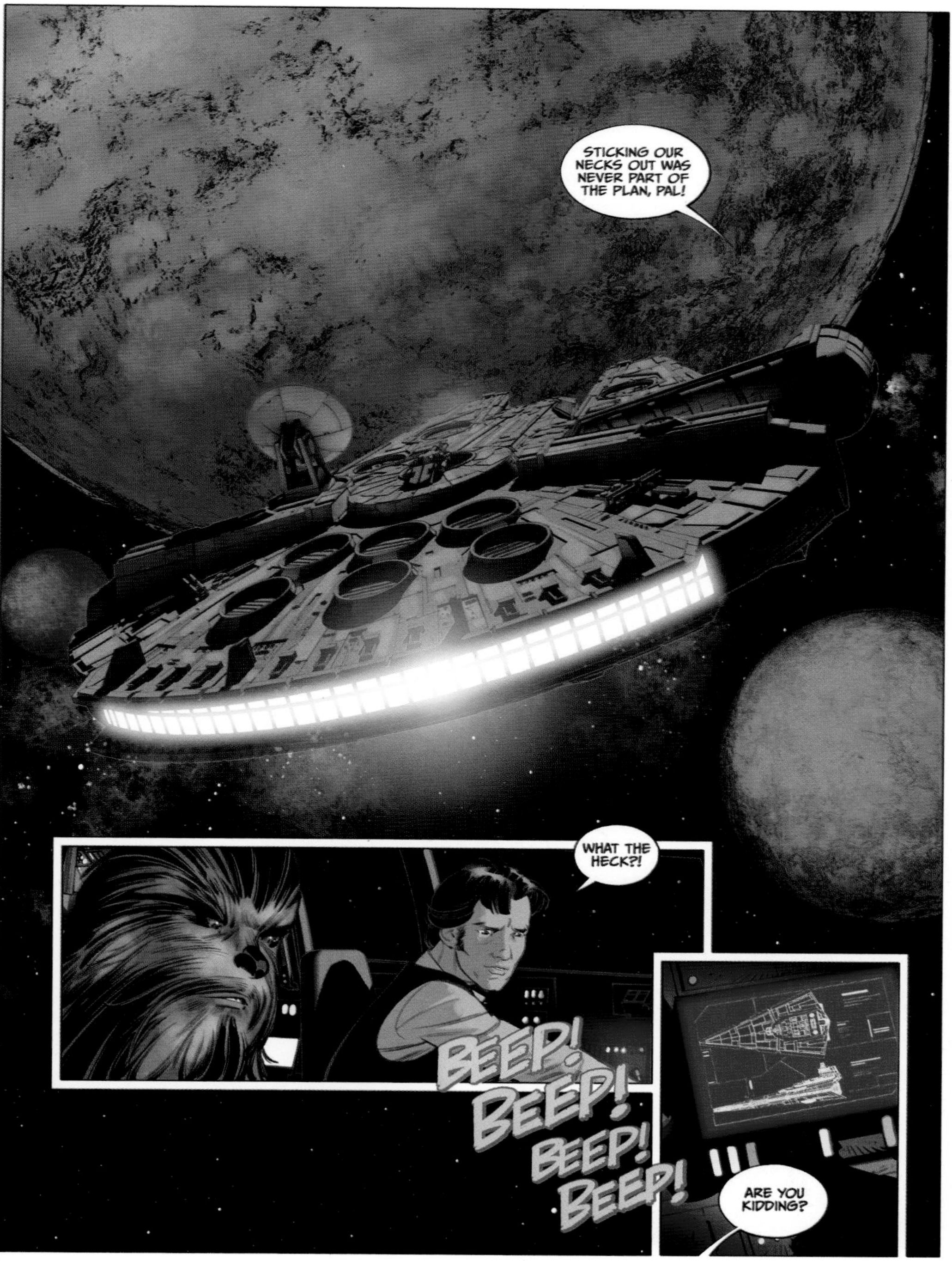
STICKING OUR NECKS OUT WAS NEVER PART OF THE PLAN, PAL!
WHAT THE HECK?!
BEEP! BEEP! BEEP! BEEP!
ARE YOU KIDDING?

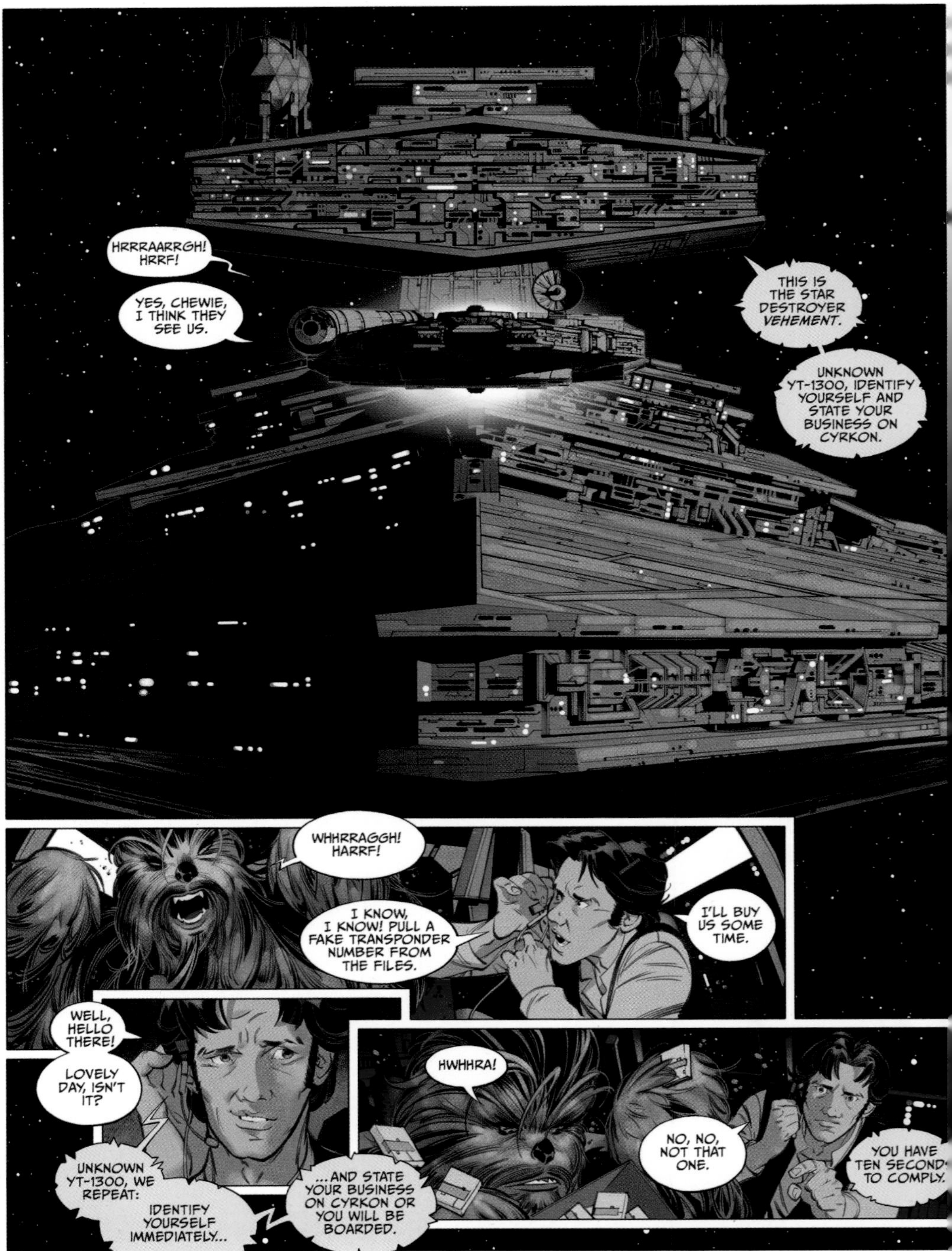

HRRRAARRGH! HRRF!
YES, CHEWIE, I THINK THEY SEE US.
THIS IS THE STAR DESTROYER *VEHEMENT.*
UNKNOWN YT-1300, IDENTIFY YOURSELF AND STATE YOUR BUSINESS ON CYRKON.
WHHRRAGGH! HARRF!
I KNOW, I KNOW! PULL A FAKE TRANSPONDER NUMBER FROM THE FILES.
I'LL BUY US SOME TIME.
WELL, HELLO THERE!
LOVELY DAY, ISN'T IT?
UNKNOWN YT-1300, WE REPEAT:
IDENTIFY YOURSELF IMMEDIATELY...
...AND STATE YOUR BUSINESS ON CYRKON OR YOU WILL BE BOARDED.
HWHHRA!
NO, NO, NOT THAT ONE.
YOU HAVE TEN SECOND TO COMPLY.

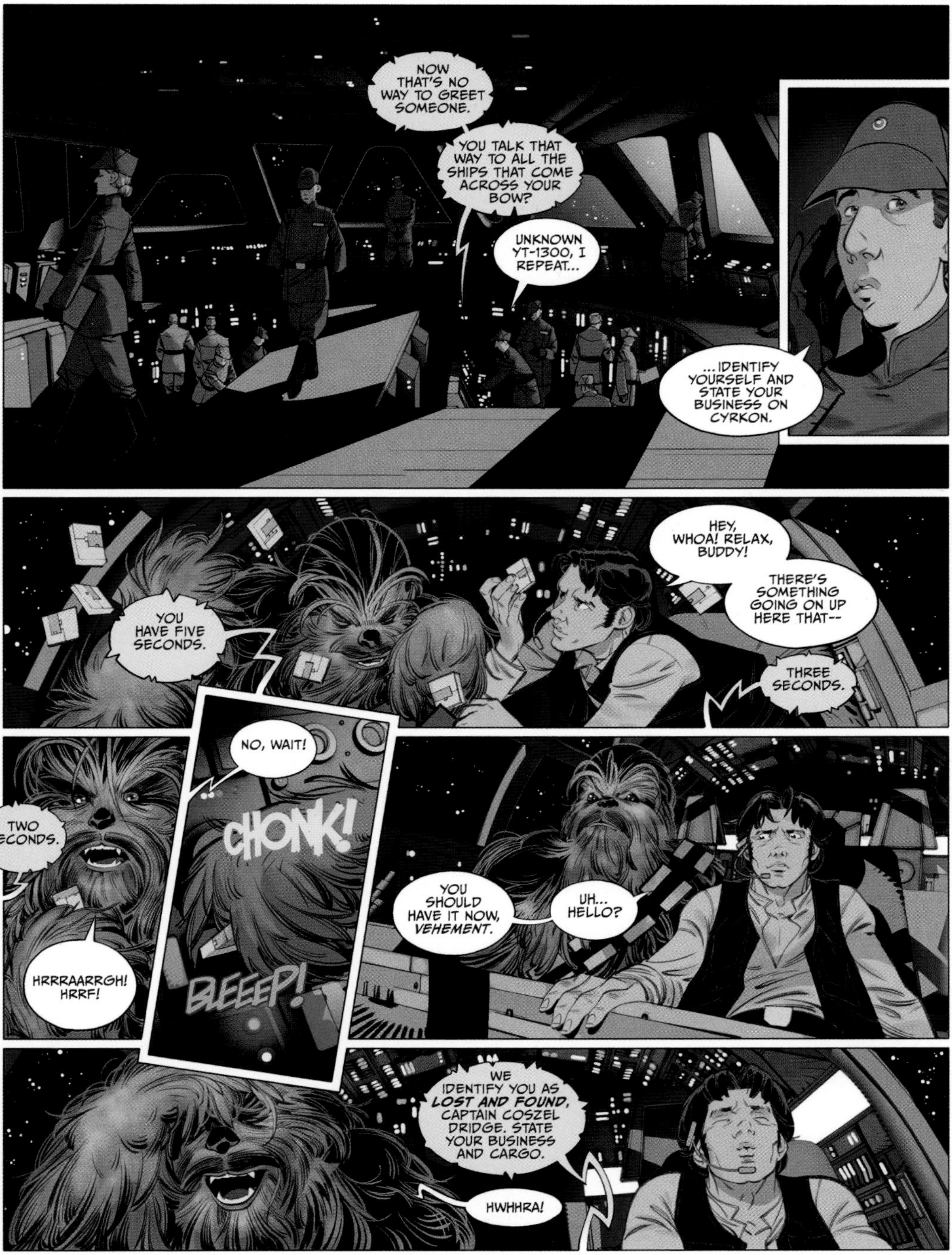

NOW THAT'S NO WAY TO GREET SOMEONE.
YOU TALK THAT WAY TO ALL THE SHIPS THAT COME ACROSS YOUR BOW?
UNKNOWN YT-1300, I REPEAT...
...IDENTIFY YOURSELF AND STATE YOUR BUSINESS ON CYRKON.
YOU HAVE FIVE SECONDS.
HEY, WHOA! RELAX, BUDDY!
THERE'S SOMETHING GOING ON UP HERE THAT--
THREE SECONDS.
TWO ECONDS.
HRRRAARRGH! HRRF!
NO, WAIT!
CHONK!
BLEEEP!
YOU SHOULD HAVE IT NOW, *VEHEMENT*.
UH... HELLO?
WE IDENTIFY YOU AS ***LOST AND FOUND***, CAPTAIN COSZEL DRIDGE. STATE YOUR BUSINESS AND CARGO.
HWHHRA!

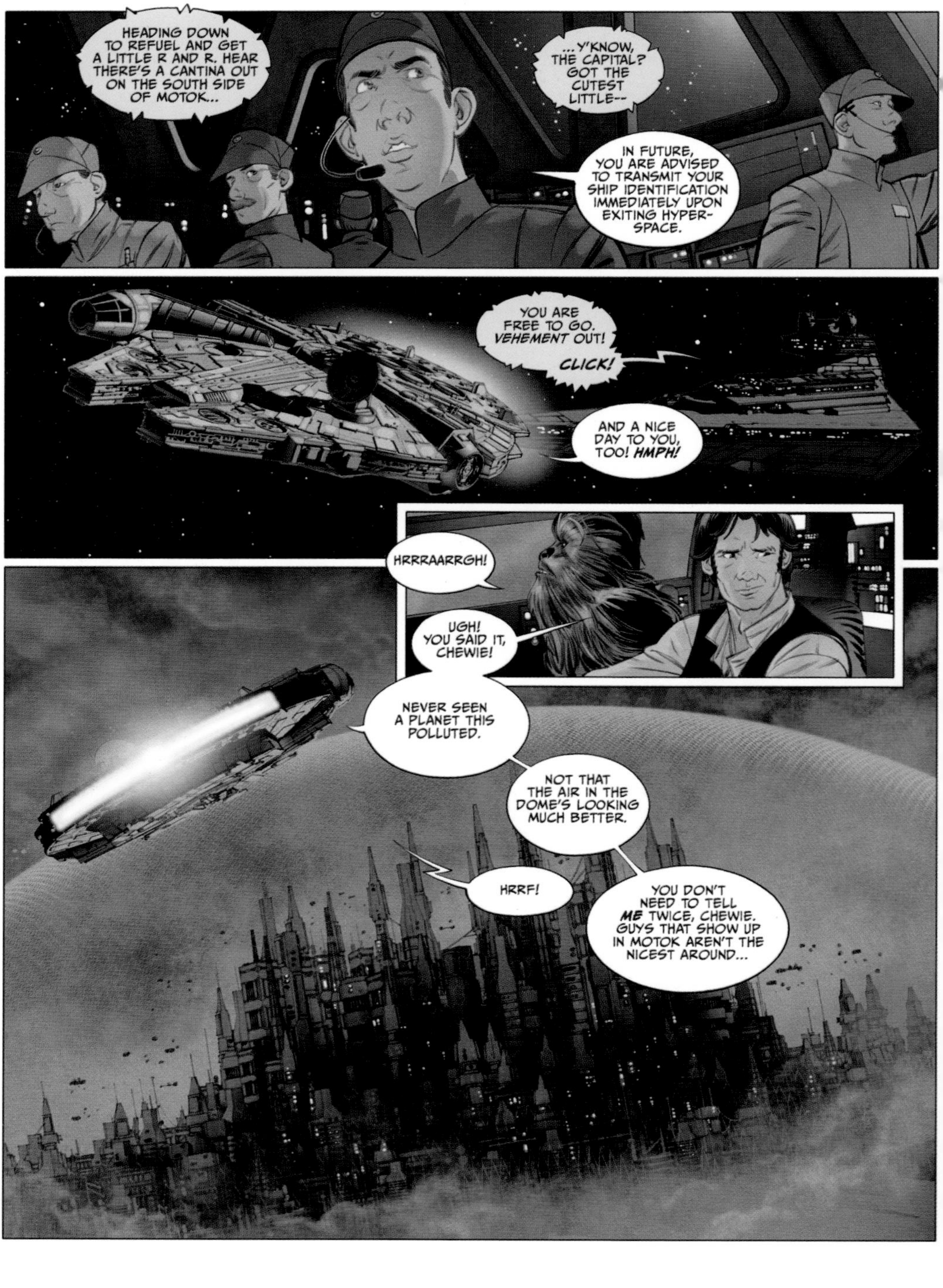
HEADING DOWN TO REFUEL AND GET A LITTLE R AND R. HEAR THERE'S A CANTINA OUT ON THE SOUTH SIDE OF MOTOK...
...Y'KNOW, THE CAPITAL? GOT THE CUTEST LITTLE--
IN FUTURE, YOU ARE ADVISED TO TRANSMIT YOUR SHIP IDENTIFICATION IMMEDIATELY UPON EXITING HYPER-SPACE.
YOU ARE FREE TO GO. *VEHEMENT* OUT!
CLICK!
AND A NICE DAY TO YOU, TOO! **HMPH!**
HRRRAARRGH!
UGH! YOU SAID IT, CHEWIE!
NEVER SEEN A PLANET THIS POLLUTED.
NOT THAT THE AIR IN THE DOME'S LOOKING MUCH BETTER.
HRRF!
YOU DON'T NEED TO TELL **ME** TWICE, CHEWIE. GUYS THAT SHOW UP IN MOTOK AREN'T THE NICEST AROUND...

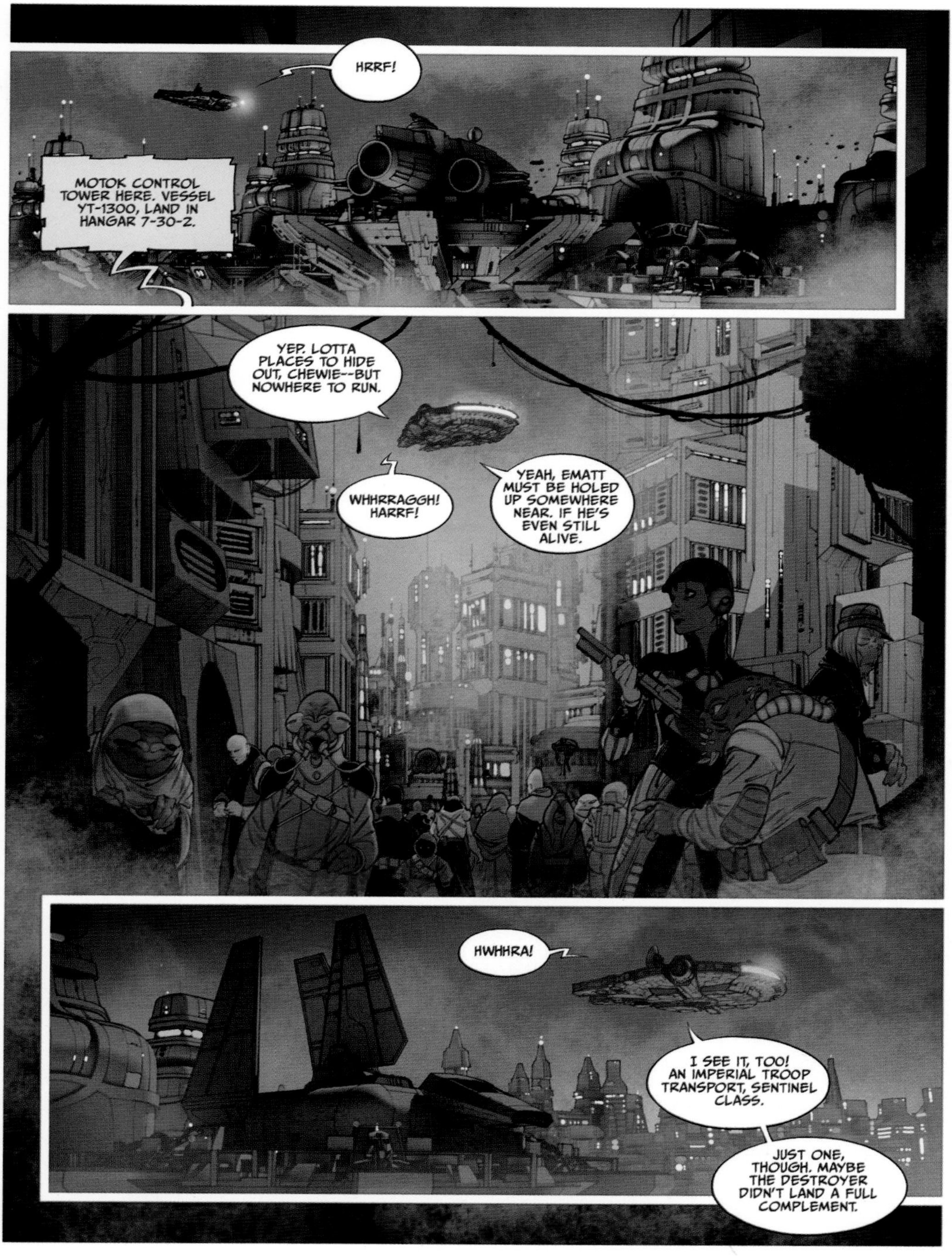
HRRF!
MOTOK CONTROL TOWER HERE. VESSEL YT-1300, LAND IN HANGAR 7-30-2.
YEP. LOTTA PLACES TO HIDE OUT, CHEWIE--BUT NOWHERE TO RUN.
WHHRRAGGH! HARRF!
YEAH, EMATT MUST BE HOLED UP SOMEWHERE NEAR. IF HE'S EVEN STILL ALIVE.
HWHHRA!
I SEE IT, TOO! AN IMPERIAL TROOP TRANSPORT, SENTINEL CLASS.
JUST ONE, THOUGH. MAYBE THE DESTROYER DIDN'T LAND A FULL COMPLEMENT.

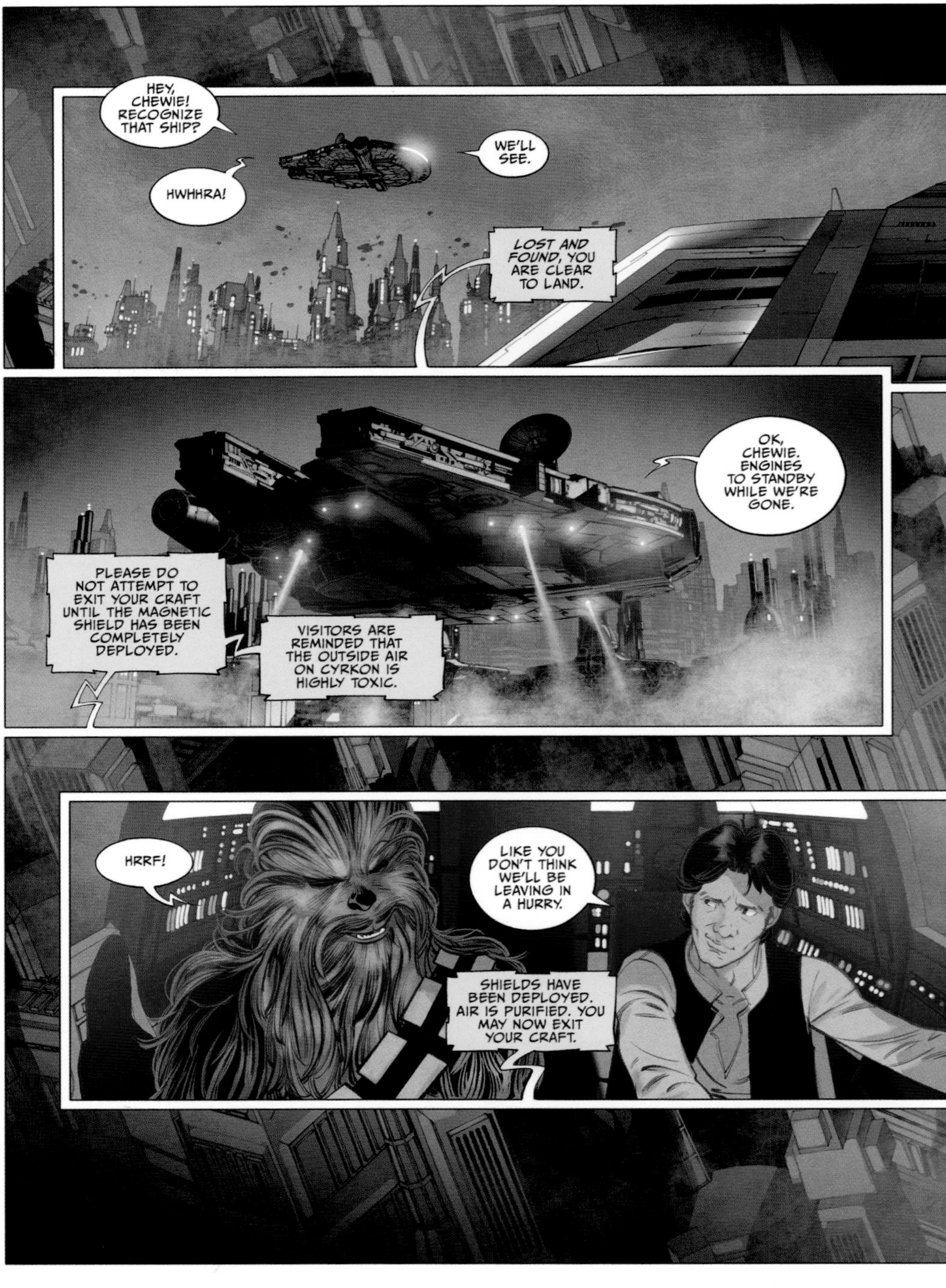
HEY, CHEWIE! RECOGNIZE THAT SHIP?
HWHHRA!
WE'LL SEE.
LOST AND FOUND, YOU ARE CLEAR TO LAND.
OK, CHEWIE. ENGINES TO STANDBY WHILE WE'RE GONE.
PLEASE DO NOT ATTEMPT TO EXIT YOUR CRAFT UNTIL THE MAGNETIC SHIELD HAS BEEN COMPLETELY DEPLOYED.
VISITORS ARE REMINDED THAT THE OUTSIDE AIR ON CYRKON IS HIGHLY TOXIC.
HRRF!
LIKE YOU DON'T THINK WE'LL BE LEAVING IN A HURRY.
SHIELDS HAVE BEEN DEPLOYED. AIR IS PURIFIED. YOU MAY NOW EXIT YOUR CRAFT.

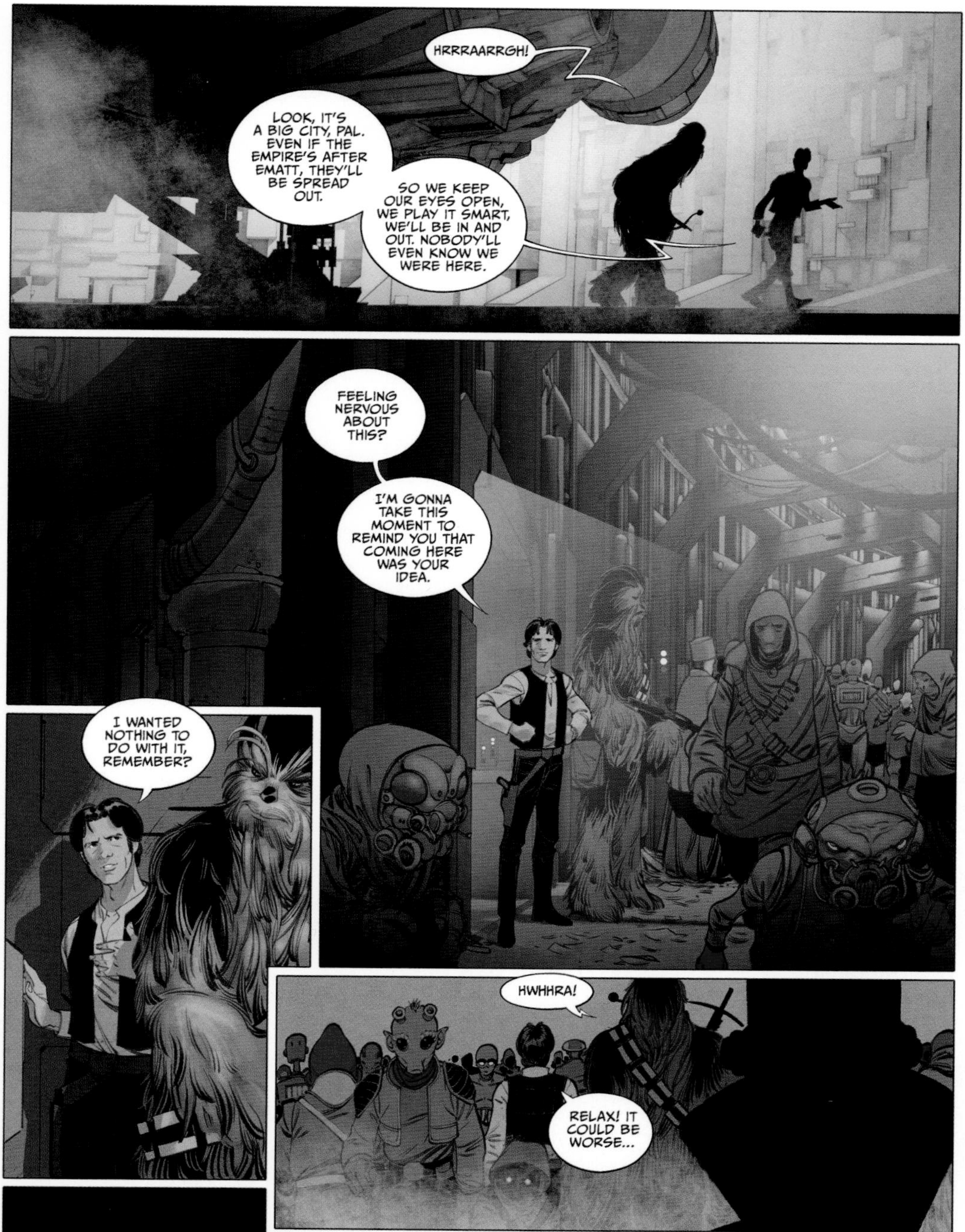
HRRRAARRGH!
LOOK, IT'S A BIG CITY, PAL. EVEN IF THE EMPIRE'S AFTER EMATT, THEY'LL BE SPREAD OUT.
SO WE KEEP OUR EYES OPEN, WE PLAY IT SMART, WE'LL BE IN AND OUT. NOBODY'LL EVEN KNOW WE WERE HERE.
FEELING NERVOUS ABOUT THIS?
I'M GONNA TAKE THIS MOMENT TO REMIND YOU THAT COMING HERE WAS YOUR IDEA.
I WANTED NOTHING TO DO WITH IT, REMEMBER?
HWHHRA!
RELAX! IT COULD BE WORSE...

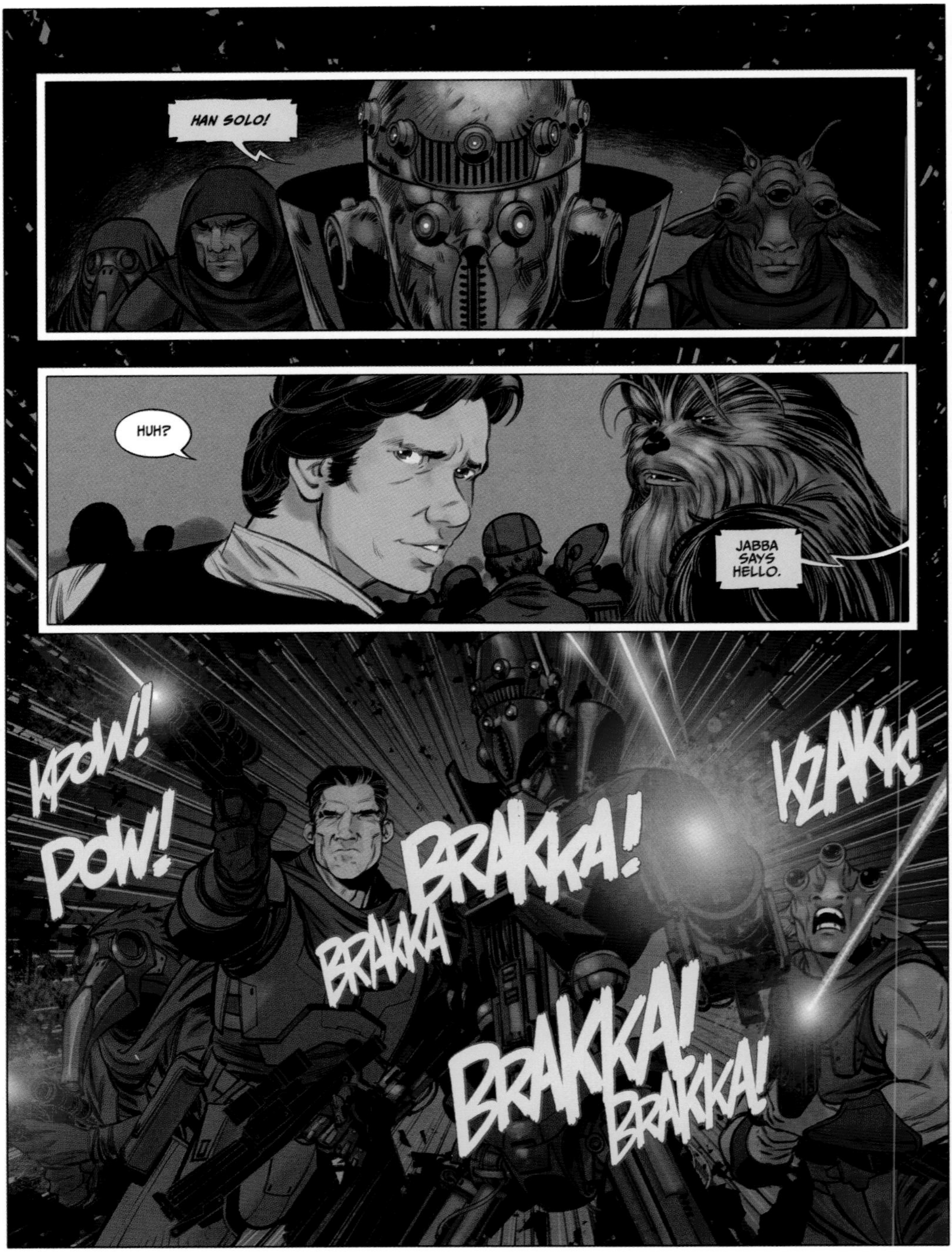
HAN SOLO!
HUH?
JABBA SAYS HELLO.
KPOW!
POW!
BRAKKA!
BRAKKA
KZAKK!
BRAKKA!
BRAKKA!

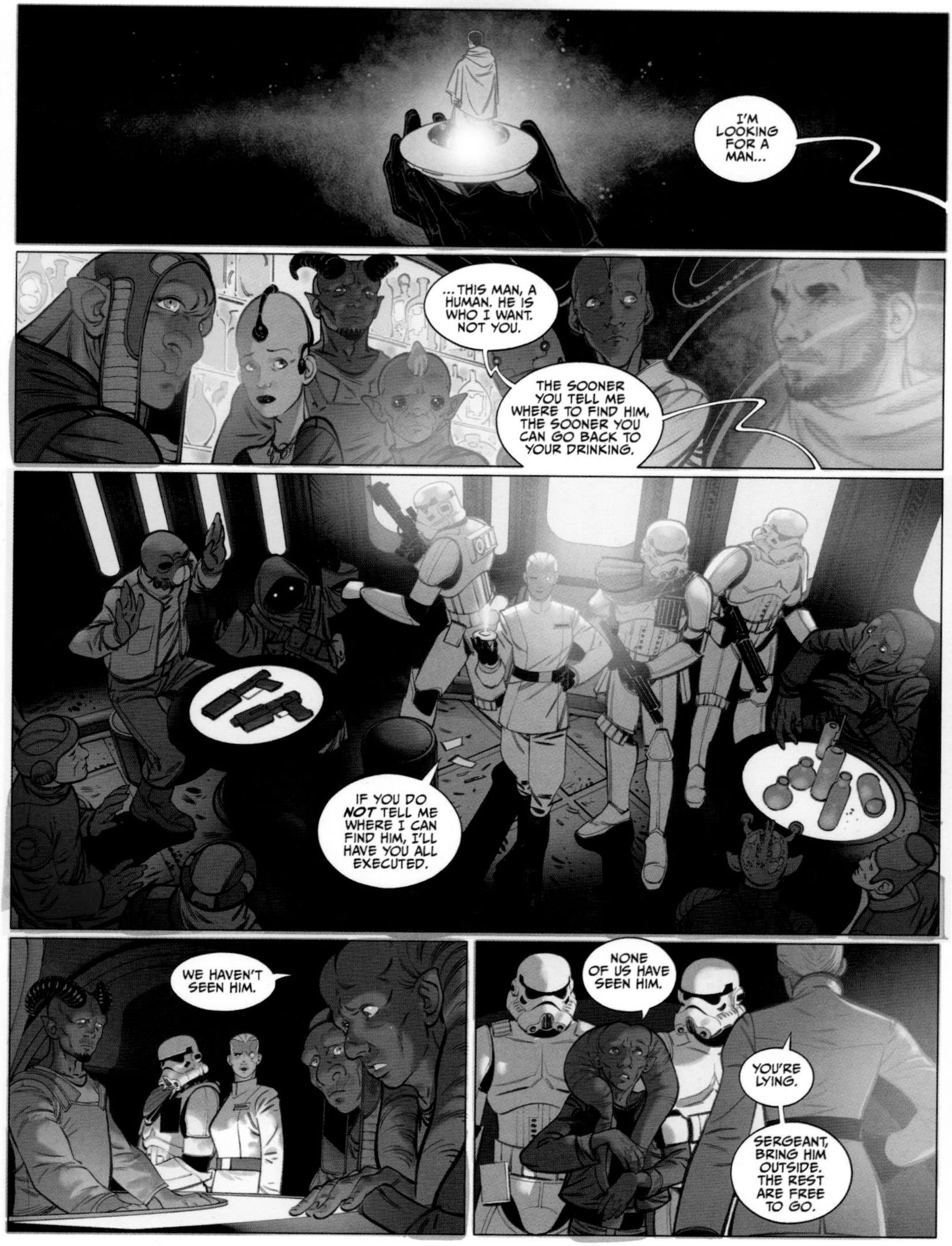
I'M LOOKING FOR A MAN...
...THIS MAN, A HUMAN. HE IS WHO I WANT. NOT YOU.
THE SOONER YOU TELL ME WHERE TO FIND HIM, THE SOONER YOU CAN GO BACK TO YOUR DRINKING.
IF YOU DO NOT TELL ME WHERE I CAN FIND HIM, I'LL HAVE YOU ALL EXECUTED.
WE HAVEN'T SEEN HIM.
NONE OF US HAVE SEEN HIM.
YOU'RE LYING.
SERGEANT, BRING HIM OUTSIDE. THE REST ARE FREE TO GO.

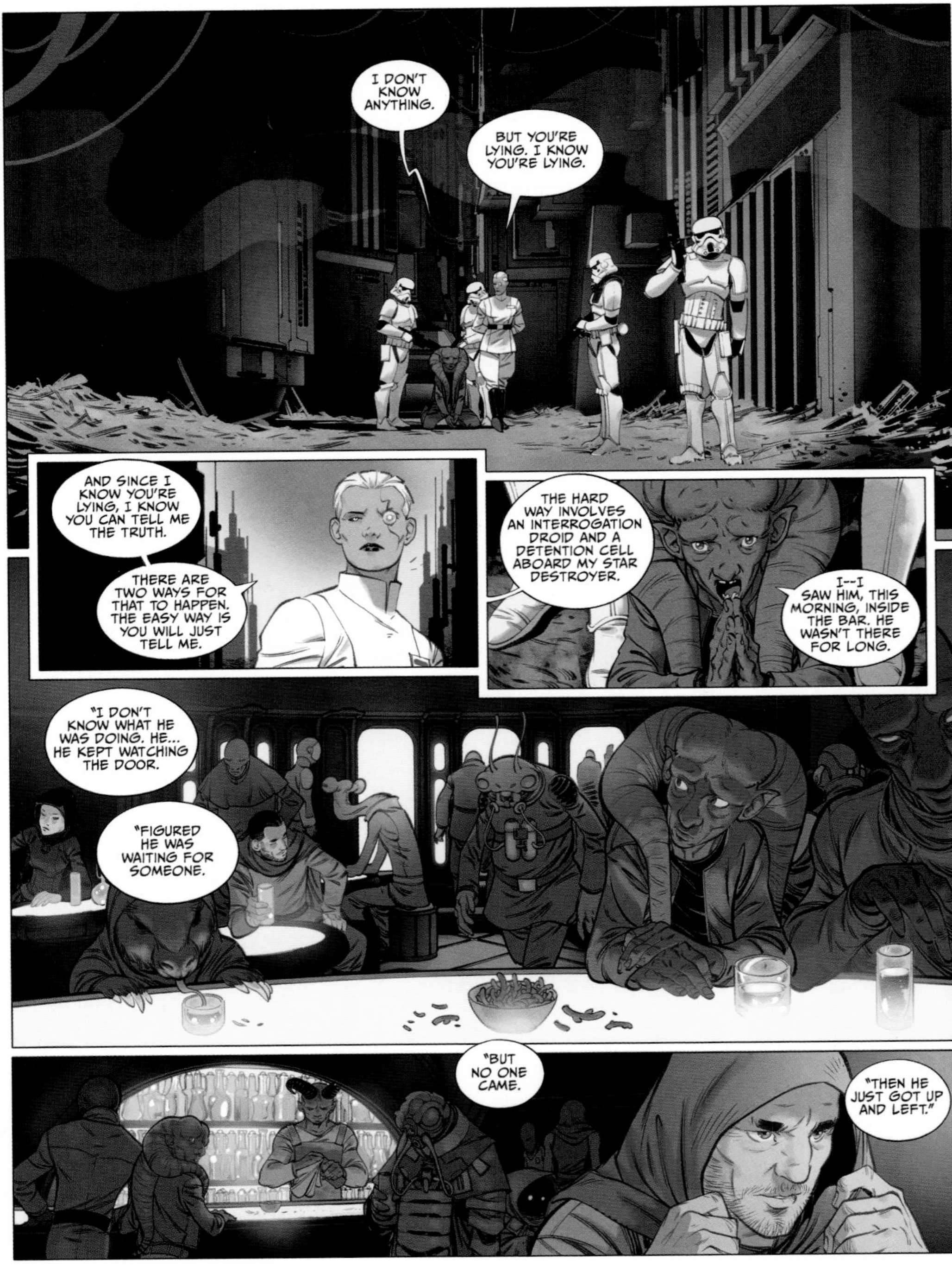
I DON'T KNOW ANYTHING.
BUT YOU'RE LYING. I KNOW YOU'RE LYING.
AND SINCE I KNOW YOU'RE LYING, I KNOW YOU CAN TELL ME THE TRUTH.
THERE ARE TWO WAYS FOR THAT TO HAPPEN. THE EASY WAY IS YOU WILL JUST TELL ME.
THE HARD WAY INVOLVES AN INTERROGATION DROID AND A DETENTION CELL ABOARD MY STAR DESTROYER.
I--I SAW HIM, THIS MORNING, INSIDE THE BAR. HE WASN'T THERE FOR LONG.
"I DON'T KNOW WHAT HE WAS DOING. HE... HE KEPT WATCHING THE DOOR.
"FIGURED HE WAS WAITING FOR SOMEONE.
"BUT NO ONE CAME.
"THEN HE JUST GOT UP AND LEFT."

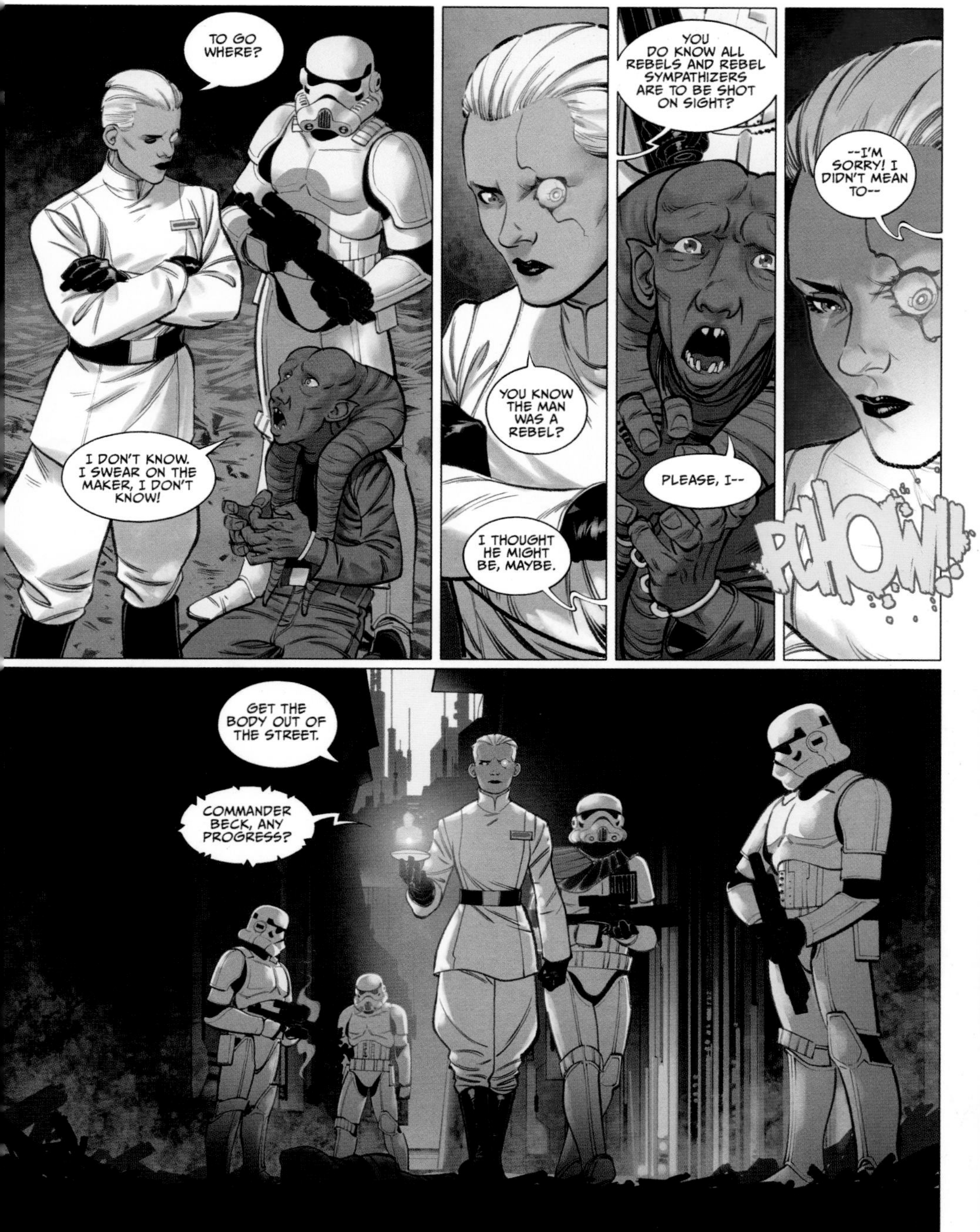
TO GO WHERE?
I DON'T KNOW. I SWEAR ON THE MAKER, I DON'T KNOW!
YOU KNOW THE MAN WAS A REBEL?
I THOUGHT HE MIGHT BE, MAYBE.
YOU DO KNOW ALL REBELS AND REBEL SYMPATHIZERS ARE TO BE SHOT ON SIGHT?
PLEASE, I--
--I'M SORRY! I DIDN'T MEAN TO--
PCHOW!!
GET THE BODY OUT OF THE STREET.
COMMANDER BECK, ANY PROGRESS?

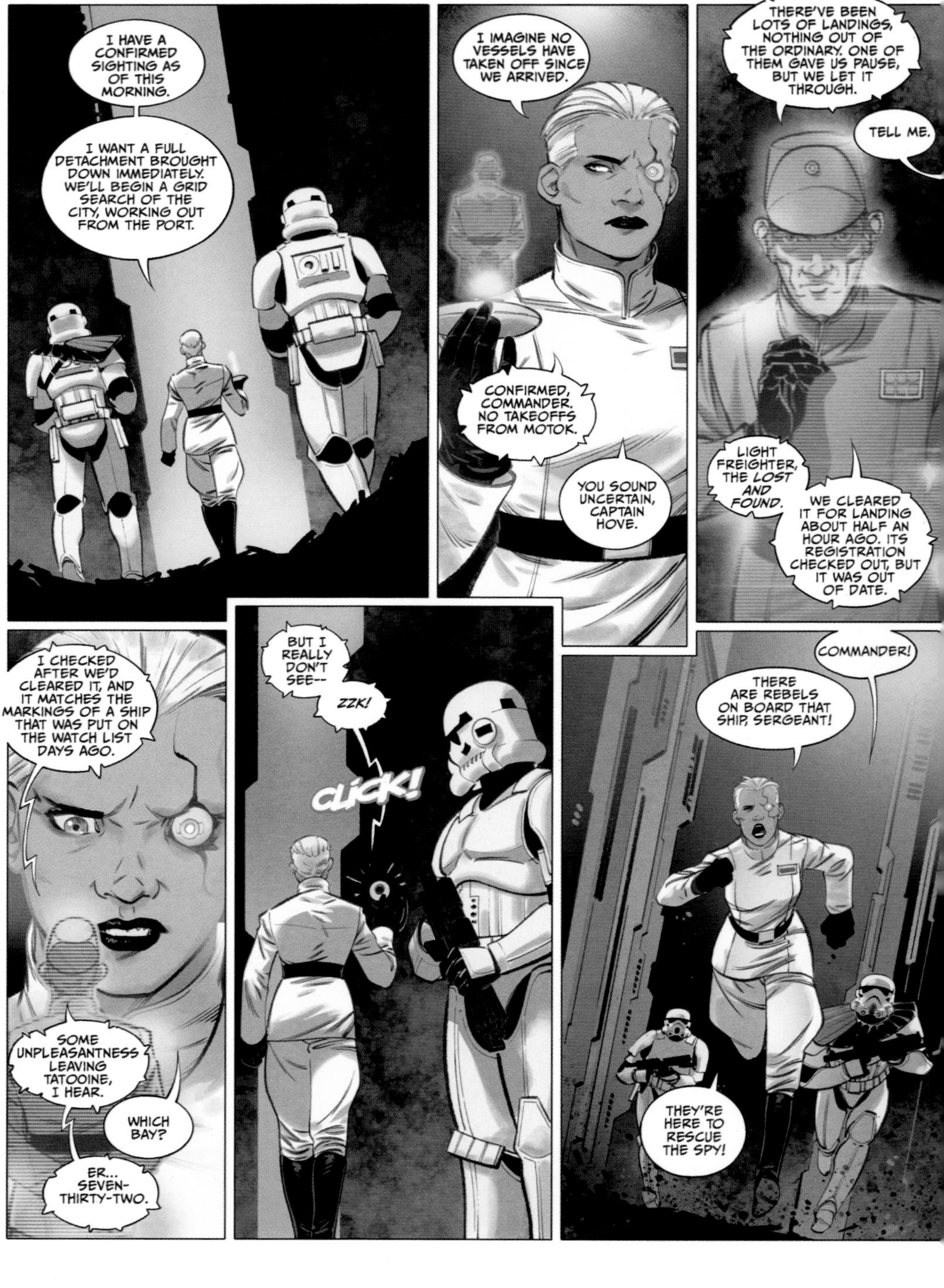
I HAVE A CONFIRMED SIGHTING AS OF THIS MORNING.
I WANT A FULL DETACHMENT BROUGHT DOWN IMMEDIATELY. WE'LL BEGIN A GRID SEARCH OF THE CITY, WORKING OUT FROM THE PORT.
I IMAGINE NO VESSELS HAVE TAKEN OFF SINCE WE ARRIVED.
CONFIRMED, COMMANDER. NO TAKEOFFS FROM MOTOK.
YOU SOUND UNCERTAIN, CAPTAIN HOVE.
THERE'VE BEEN LOTS OF LANDINGS, NOTHING OUT OF THE ORDINARY. ONE OF THEM GAVE US PAUSE, BUT WE LET IT THROUGH.
TELL ME.
LIGHT FREIGHTER, THE *LOST AND FOUND.*
WE CLEARED IT FOR LANDING ABOUT HALF AN HOUR AGO. ITS REGISTRATION CHECKED OUT, BUT IT WAS OUT OF DATE.
I CHECKED AFTER WE'D CLEARED IT, AND IT MATCHES THE MARKINGS OF A SHIP THAT WAS PUT ON THE WATCH LIST DAYS AGO.
SOME UNPLEASANTNESS LEAVING TATOOINE, I HEAR.
WHICH BAY?
ER... SEVEN-THIRTY-TWO.
BUT I REALLY DON'T SEE--
ZZK!
CLICK!
COMMANDER!
THERE ARE REBELS ON BOARD THAT SHIP, SERGEANT!
THEY'RE HERE TO RESCUE THE SPY!

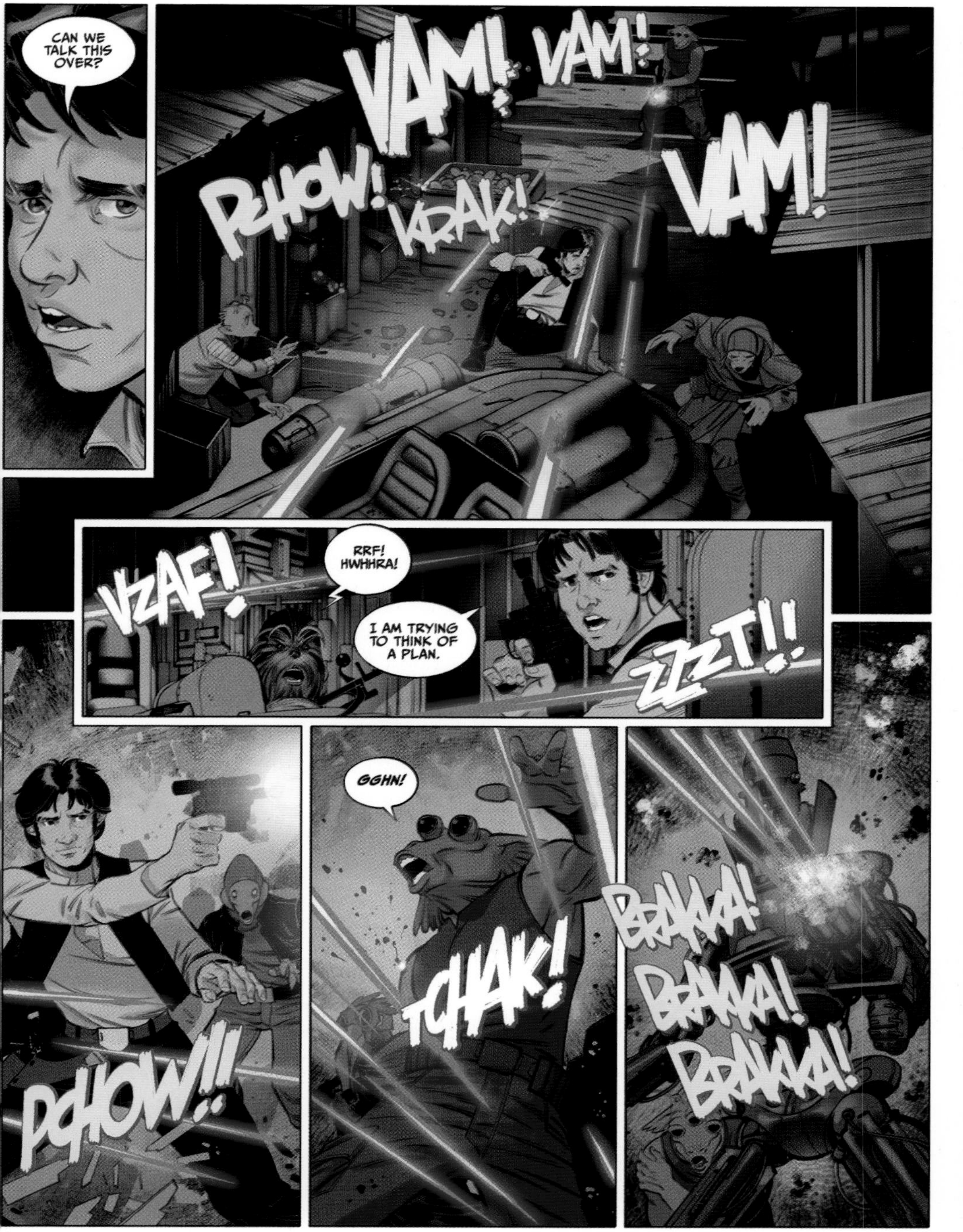
CAN WE TALK THIS OVER?
VAM! VAM!
PCHOW!
KRAK!
VAM!
VZAF!
RRF! HWHHRA!
I AM TRYING TO THINK OF A PLAN.
ZZZT!!
PCHOW!!
GGHN!
TCHAK!
BRAKKA!
BRAKKA!
BRAKKA!

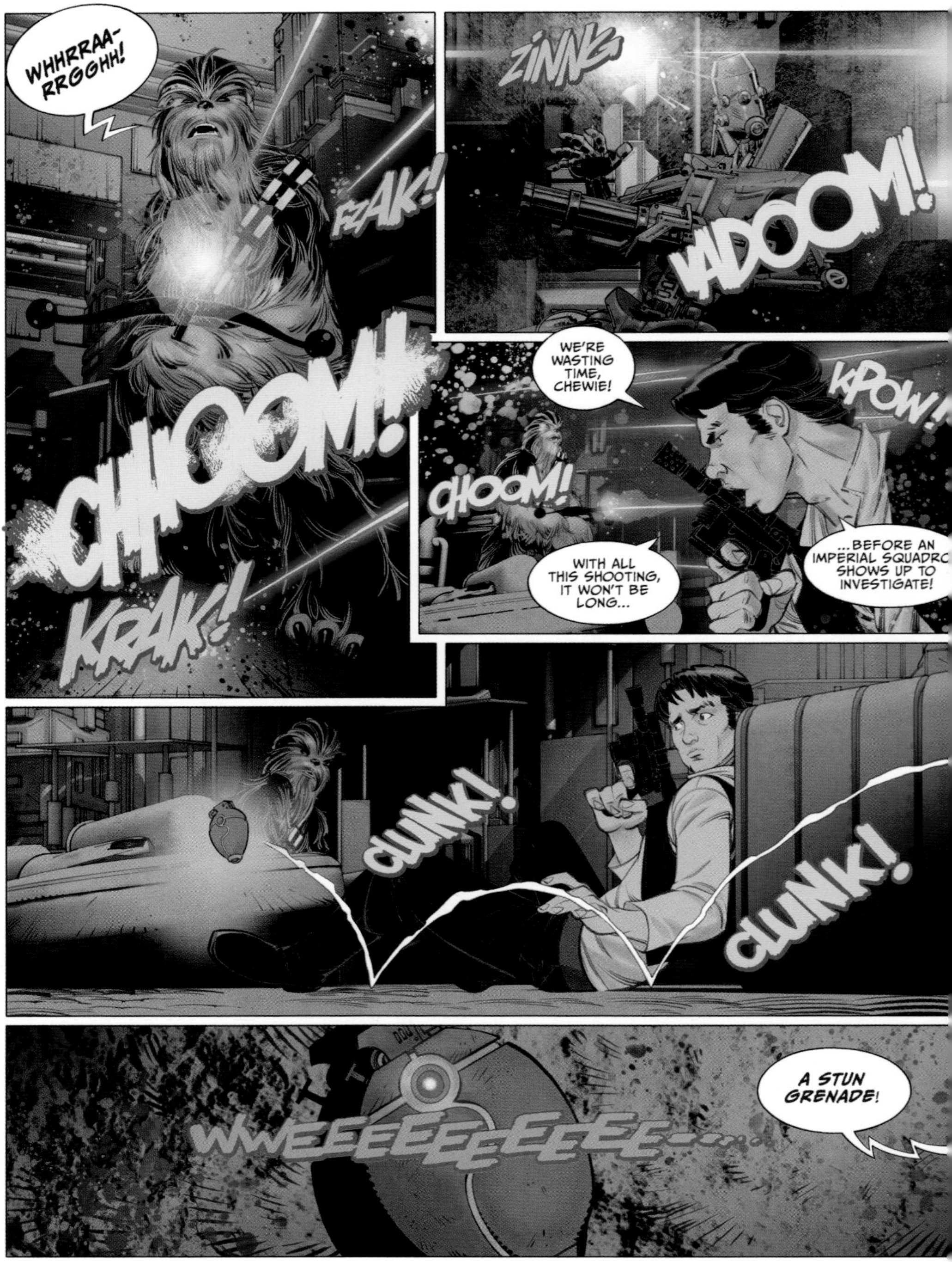
WHHRRAA-RRGGHH!
FZAK!
CHOOM!
KRAK!
ZINNG
KADOOM!
WE'RE WASTING TIME, CHEWIE!
KPOW!
CHOOM!
WITH ALL THIS SHOOTING, IT WON'T BE LONG...
...BEFORE AN IMPERIAL SQUADRO SHOWS UP TO INVESTIGATE!
CLUNK!
CLUNK!
WWEEEEEEEEEEEE...
A STUN GRENADE!

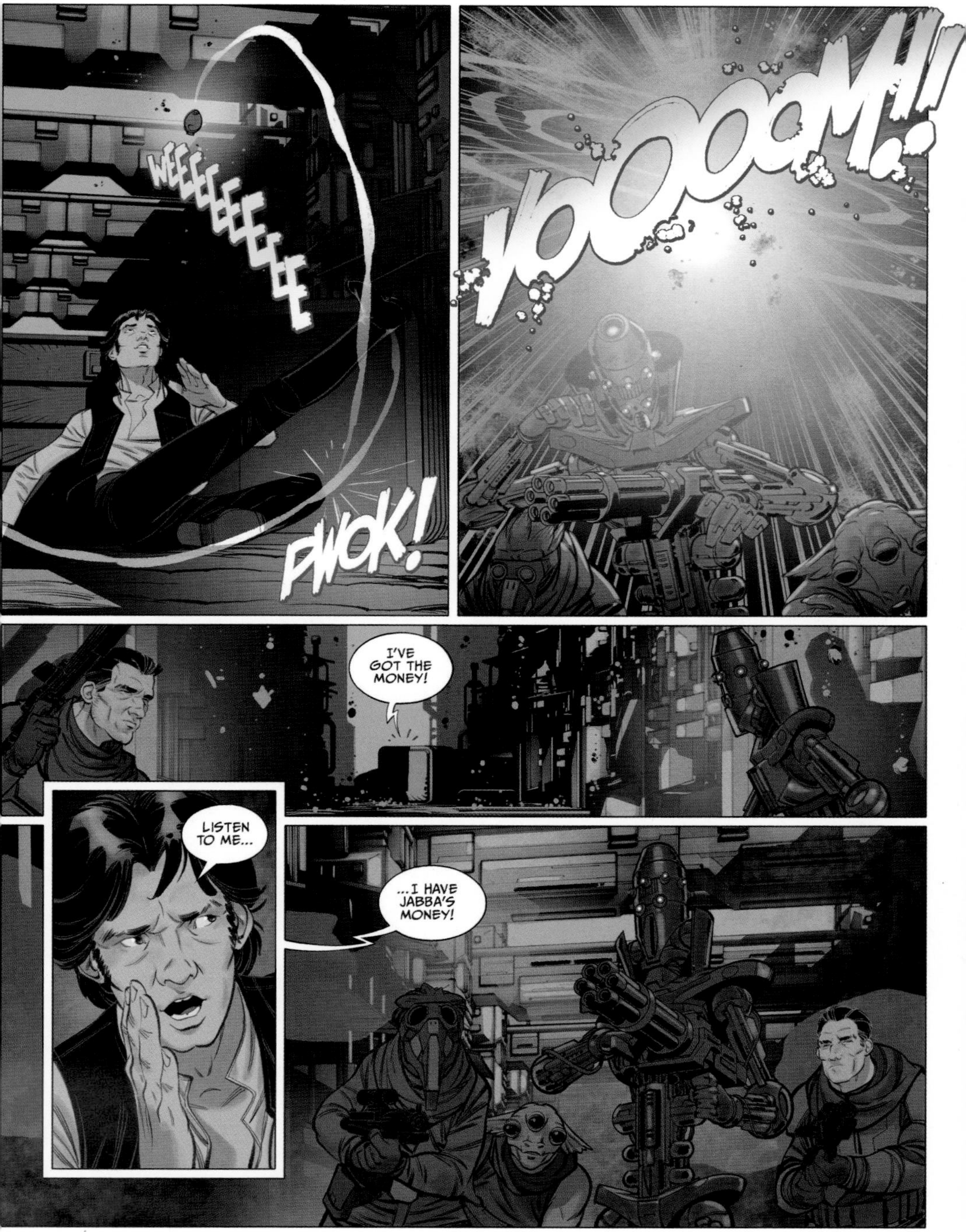
WEEEEEEEEEE
PWOK!
VOOOOOM!!
I'VE GOT THE MONEY!
LISTEN TO ME...
...I HAVE JABBA'S MONEY!

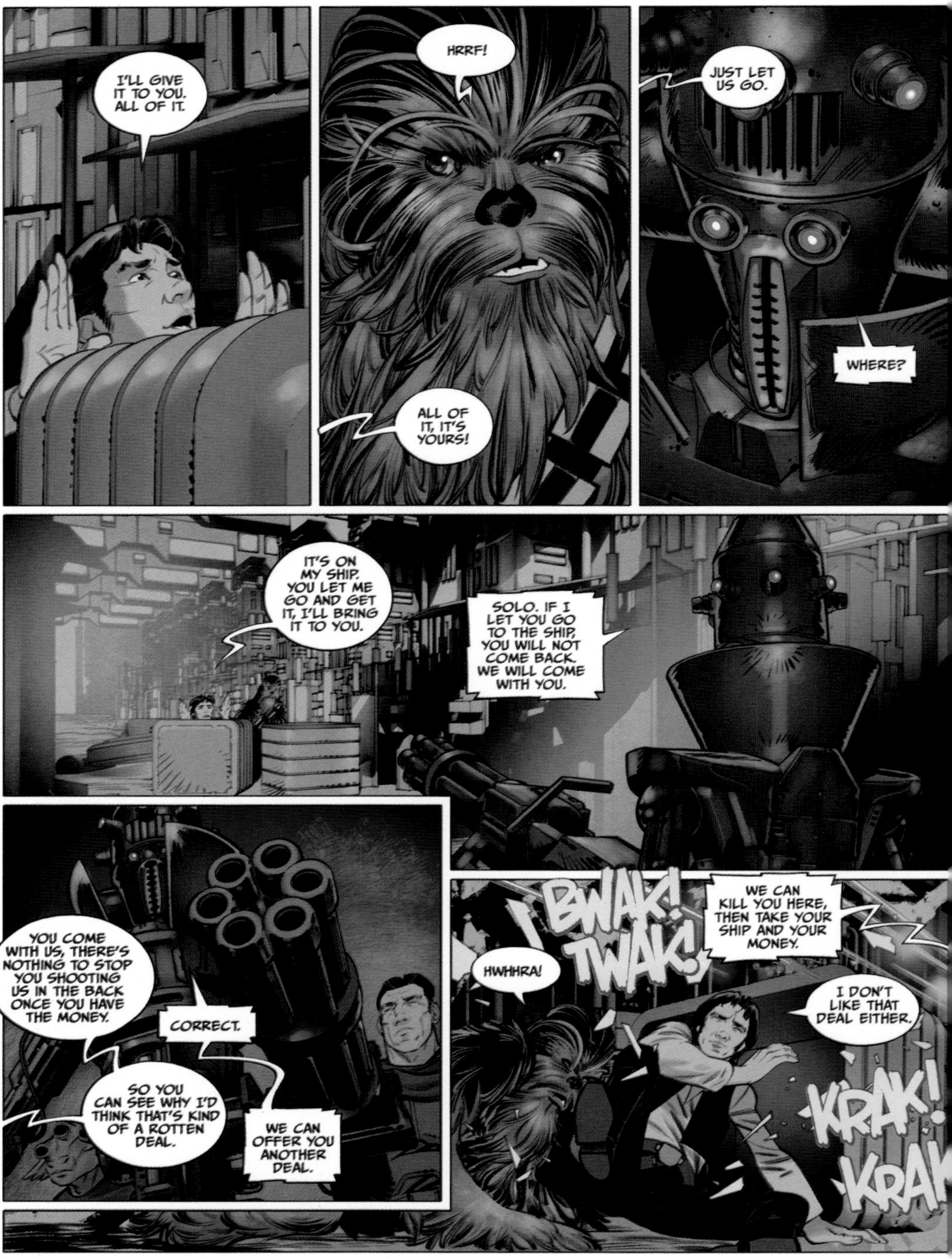
I'LL GIVE IT TO YOU. ALL OF IT.
HRRF!
ALL OF IT, IT'S YOURS!
JUST LET US GO.
WHERE?
IT'S ON MY SHIP. YOU LET ME GO AND GET IT, I'LL BRING IT TO YOU.
SOLO. IF I LET YOU GO TO THE SHIP, YOU WILL NOT COME BACK. WE WILL COME WITH YOU.
YOU COME WITH US, THERE'S NOTHING TO STOP YOU SHOOTING US IN THE BACK ONCE YOU HAVE THE MONEY.
CORRECT.
SO YOU CAN SEE WHY I'D THINK THAT'S KIND OF A ROTTEN DEAL.
WE CAN OFFER YOU ANOTHER DEAL.
BWAK!
TWAK!
WE CAN KILL YOU HERE, THEN TAKE YOUR SHIP AND YOUR MONEY.
HWHHRA!
I DON'T LIKE THAT DEAL EITHER.
KRAK!

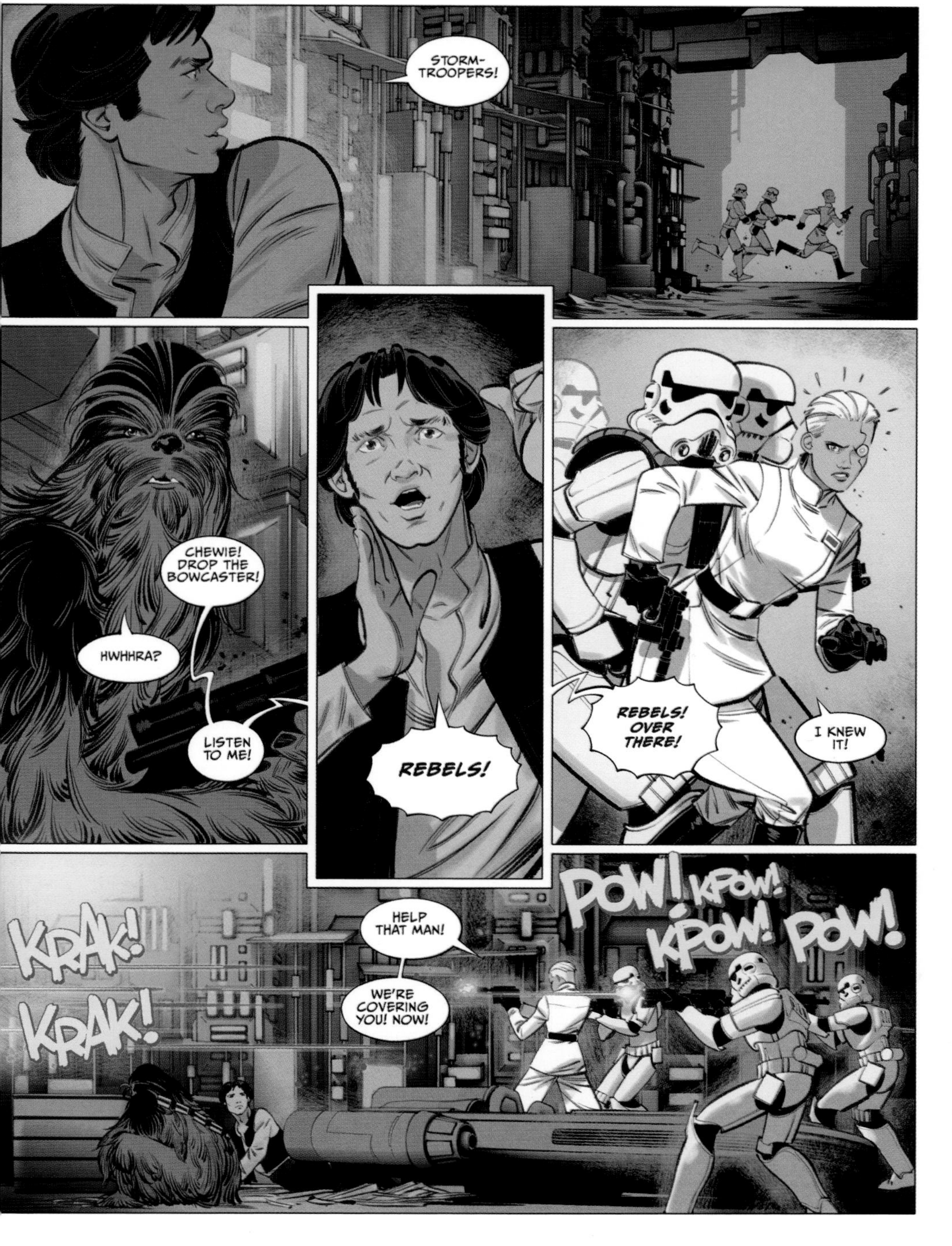
STORM-TROOPERS!
CHEWIE! DROP THE BOWCASTER!
HWHHRA?
LISTEN TO ME!
REBELS!
REBELS! OVER THERE!
I KNEW IT!
KRAK! KRAK!
HELP THAT MAN!
WE'RE COVERING YOU! NOW!
POW! KPOW! KPOW! POW!

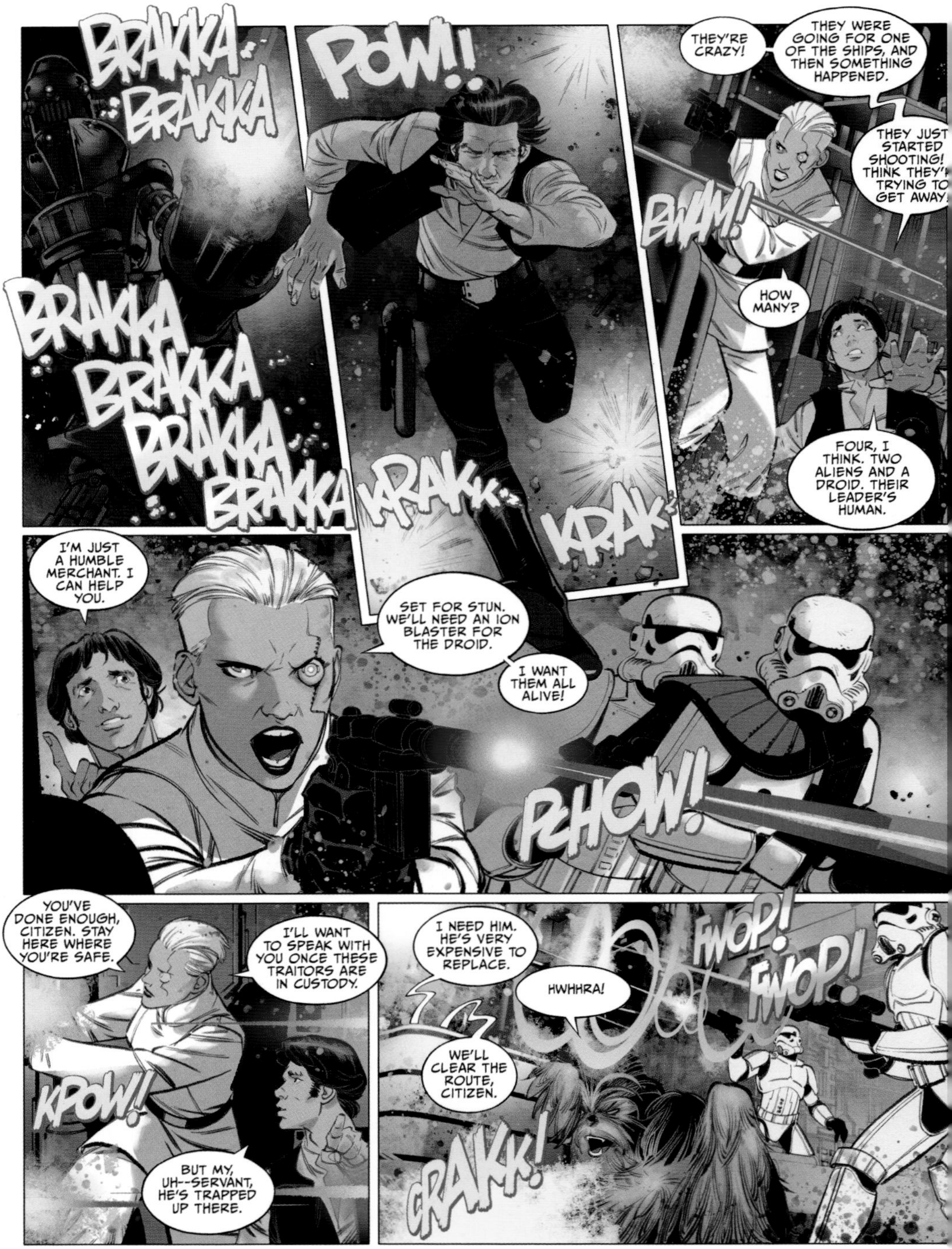
BRAKKA BRAKKA
POW!
THEY'RE CRAZY!
THEY WERE GOING FOR ONE OF THE SHIPS, AND THEN SOMETHING HAPPENED.
THEY JUST STARTED SHOOTING! THINK THEY'RE TRYING TO GET AWAY!
BWAM!
HOW MANY?
FOUR, I THINK. TWO ALIENS AND A DROID. THEIR LEADER'S HUMAN.
BRAKKA BRAKKA BRAKKA BRAKKA
KRAKK
KRAK
I'M JUST A HUMBLE MERCHANT. I CAN HELP YOU.
SET FOR STUN. WE'LL NEED AN ION BLASTER FOR THE DROID.
I WANT THEM ALL ALIVE!
PCHOW!
YOU'VE DONE ENOUGH, CITIZEN. STAY HERE WHERE YOU'RE SAFE.
I'LL WANT TO SPEAK WITH YOU ONCE THESE TRAITORS ARE IN CUSTODY.
KPOW!
BUT MY, UH--SERVANT, HE'S TRAPPED UP THERE.
I NEED HIM. HE'S VERY EXPENSIVE TO REPLACE.
HWHHRA!
WE'LL CLEAR THE ROUTE, CITIZEN.
FWOP! FWOP!
CRAKK!

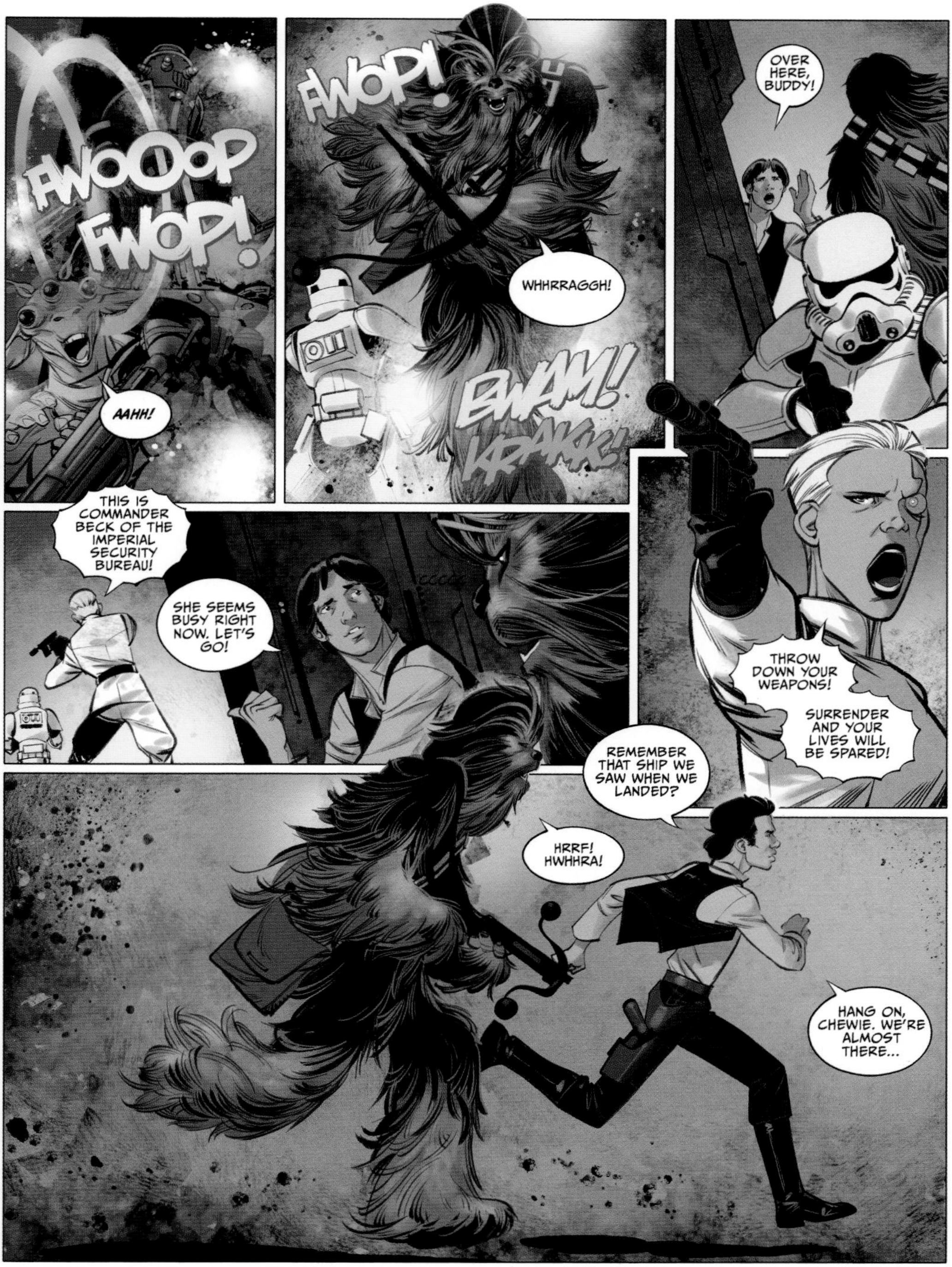

FWOOOP
FWOP!
AAHH!
FWOP!
WHHRRAGGH!
BWAM!
KRAKK!
OVER HERE, BUDDY!
THROW DOWN YOUR WEAPONS!
SURRENDER AND YOUR LIVES WILL BE SPARED!
THIS IS COMMANDER BECK OF THE IMPERIAL SECURITY BUREAU!
SHE SEEMS BUSY RIGHT NOW. LET'S GO!
REMEMBER THAT SHIP WE SAW WHEN WE LANDED?
HRRF! HWHHRA!
HANG ON, CHEWIE. WE'RE ALMOST THERE...

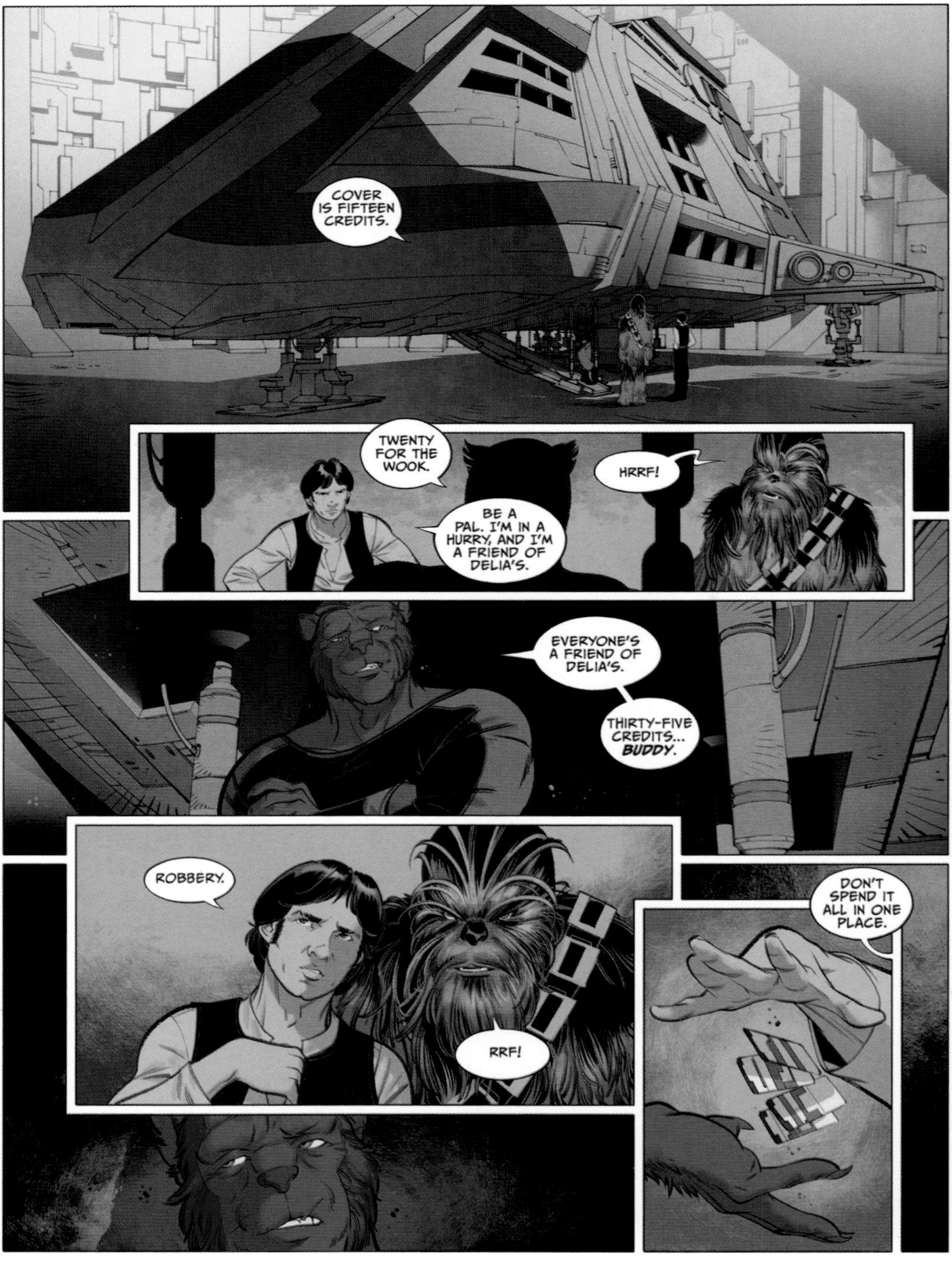
COVER IS FIFTEEN CREDITS.
TWENTY FOR THE WOOK.
BE A PAL. I'M IN A HURRY, AND I'M A FRIEND OF DELIA'S.
HRRF!
EVERYONE'S A FRIEND OF DELIA'S.
THIRTY-FIVE CREDITS... *BUDDY*.
ROBBERY.
RRF!
DON'T SPEND IT ALL IN ONE PLACE.

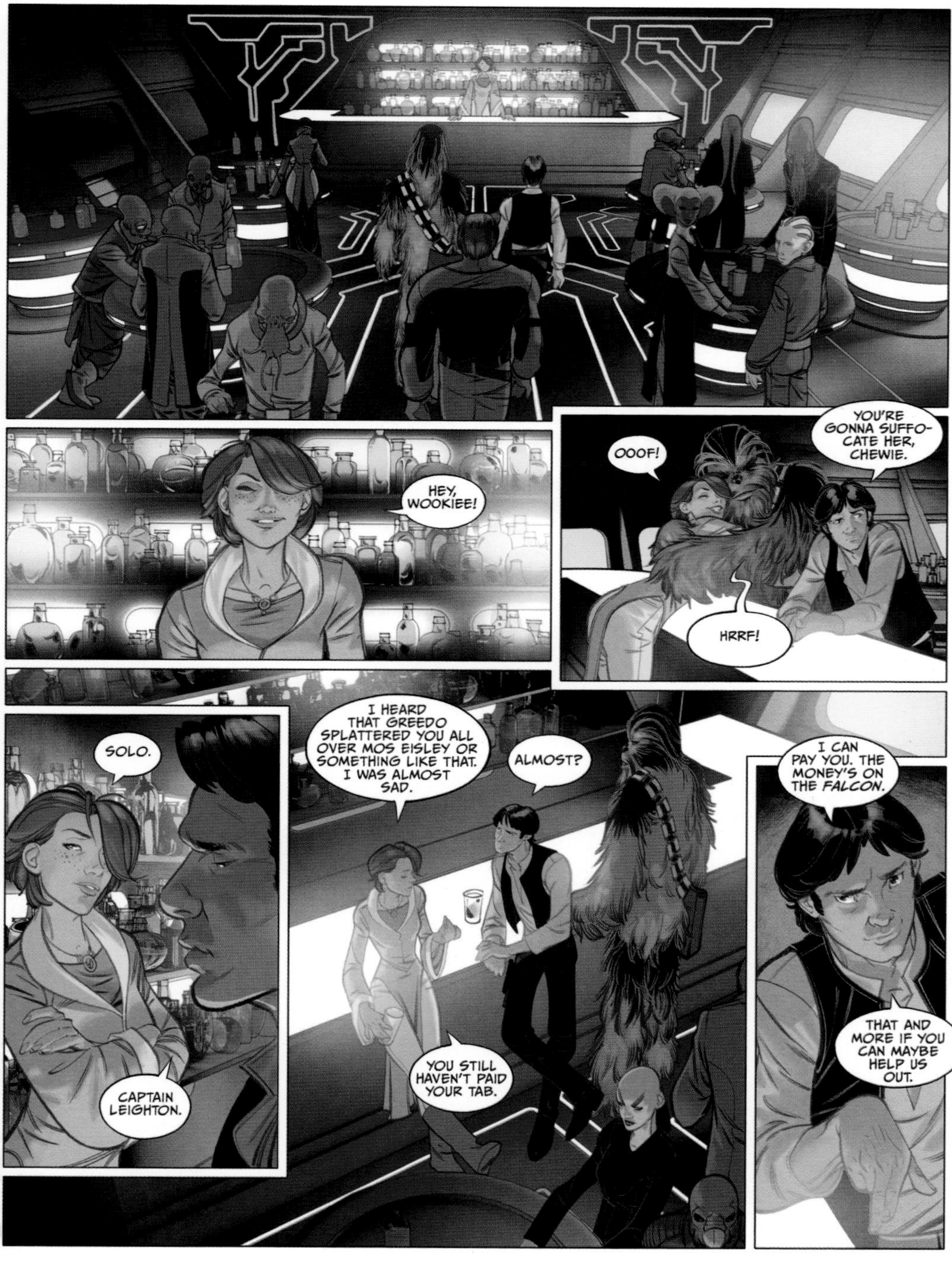
HEY, WOOKIEE!
OOOF!
YOU'RE GONNA SUFFOCATE HER, CHEWIE.
HRRF!
SOLO.
CAPTAIN LEIGHTON.
I HEARD THAT GREEDO SPLATTERED YOU ALL OVER MOS EISLEY OR SOMETHING LIKE THAT. I WAS ALMOST SAD.
ALMOST?
YOU STILL HAVEN'T PAID YOUR TAB.
I CAN PAY YOU. THE MONEY'S ON THE *FALCON*.
THAT AND MORE IF YOU CAN MAYBE HELP US OUT.

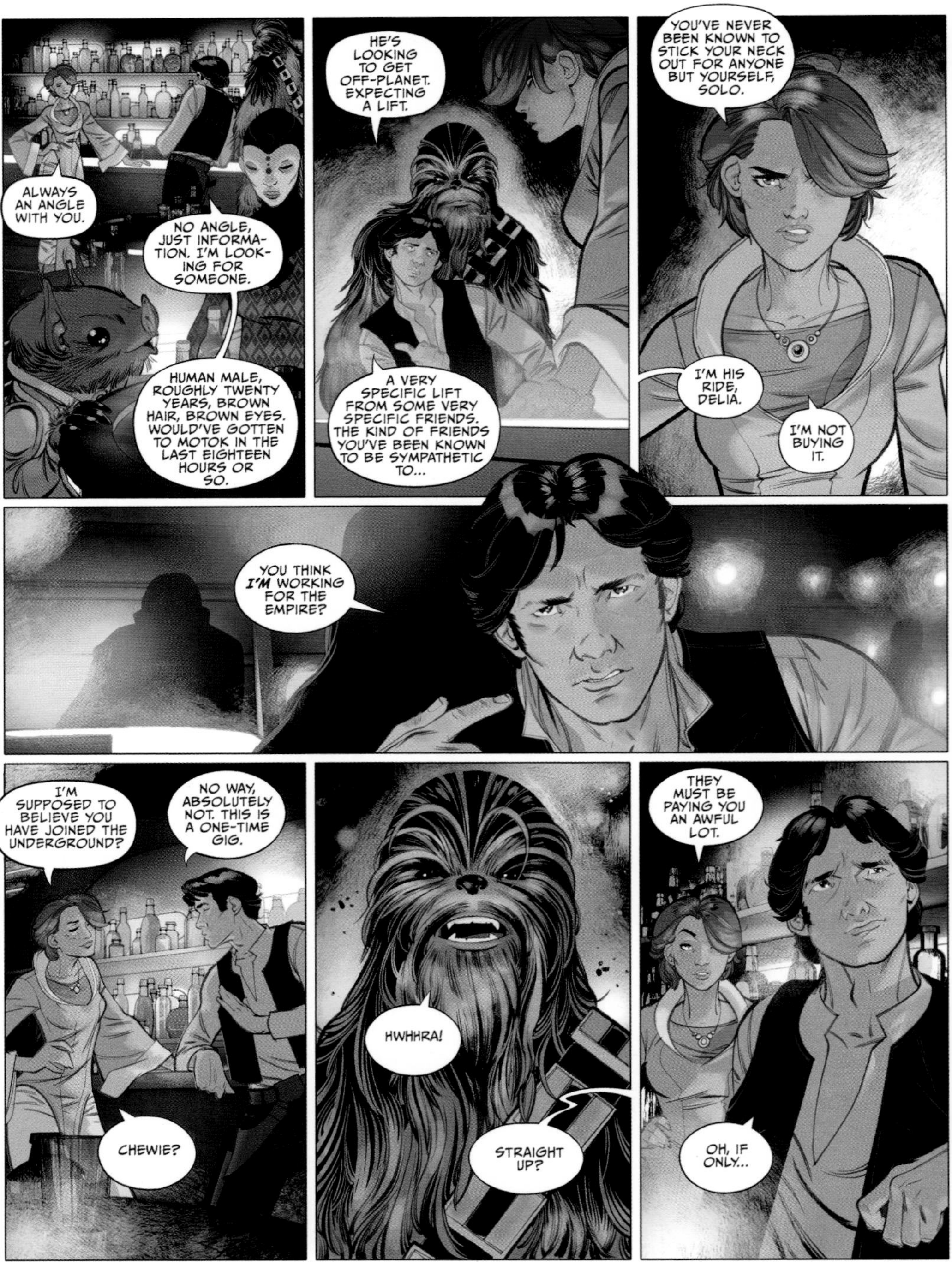
ALWAYS AN ANGLE WITH YOU.
NO ANGLE, JUST INFORMATION. I'M LOOKING FOR SOMEONE.
HUMAN MALE, ROUGHLY TWENTY YEARS, BROWN HAIR, BROWN EYES. WOULD'VE GOTTEN TO MOTOK IN THE LAST EIGHTEEN HOURS OR SO.
HE'S LOOKING TO GET OFF-PLANET. EXPECTING A LIFT.
A VERY SPECIFIC LIFT FROM SOME VERY SPECIFIC FRIENDS. THE KIND OF FRIENDS YOU'VE BEEN KNOWN TO BE SYMPATHETIC TO...
YOU'VE NEVER BEEN KNOWN TO STICK YOUR NECK OUT FOR ANYONE BUT YOURSELF, SOLO.
I'M HIS RIDE, DELIA.
I'M NOT BUYING IT.
YOU THINK I'M WORKING FOR THE EMPIRE?
I'M SUPPOSED TO BELIEVE YOU HAVE JOINED THE UNDERGROUND?
NO WAY, ABSOLUTELY NOT. THIS IS A ONE-TIME GIG.
CHEWIE?
HWHHRA!
STRAIGHT UP?
THEY MUST BE PAYING YOU AN AWFUL LOT.
OH, IF ONLY...

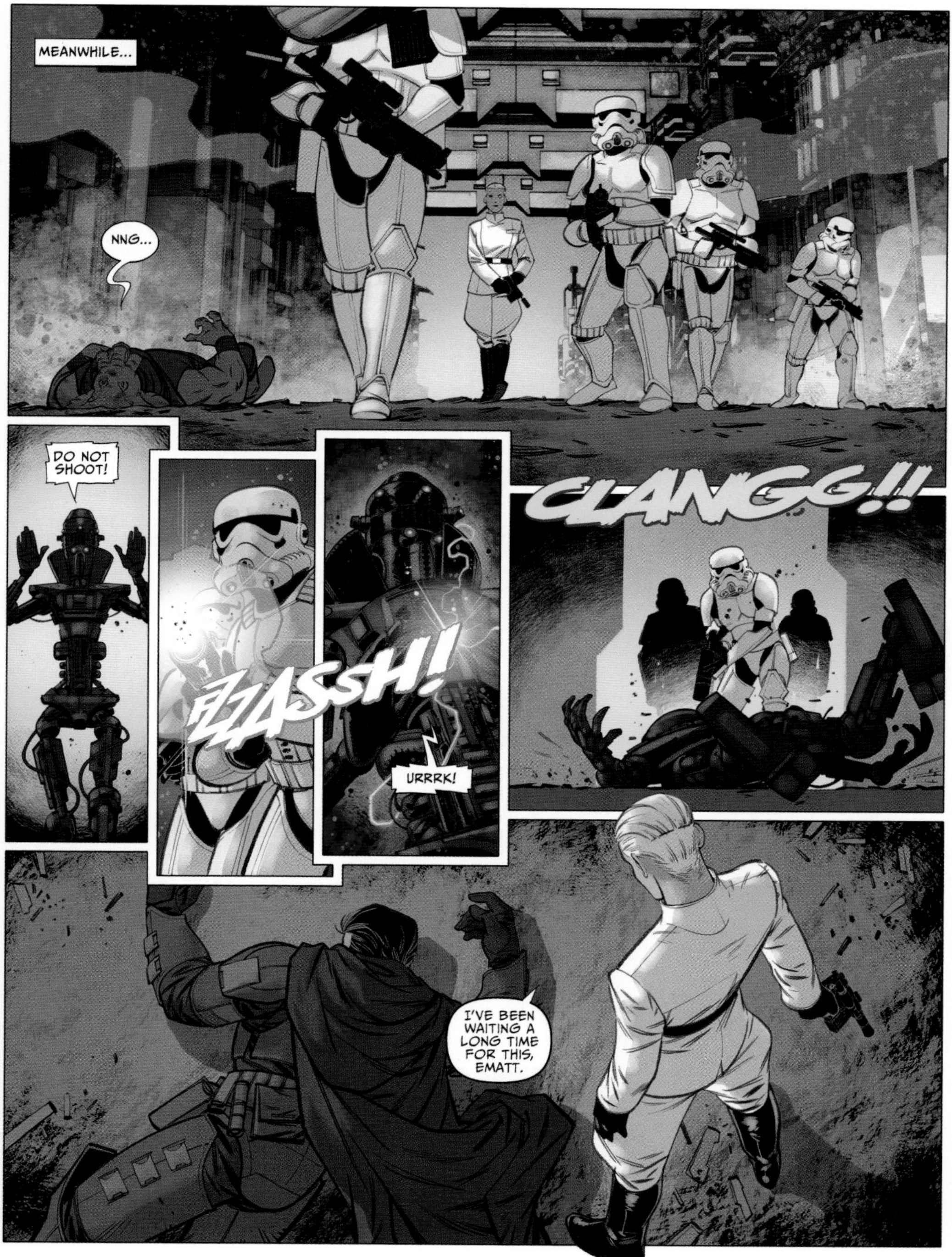
MEANWHILE...
NNG...
DO NOT SHOOT!
FZZASSH!
URRRK!
CLANGG!!
I'VE BEEN WAITING A LONG TIME FOR THIS, EMATT.

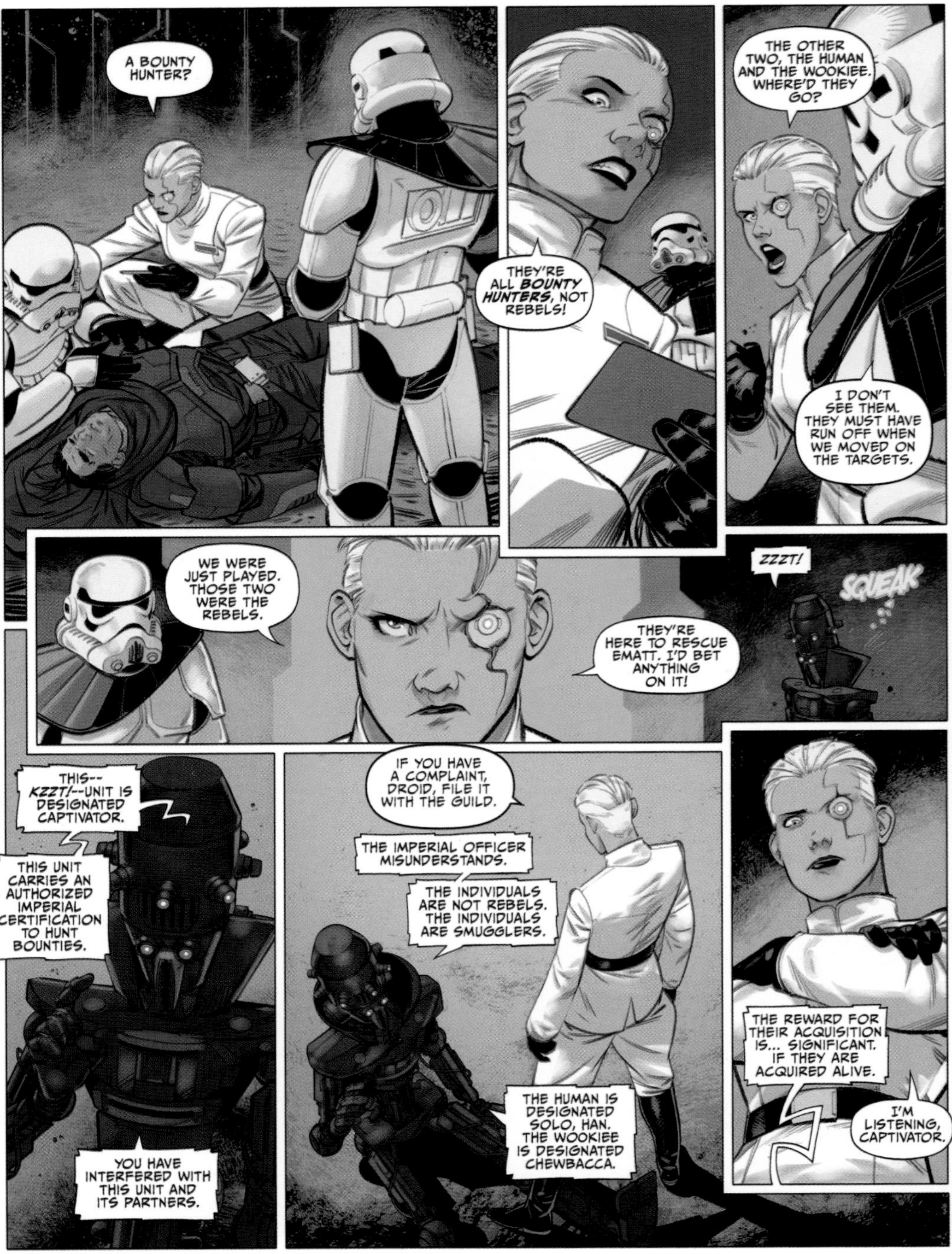

A BOUNTY HUNTER?
THEY'RE ALL ***BOUNTY HUNTERS***, NOT REBELS!
THE OTHER TWO, THE HUMAN AND THE WOOKIEE. WHERE'D THEY GO?
I DON'T SEE THEM. THEY MUST HAVE RUN OFF WHEN WE MOVED ON THE TARGETS.
WE WERE JUST PLAYED. THOSE TWO WERE THE REBELS.
THEY'RE HERE TO RESCUE EMATT. I'D BET ANYTHING ON IT!
ZZZT!
SQUEAK
THIS-- *KZZT!*--UNIT IS DESIGNATED CAPTIVATOR.
THIS UNIT CARRIES AN AUTHORIZED IMPERIAL CERTIFICATION TO HUNT BOUNTIES.
YOU HAVE INTERFERED WITH THIS UNIT AND ITS PARTNERS.
IF YOU HAVE A COMPLAINT, DROID, FILE IT WITH THE GUILD.
THE IMPERIAL OFFICER MISUNDERSTANDS.
THE INDIVIDUALS ARE NOT REBELS. THE INDIVIDUALS ARE SMUGGLERS.
THE HUMAN IS DESIGNATED SOLO, HAN. THE WOOKIEE IS DESIGNATED CHEWBACCA.
THE REWARD FOR THEIR ACQUISITION IS... SIGNIFICANT. IF THEY ARE ACQUIRED ALIVE.
I'M LISTENING, CAPTIVATOR.

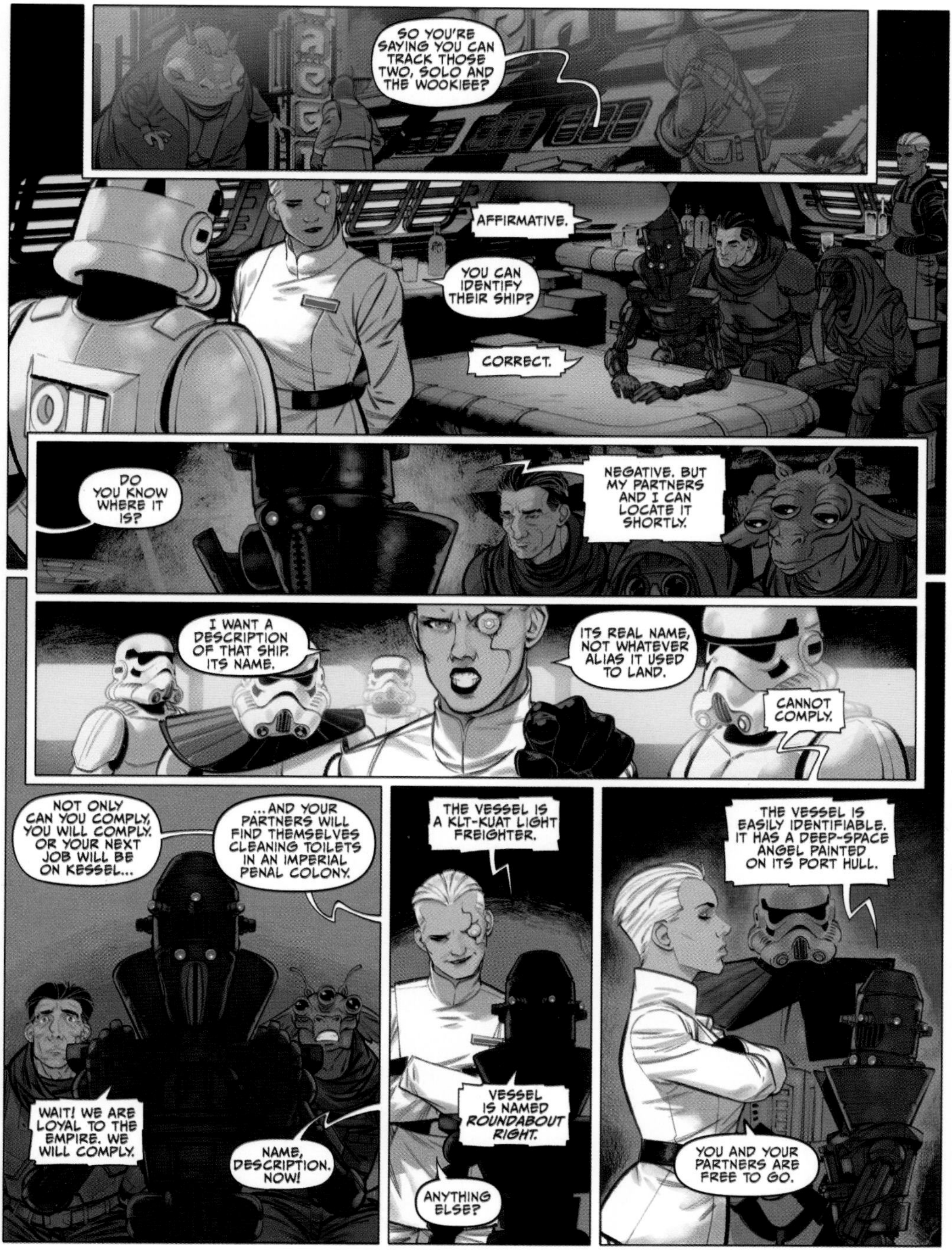
SO YOU'RE SAYING YOU CAN TRACK THOSE TWO, SOLO AND THE WOOKIEE?
AFFIRMATIVE.
YOU CAN IDENTIFY THEIR SHIP?
CORRECT.
DO YOU KNOW WHERE IT IS?
NEGATIVE. BUT MY PARTNERS AND I CAN LOCATE IT SHORTLY.
I WANT A DESCRIPTION OF THAT SHIP. ITS NAME.
ITS REAL NAME, NOT WHATEVER ALIAS IT USED TO LAND.
CANNOT COMPLY.
NOT ONLY CAN YOU COMPLY, YOU WILL COMPLY. OR YOUR NEXT JOB WILL BE ON KESSEL...
...AND YOUR PARTNERS WILL FIND THEMSELVES CLEANING TOILETS IN AN IMPERIAL PENAL COLONY.
WAIT! WE ARE LOYAL TO THE EMPIRE. WE WILL COMPLY.
NAME, DESCRIPTION. NOW!
THE VESSEL IS A KLT-KUAT LIGHT FREIGHTER.
VESSEL IS NAMED *ROUNDABOUT RIGHT.*
ANYTHING ELSE?
THE VESSEL IS EASILY IDENTIFIABLE. IT HAS A DEEP-SPACE ANGEL PAINTED ON ITS PORT HULL.
YOU AND YOUR PARTNERS ARE FREE TO GO.

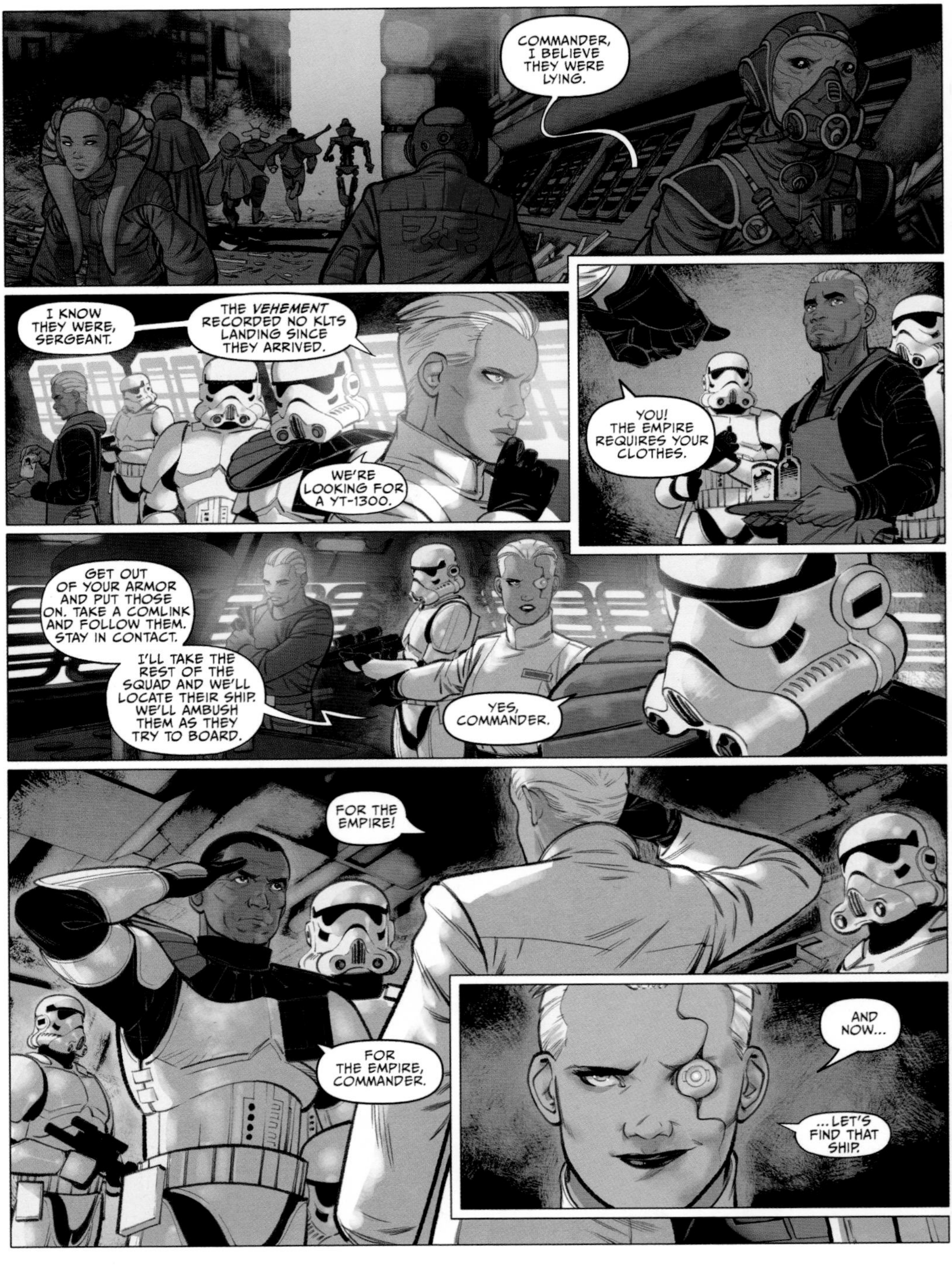
COMMANDER, I BELIEVE THEY WERE LYING.
I KNOW THEY WERE, SERGEANT.
THE *VEHEMENT* RECORDED NO KLTS LANDING SINCE THEY ARRIVED.
WE'RE LOOKING FOR A YT-1300.
YOU! THE EMPIRE REQUIRES YOUR CLOTHES.
GET OUT OF YOUR ARMOR AND PUT THOSE ON. TAKE A COMLINK AND FOLLOW THEM. STAY IN CONTACT.
I'LL TAKE THE REST OF THE SQUAD AND WE'LL LOCATE THEIR SHIP. WE'LL AMBUSH THEM AS THEY TRY TO BOARD.
YES, COMMANDER.
FOR THE EMPIRE!
FOR THE EMPIRE, COMMANDER.
AND NOW...
...LET'S FIND THAT SHIP.

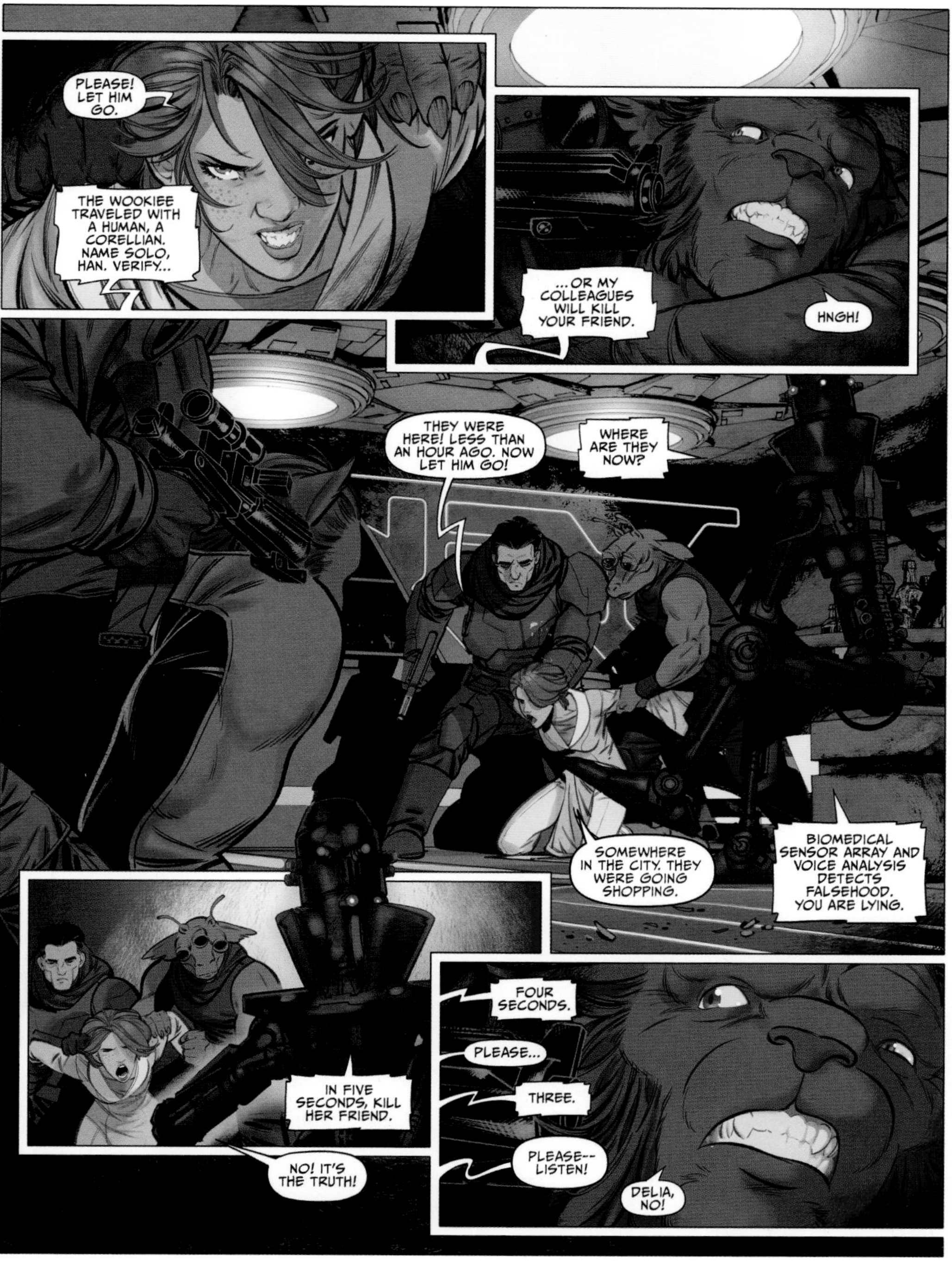
PLEASE! LET HIM GO.
THE WOOKIEE TRAVELED WITH A HUMAN, A CORELLIAN. NAME SOLO, HAN. VERIFY...
...OR MY COLLEAGUES WILL KILL YOUR FRIEND.
HNGH!
THEY WERE HERE! LESS THAN AN HOUR AGO. NOW LET HIM GO!
WHERE ARE THEY NOW?
SOMEWHERE IN THE CITY. THEY WERE GOING SHOPPING.
BIOMEDICAL SENSOR ARRAY AND VOICE ANALYSIS DETECTS FALSEHOOD. YOU ARE LYING.
IN FIVE SECONDS, KILL HER FRIEND.
NO! IT'S THE TRUTH!
FOUR SECONDS.
PLEASE...
THREE.
PLEASE-- LISTEN!
DELIA, NO!

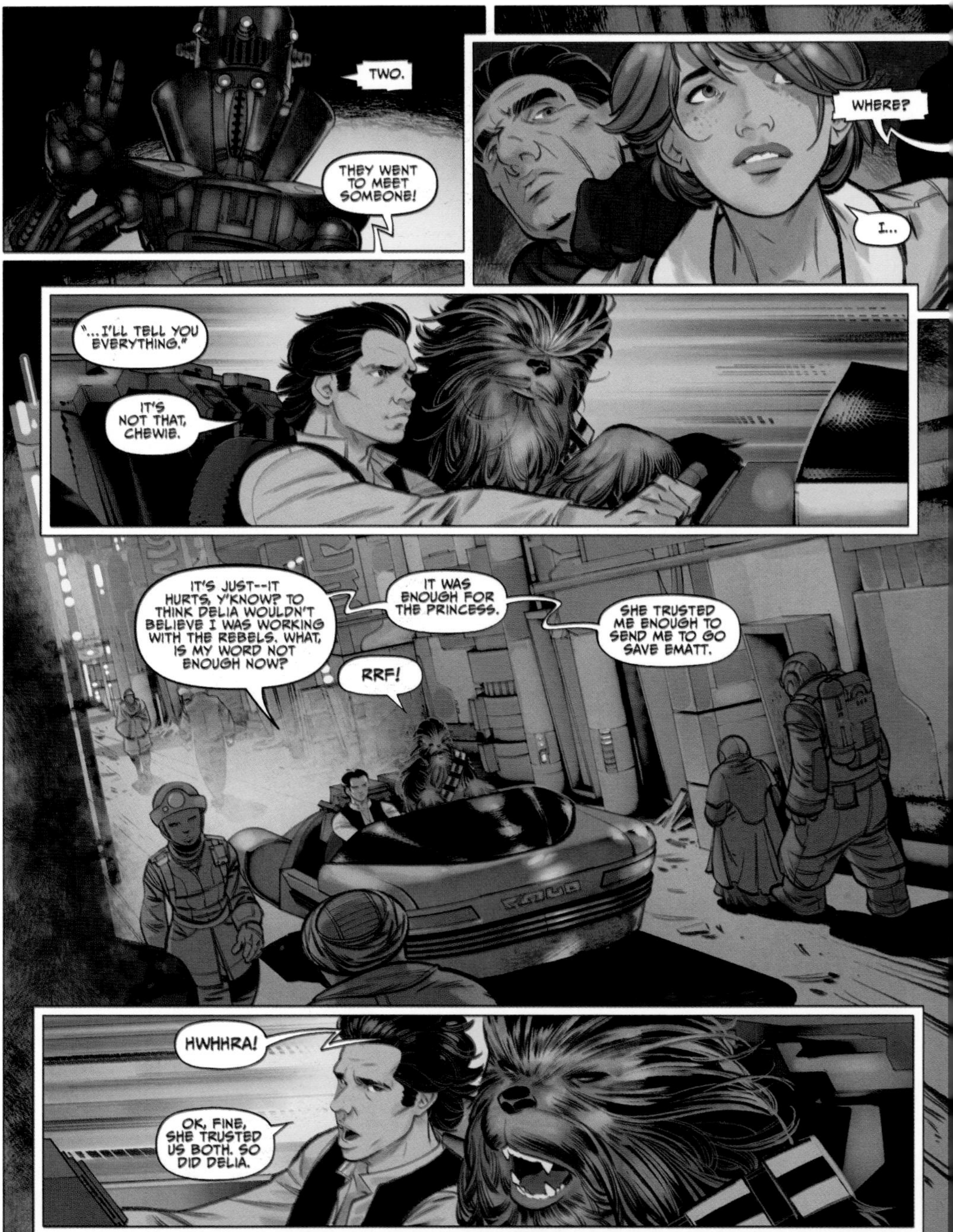
TWO.
THEY WENT TO MEET SOMEONE!
WHERE?
I...
"...I'LL TELL YOU EVERYTHING."
IT'S NOT THAT, CHEWIE.
IT'S JUST--IT HURTS, Y'KNOW? TO THINK DELIA WOULDN'T BELIEVE I WAS WORKING WITH THE REBELS. WHAT, IS MY WORD NOT ENOUGH NOW?
RRF!
IT WAS ENOUGH FOR THE PRINCESS.
SHE TRUSTED ME ENOUGH TO SEND ME TO GO SAVE EMATT.
HWHHRA!
OK, FINE, SHE TRUSTED US BOTH. SO DID DELIA.

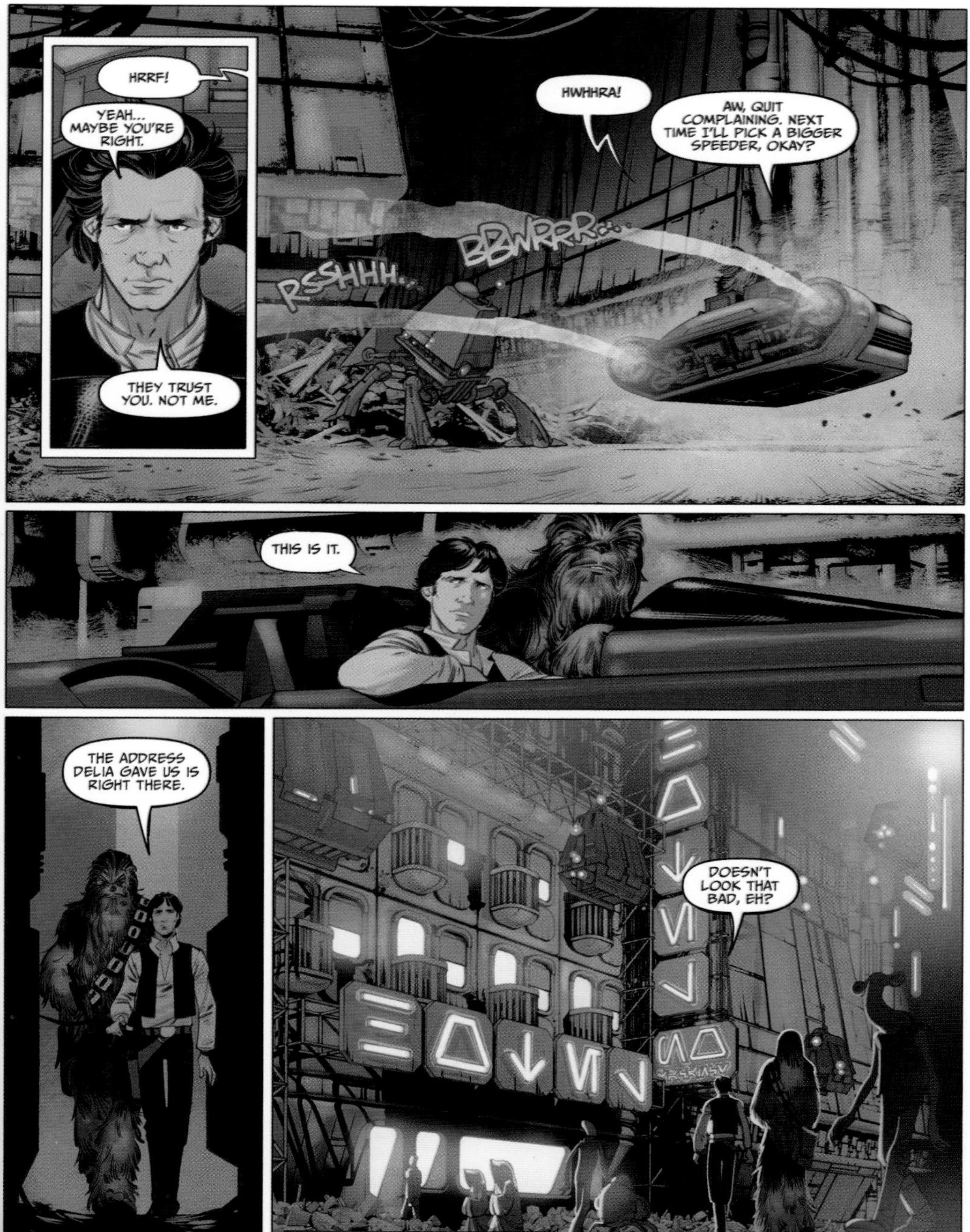
HRRF!
YEAH... MAYBE YOU'RE RIGHT.
THEY TRUST YOU. NOT ME.
HWHHRA!
AW, QUIT COMPLAINING. NEXT TIME I'LL PICK A BIGGER SPEEDER, OKAY?
BBWRRR...
RSSHHH...
THIS IS IT.
THE ADDRESS DELIA GAVE US IS RIGHT THERE.
DOESN'T LOOK THAT BAD, EH?
SIGN: HOTEL, NO VACANCY

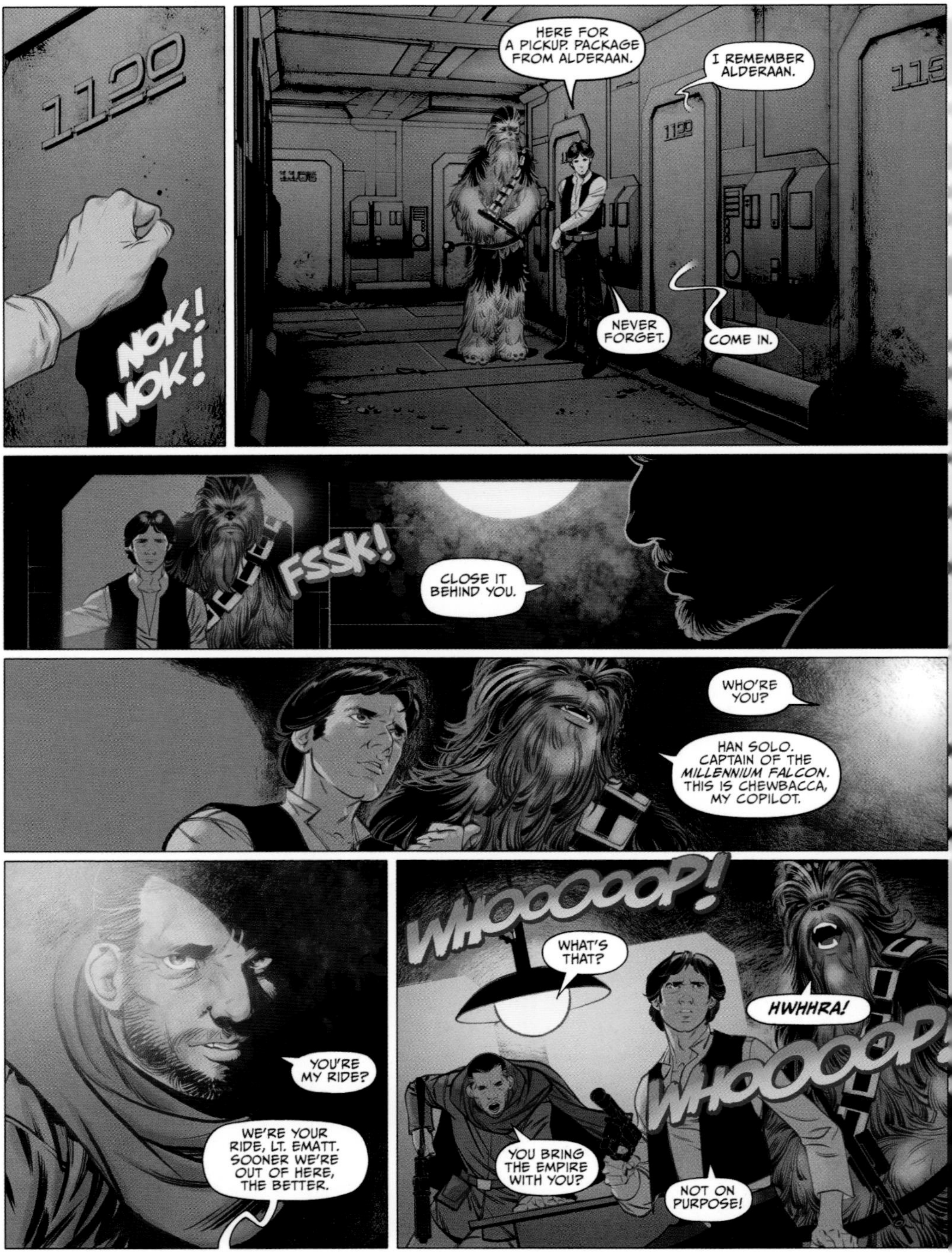
NOK! NOK!
HERE FOR A PICKUP. PACKAGE FROM ALDERAAN.
I REMEMBER ALDERAAN.
NEVER FORGET.
COME IN.
FSSK!
CLOSE IT BEHIND YOU.
WHO'RE YOU?
HAN SOLO. CAPTAIN OF THE *MILLENNIUM FALCON*. THIS IS CHEWBACCA, MY COPILOT.
YOU'RE MY RIDE?
WE'RE YOUR RIDE, LT. EMATT. SOONER WE'RE OUT OF HERE, THE BETTER.
WHOOOOOP!
WHAT'S THAT?
HWHHRA!
WHOOOOP!
YOU BRING THE EMPIRE WITH YOU?
NOT ON PURPOSE!

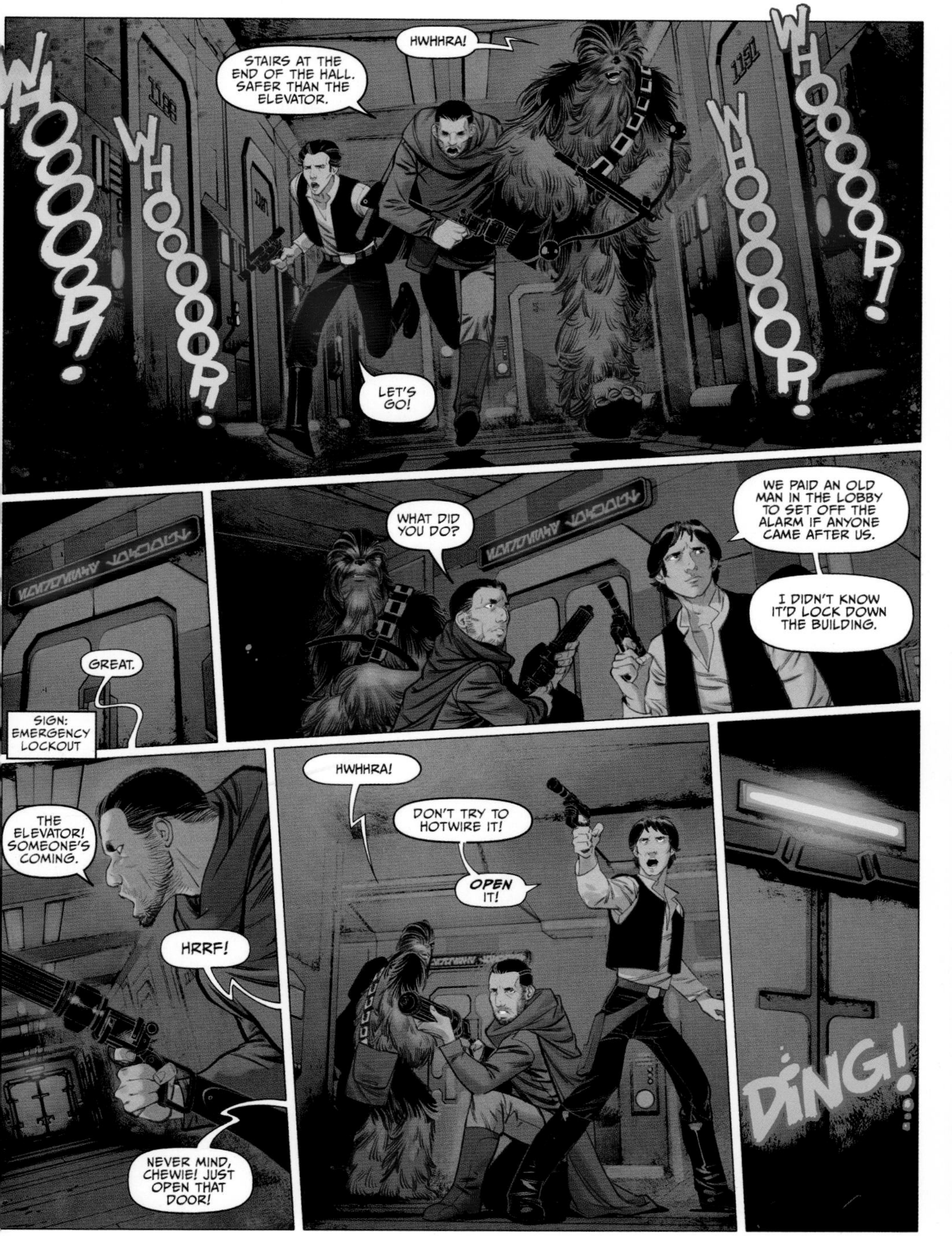
WHOOOOOR!
WHOOOOOR!
STAIRS AT THE END OF THE HALL. SAFER THAN THE ELEVATOR.
HWHHRA!
WHOOOOOR!
WHOOOOOR!
LET'S GO!
SIGN: EMERGENCY LOCKOUT
GREAT.
WHAT DID YOU DO?
WE PAID AN OLD MAN IN THE LOBBY TO SET OFF THE ALARM IF ANYONE CAME AFTER US.
I DIDN'T KNOW IT'D LOCK DOWN THE BUILDING.
THE ELEVATOR! SOMEONE'S COMING.
HRRF!
NEVER MIND, CHEWIE! JUST OPEN THAT DOOR!
HWHHRA!
DON'T TRY TO HOTWIRE IT!
OPEN IT!
DING!

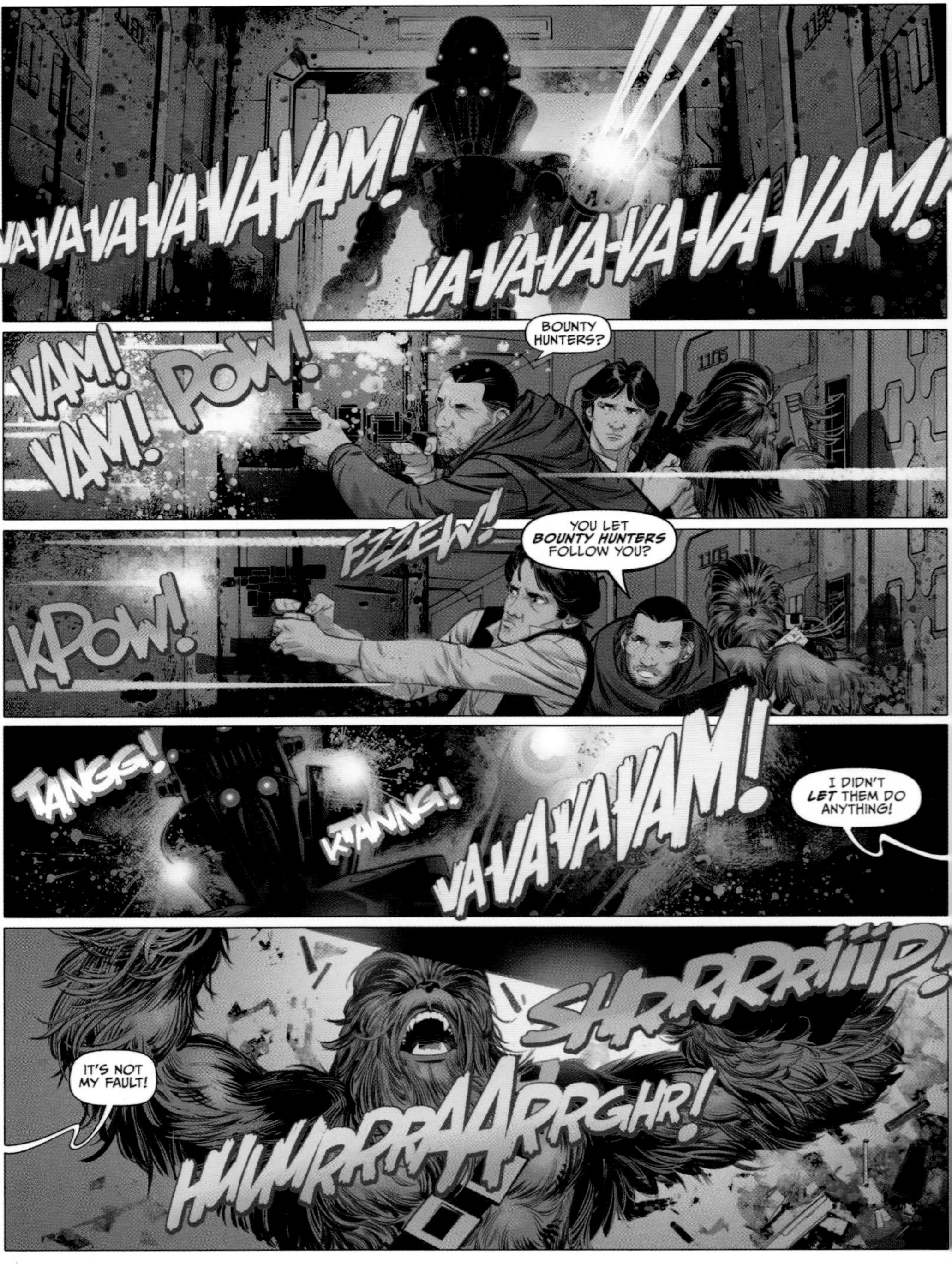
VA-VA-VA-VA-VA-VAM!
VA-VA-VA-VA-VA-VA-VAM!
VAM!
VAM!
POW!
BOUNTY HUNTERS?
FZZEW!
KPOW!
YOU LET *BOUNTY HUNTERS* FOLLOW YOU?
TANGG!
K'TANNG!
VA-VA-VA-VAM!
I DIDN'T *LET* THEM DO ANYTHING!
SHRRRRIIIP!
IT'S NOT MY FAULT!
HUURRRAARRGHR!

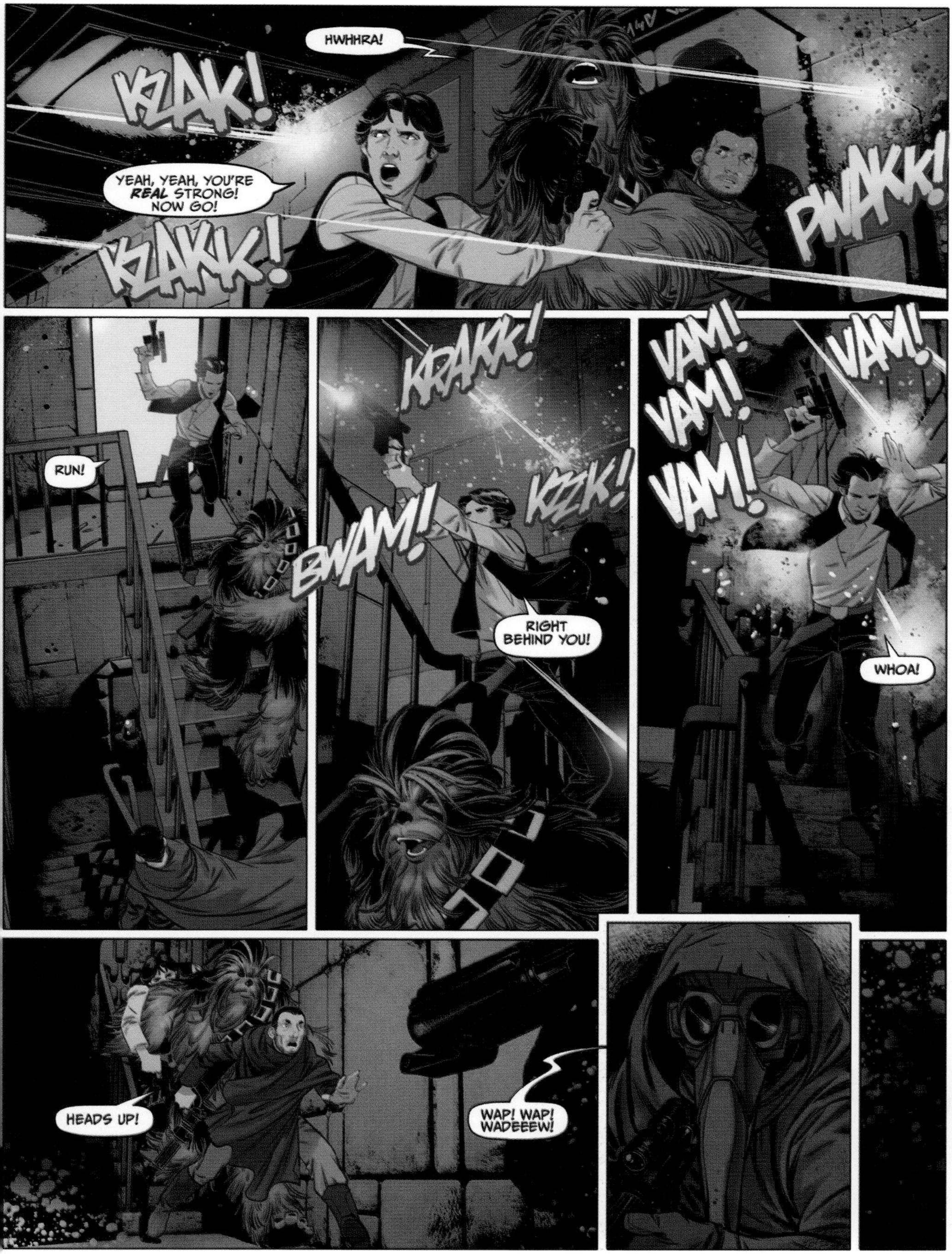
HWHHRA!
KZAK!
YEAH, YEAH, YOU'RE REAL STRONG! NOW GO!
KZAKK!
PWAKK!
RUN!
KRAKK!
BWAM!
KZZK!
RIGHT BEHIND YOU!
VAM!
VAM!
VAM!
VAM!
WHOA!
HEADS UP!
WAP! WAP! WADEEEW!

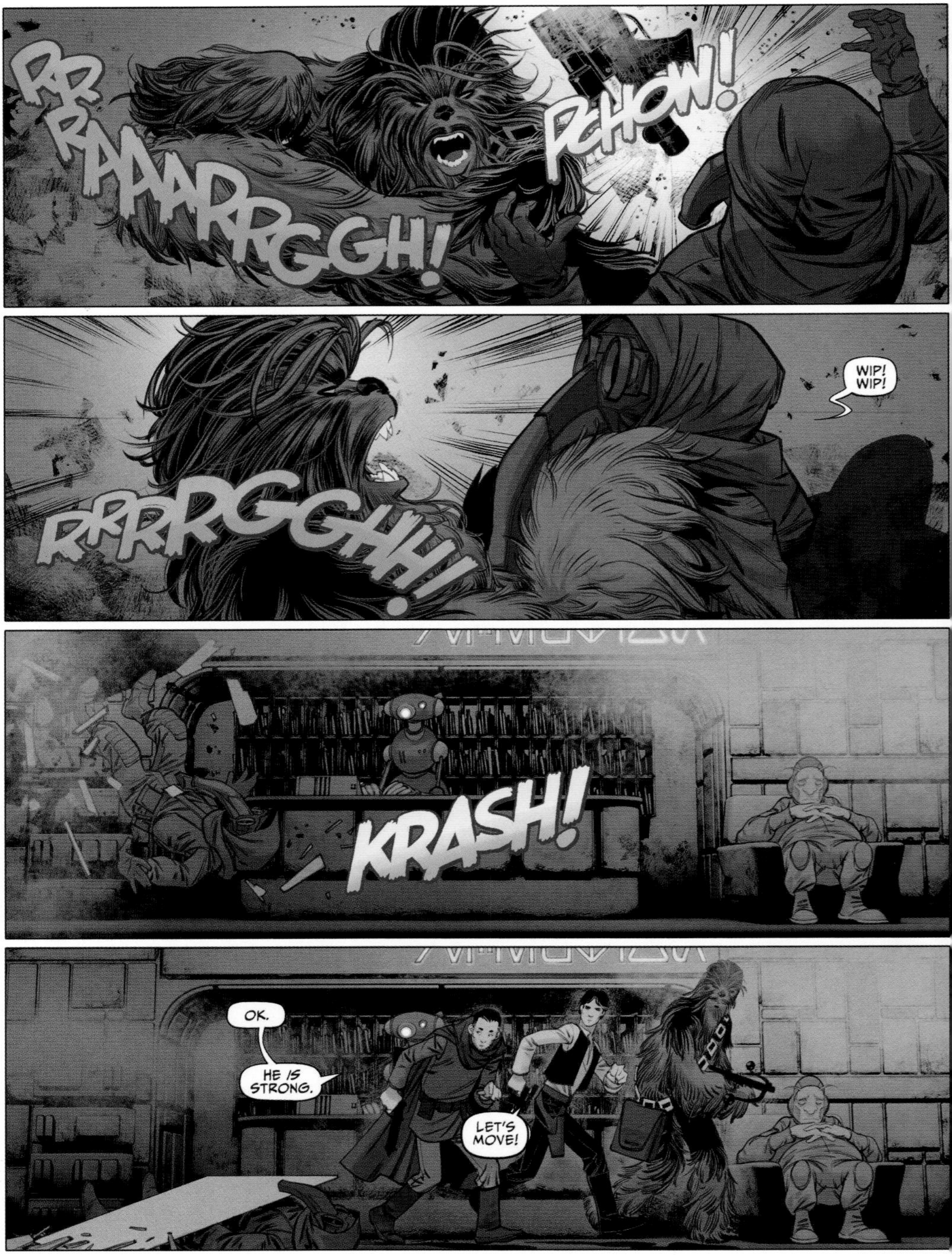
RRRAAARRGGH!
PCHOW!
RRRRGGHH!
WIP! WIP!
KRASH!
OK.
HE IS STRONG.
LET'S MOVE!

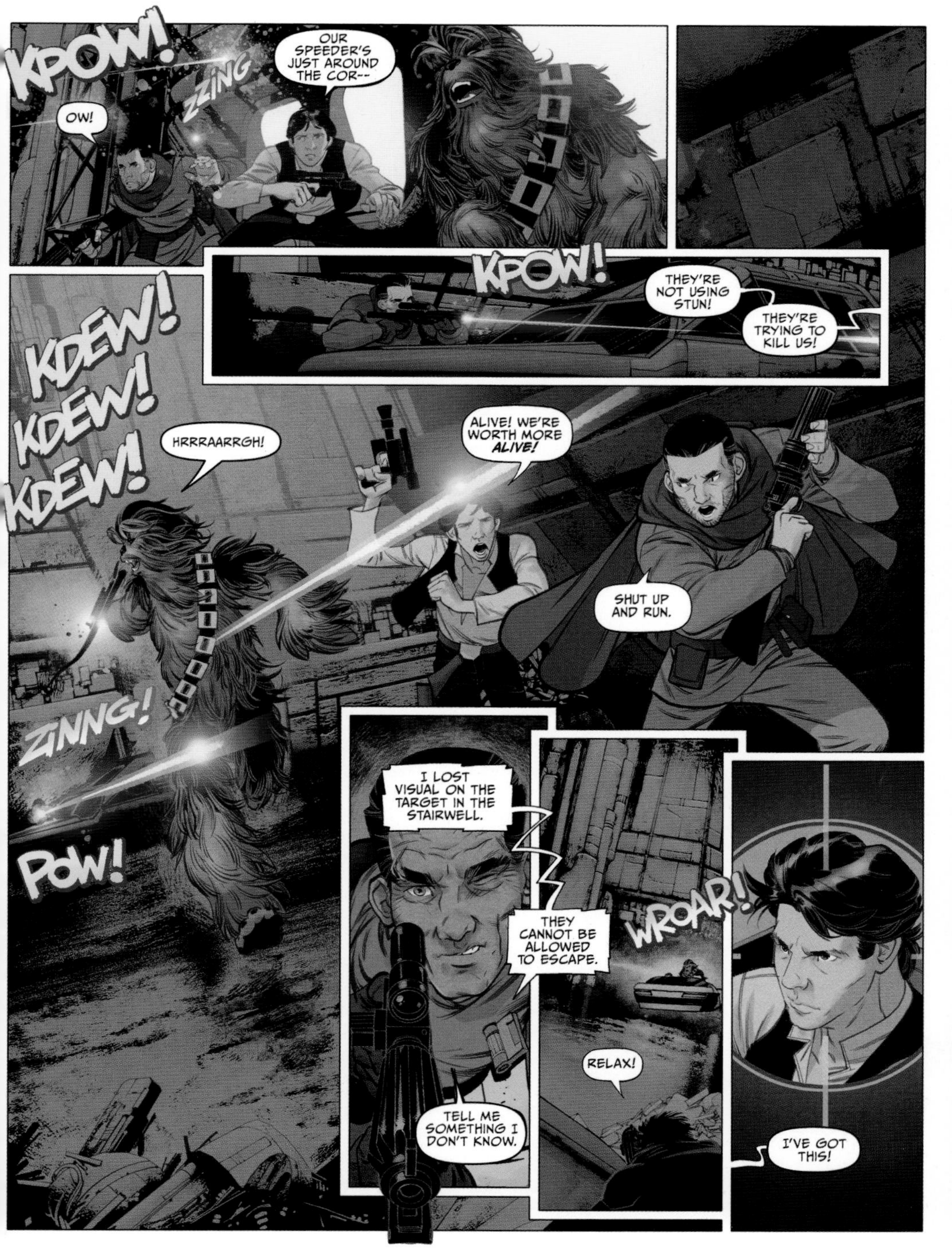
KPOW!
OW!
ZZING
OUR SPEEDER'S JUST AROUND THE COR--
KPOW!
THEY'RE NOT USING STUN!
THEY'RE TRYING TO KILL US!
KDEW! KDEW! KDEW!
HRRRAARRGH!
ALIVE! WE'RE WORTH MORE *ALIVE!*
SHUT UP AND RUN.
ZINNG!
POW!
I LOST VISUAL ON THE TARGET IN THE STAIRWELL.
THEY CANNOT BE ALLOWED TO ESCAPE.
TELL ME SOMETHING I DON'T KNOW.
WROAR!
RELAX!
I'VE GOT THIS!

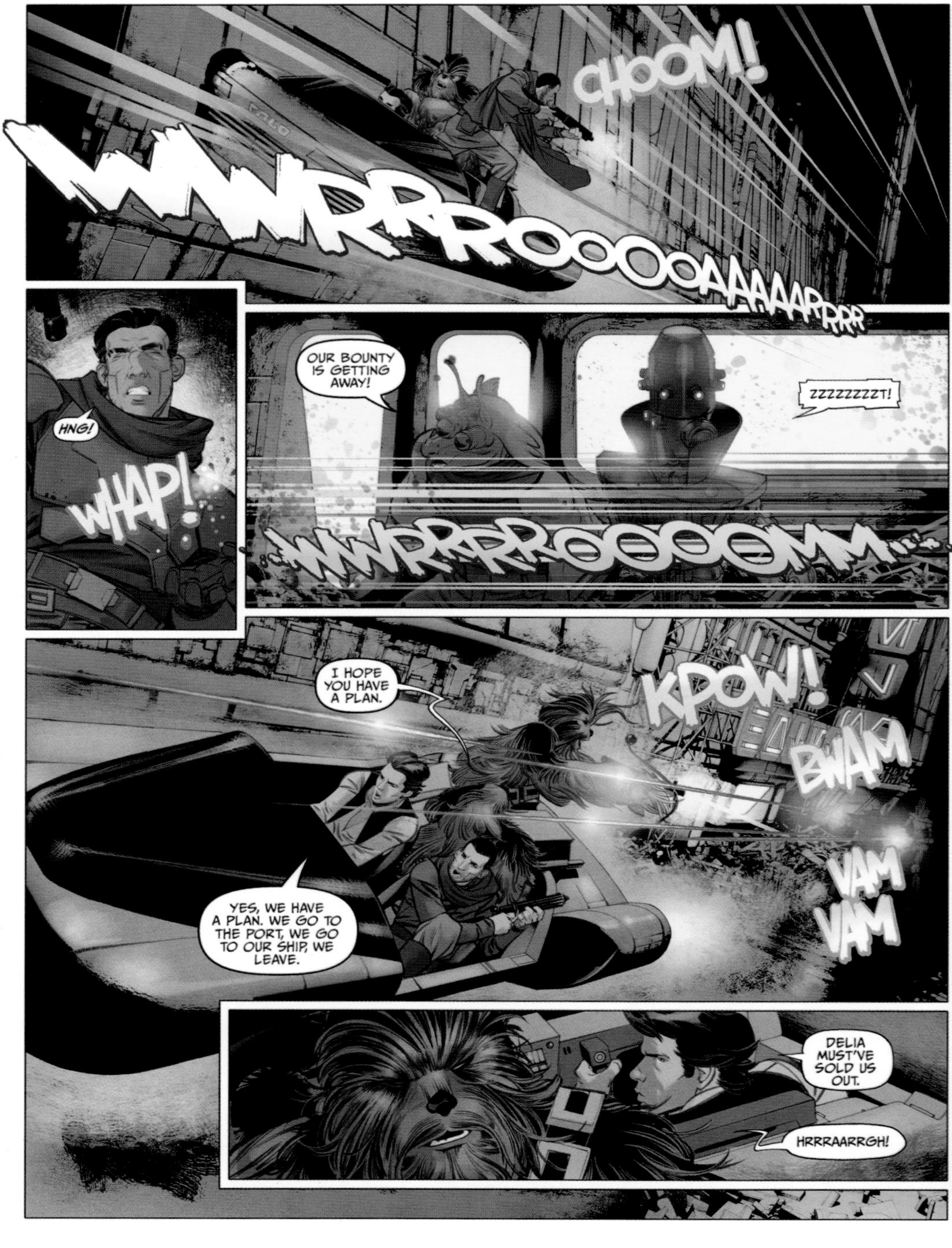
CHOOM!
WWRRROOOOOAAAAARRRR
HNG!
WHAP!
OUR BOUNTY IS GETTING AWAY!
ZZZZZZZZT!
WWRRRROOOOOMM...
I HOPE YOU HAVE A PLAN.
KPOW!
BWAM
VAM VAM
YES, WE HAVE A PLAN. WE GO TO THE PORT, WE GO TO OUR SHIP, WE LEAVE.
DELIA MUST'VE SOLD US OUT.
HRRRAARRGH!

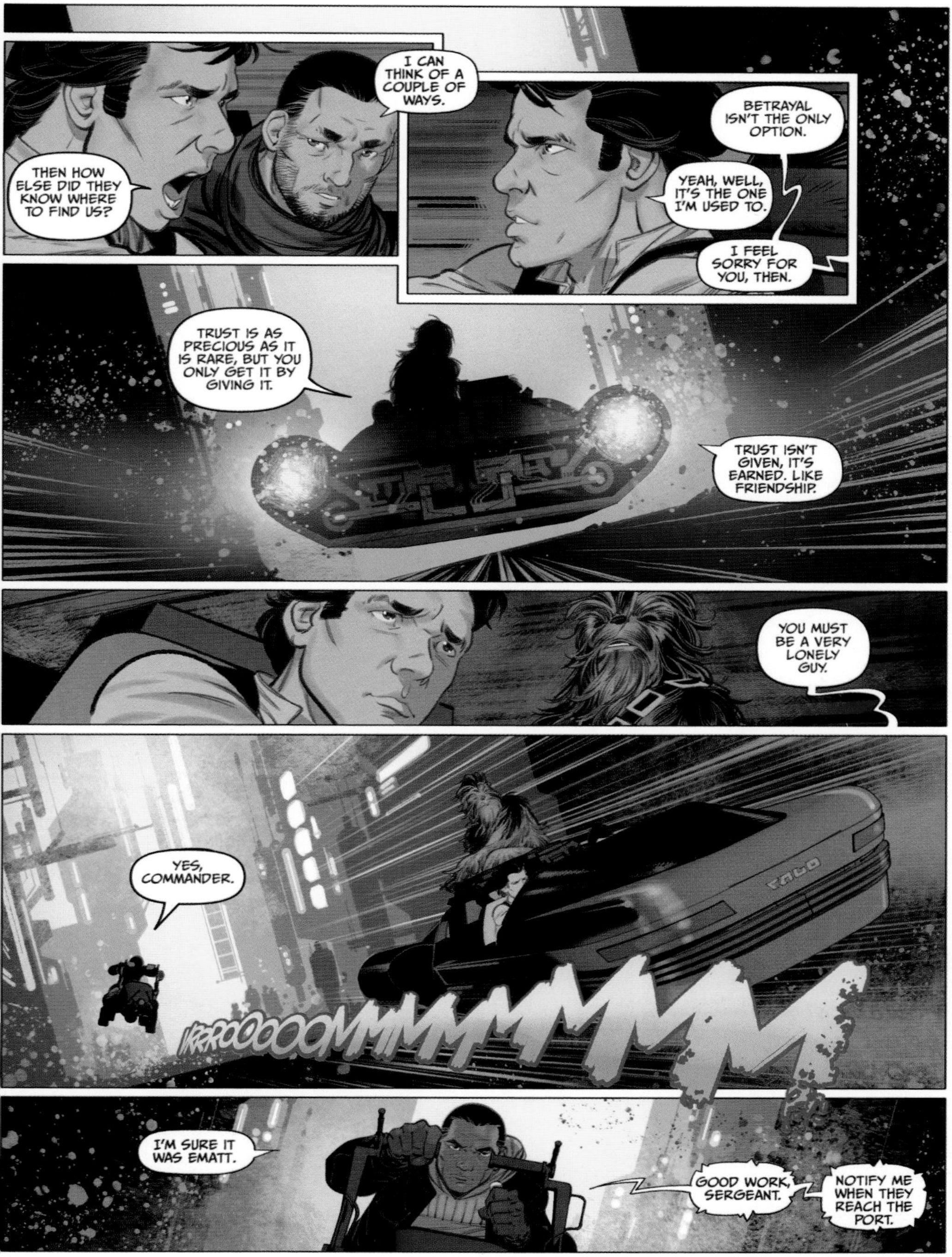
I CAN THINK OF A COUPLE OF WAYS.
THEN HOW ELSE DID THEY KNOW WHERE TO FIND US?
BETRAYAL ISN'T THE ONLY OPTION.
YEAH, WELL, IT'S THE ONE I'M USED TO.
I FEEL SORRY FOR YOU, THEN.
TRUST IS AS PRECIOUS AS IT IS RARE, BUT YOU ONLY GET IT BY GIVING IT.
TRUST ISN'T GIVEN, IT'S EARNED. LIKE FRIENDSHIP.
YOU MUST BE A VERY LONELY GUY.
YES, COMMANDER.
VRRROOOOOOMMMMMMMMM
I'M SURE IT WAS EMATT.
GOOD WORK, SERGEANT.
NOTIFY ME WHEN THEY REACH THE PORT.

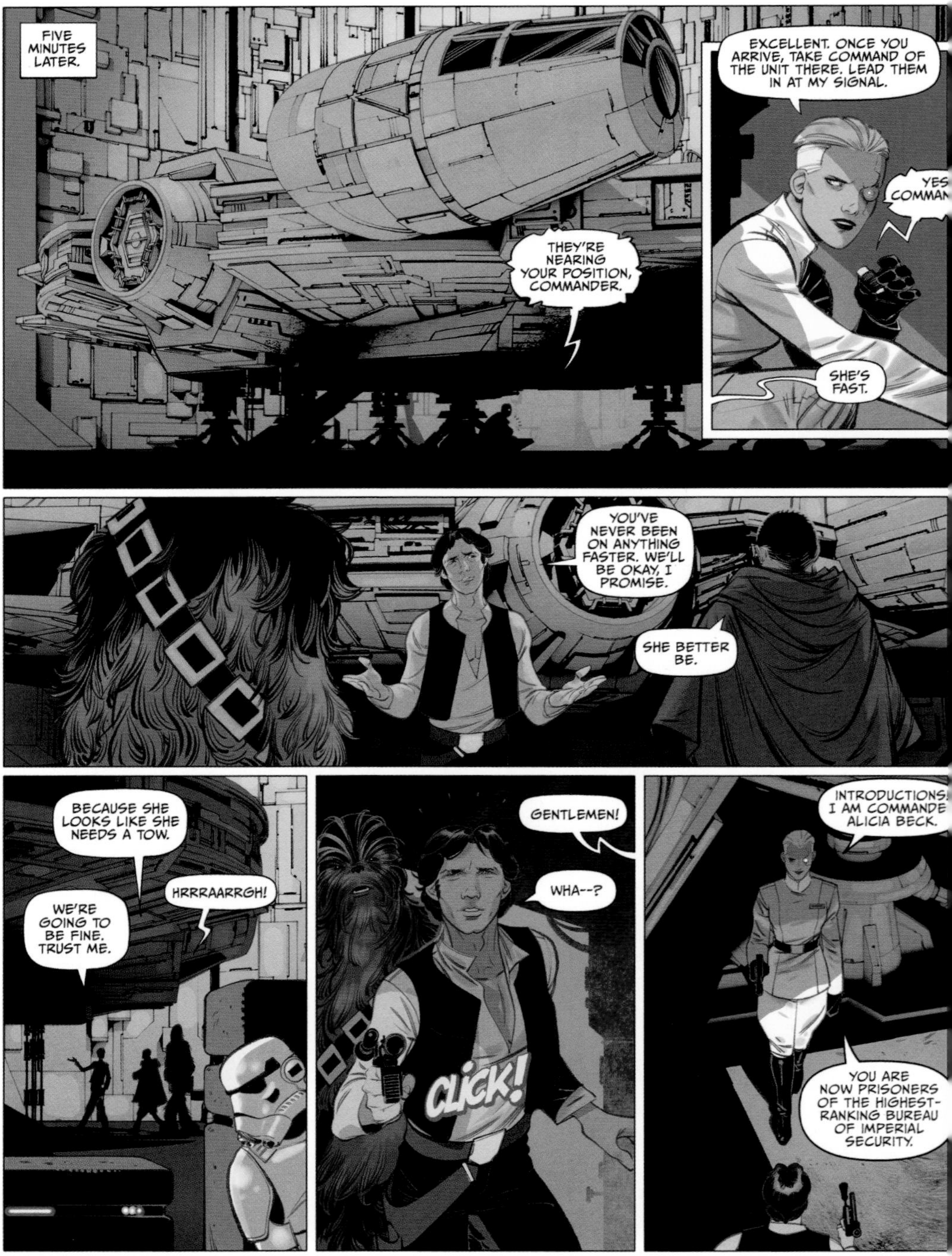
FIVE MINUTES LATER.
THEY'RE NEARING YOUR POSITION, COMMANDER.
EXCELLENT. ONCE YOU ARRIVE, TAKE COMMAND OF THE UNIT THERE. LEAD THEM IN AT MY SIGNAL.
YES COMMAN
SHE'S FAST.
YOU'VE NEVER BEEN ON ANYTHING FASTER. WE'LL BE OKAY, I PROMISE.
SHE BETTER BE.
BECAUSE SHE LOOKS LIKE SHE NEEDS A TOW.
HRRRAARRGH!
WE'RE GOING TO BE FINE. TRUST ME.
GENTLEMEN!
WHA--?
CLICK!
INTRODUCTIONS! I AM COMMANDE ALICIA BECK.
YOU ARE NOW PRISONERS OF THE HIGHEST-RANKING BUREAU OF IMPERIAL SECURITY.

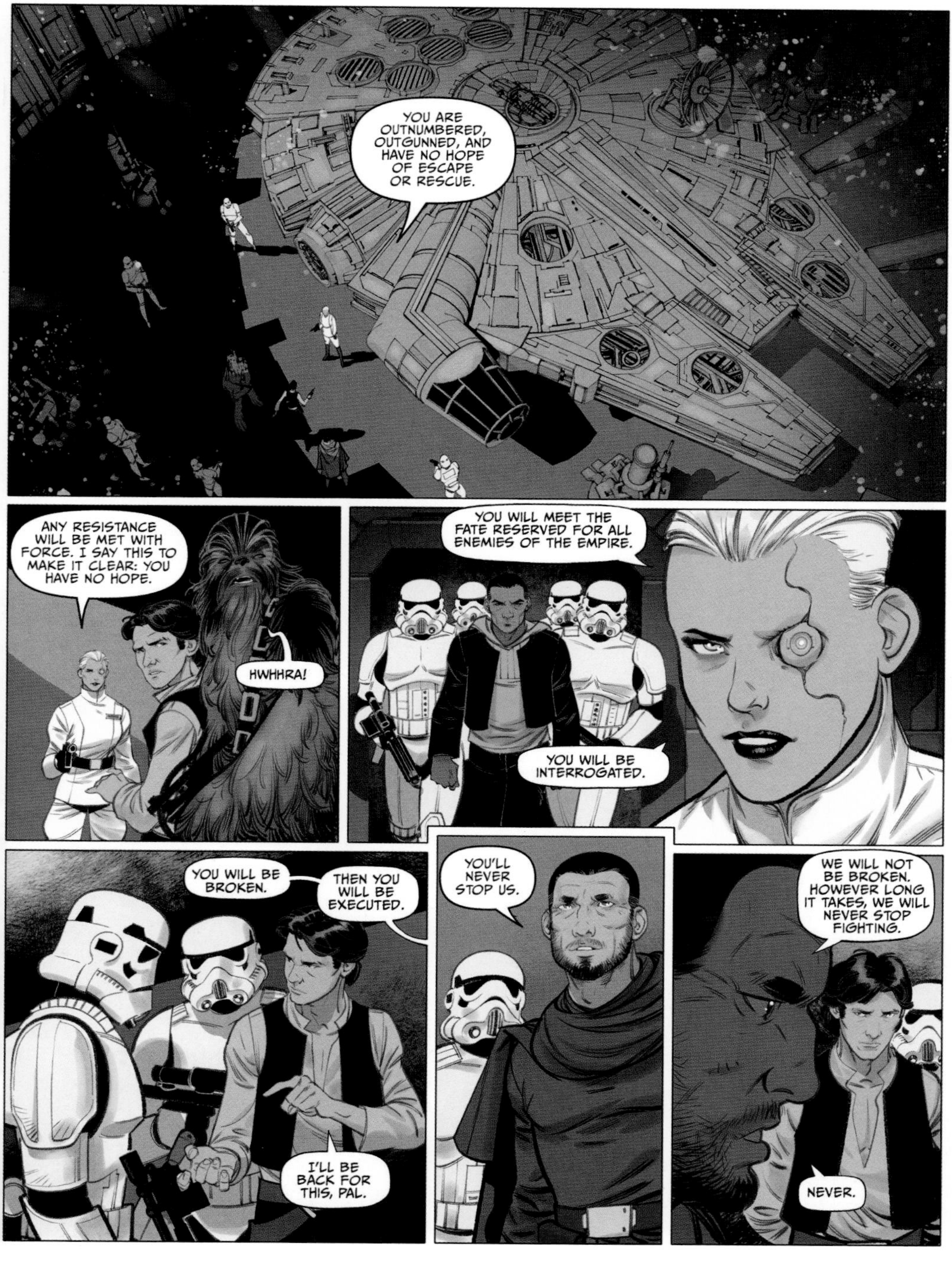
YOU ARE OUTNUMBERED, OUTGUNNED, AND HAVE NO HOPE OF ESCAPE OR RESCUE.
ANY RESISTANCE WILL BE MET WITH FORCE. I SAY THIS TO MAKE IT CLEAR: YOU HAVE NO HOPE.
HWHHRA!
YOU WILL MEET THE FATE RESERVED FOR ALL ENEMIES OF THE EMPIRE.
YOU WILL BE INTERROGATED.
YOU WILL BE BROKEN.
THEN YOU WILL BE EXECUTED.
I'LL BE BACK FOR THIS, PAL.
YOU'LL NEVER STOP US.
WE WILL NOT BE BROKEN. HOWEVER LONG IT TAKES, WE WILL NEVER STOP FIGHTING.
NEVER.

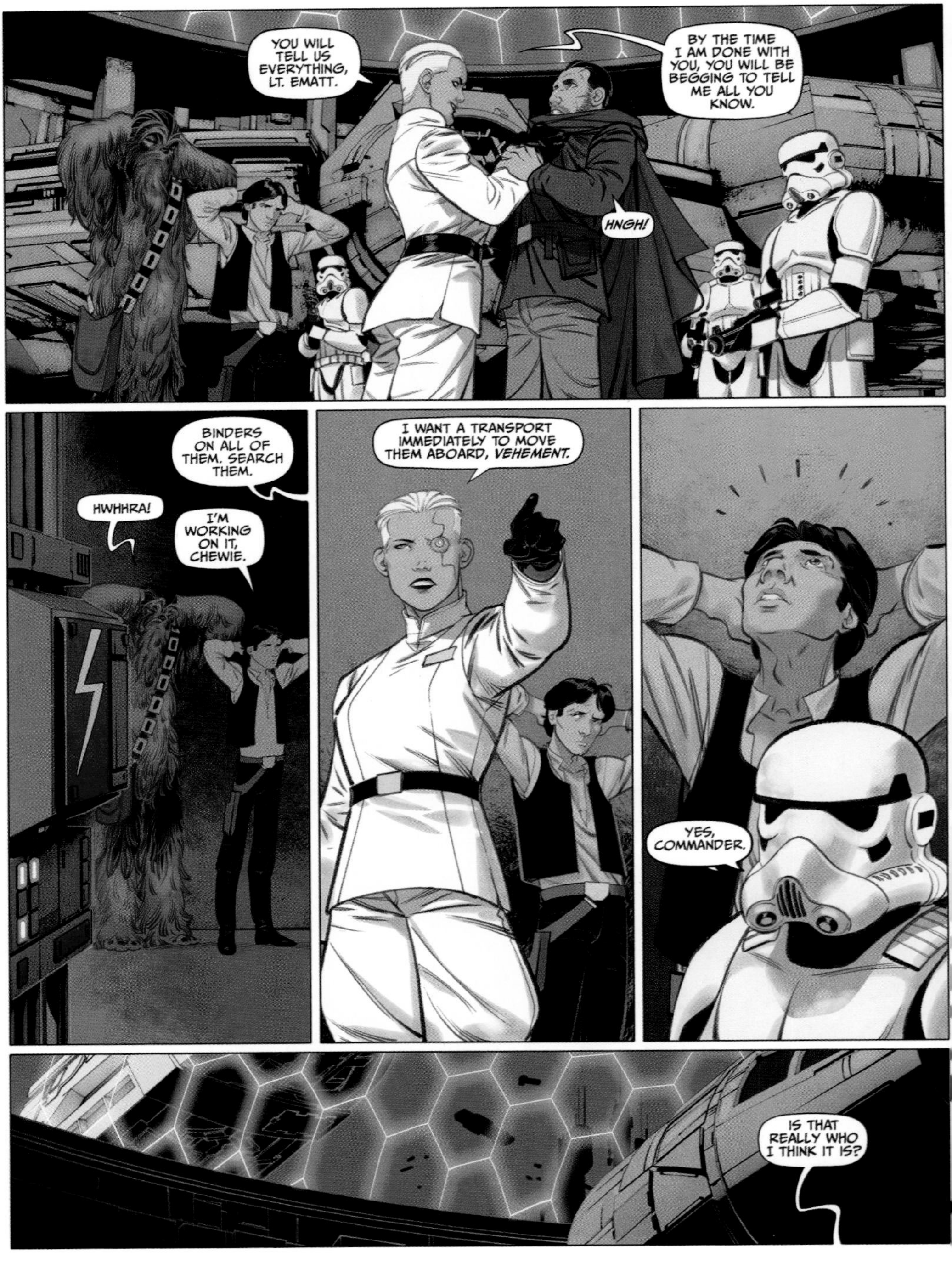
YOU WILL TELL US EVERYTHING, LT. EMATT.
BY THE TIME I AM DONE WITH YOU, YOU WILL BE BEGGING TO TELL ME ALL YOU KNOW.
HNGH!
BINDERS ON ALL OF THEM. SEARCH THEM.
HWHHRA!
I'M WORKING ON IT, CHEWIE.
I WANT A TRANSPORT IMMEDIATELY TO MOVE THEM ABOARD, VEHEMENT.
YES, COMMANDER.
IS THAT REALLY WHO I THINK IT IS?

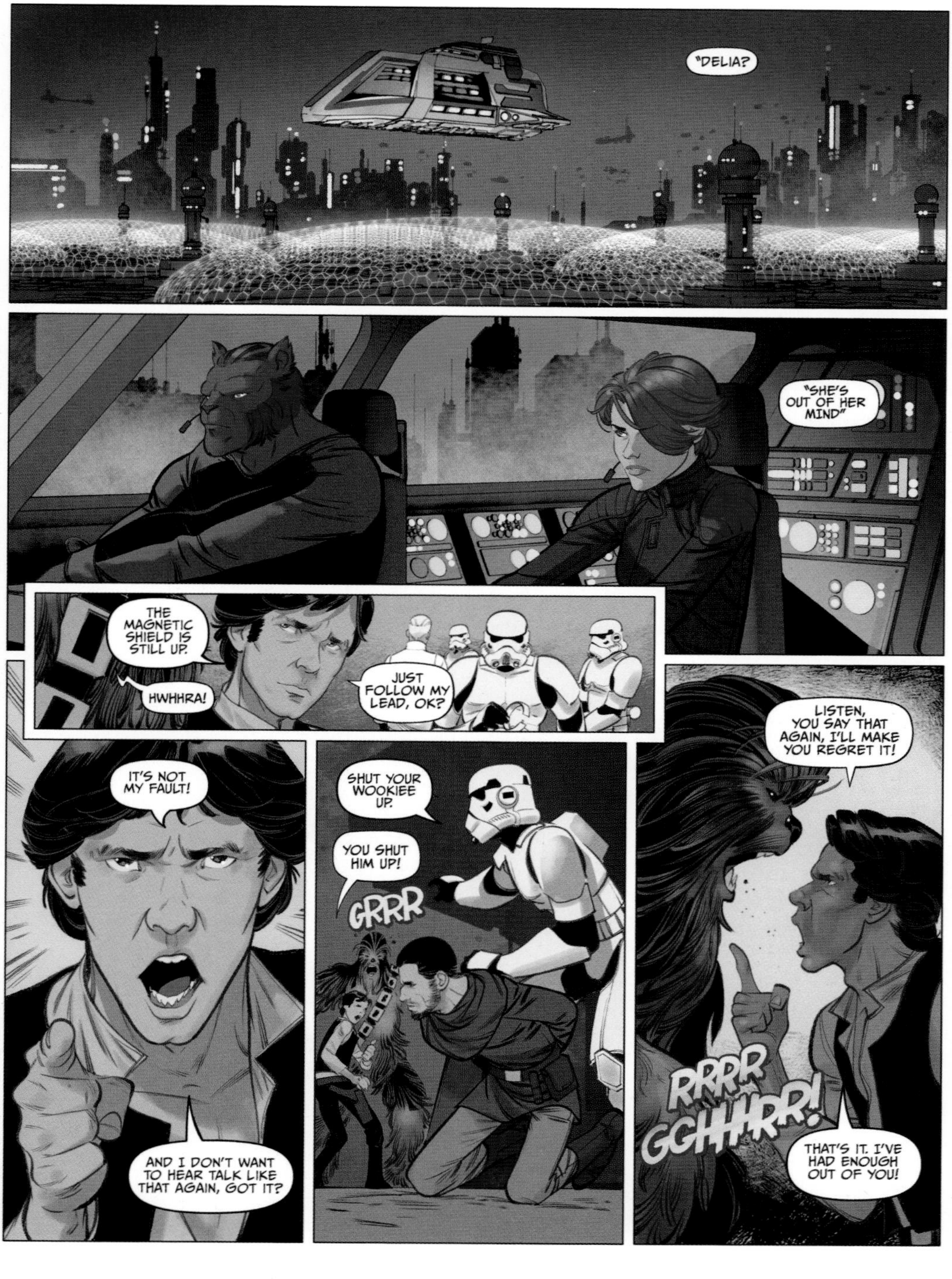
"DELIA?
"SHE'S OUT OF HER MIND"
THE MAGNETIC SHIELD IS STILL UP.
HWHHRA!
JUST FOLLOW MY LEAD, OK?
IT'S NOT MY FAULT!
AND I DON'T WANT TO HEAR TALK LIKE THAT AGAIN, GOT IT?
SHUT YOUR WOOKIEE UP.
YOU SHUT HIM UP!
GRRR
LISTEN, YOU SAY THAT AGAIN, I'LL MAKE YOU REGRET IT!
RRRR GGHHRR!
THAT'S IT. I'VE HAD ENOUGH OUT OF YOU!

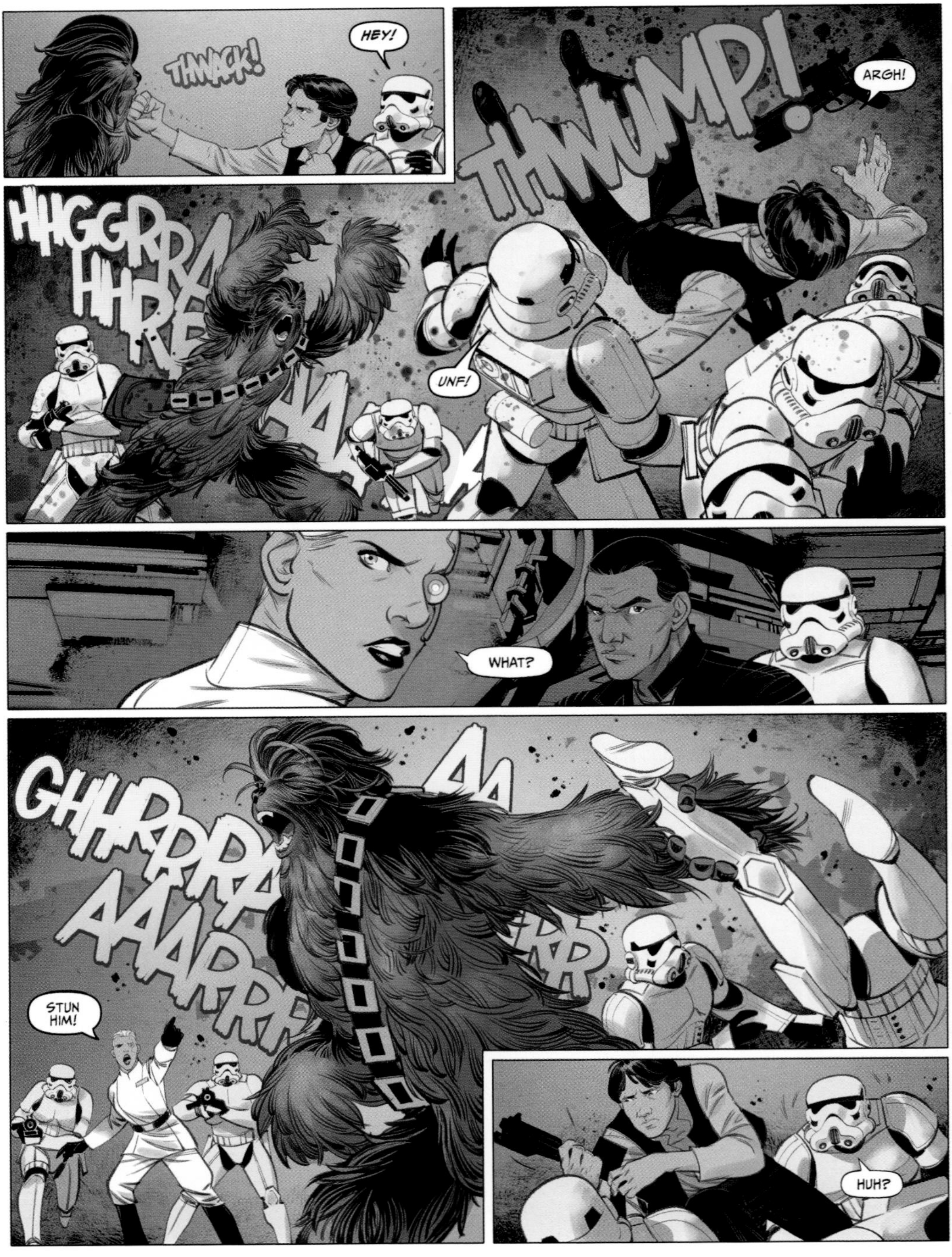
THWACK!
HEY!
THWUMP!
ARGH!
HHGGRRAHHRE
UNF!
WHAT?
GHHRRRRAAAARRRRRR
STUN HIM!
HUH?

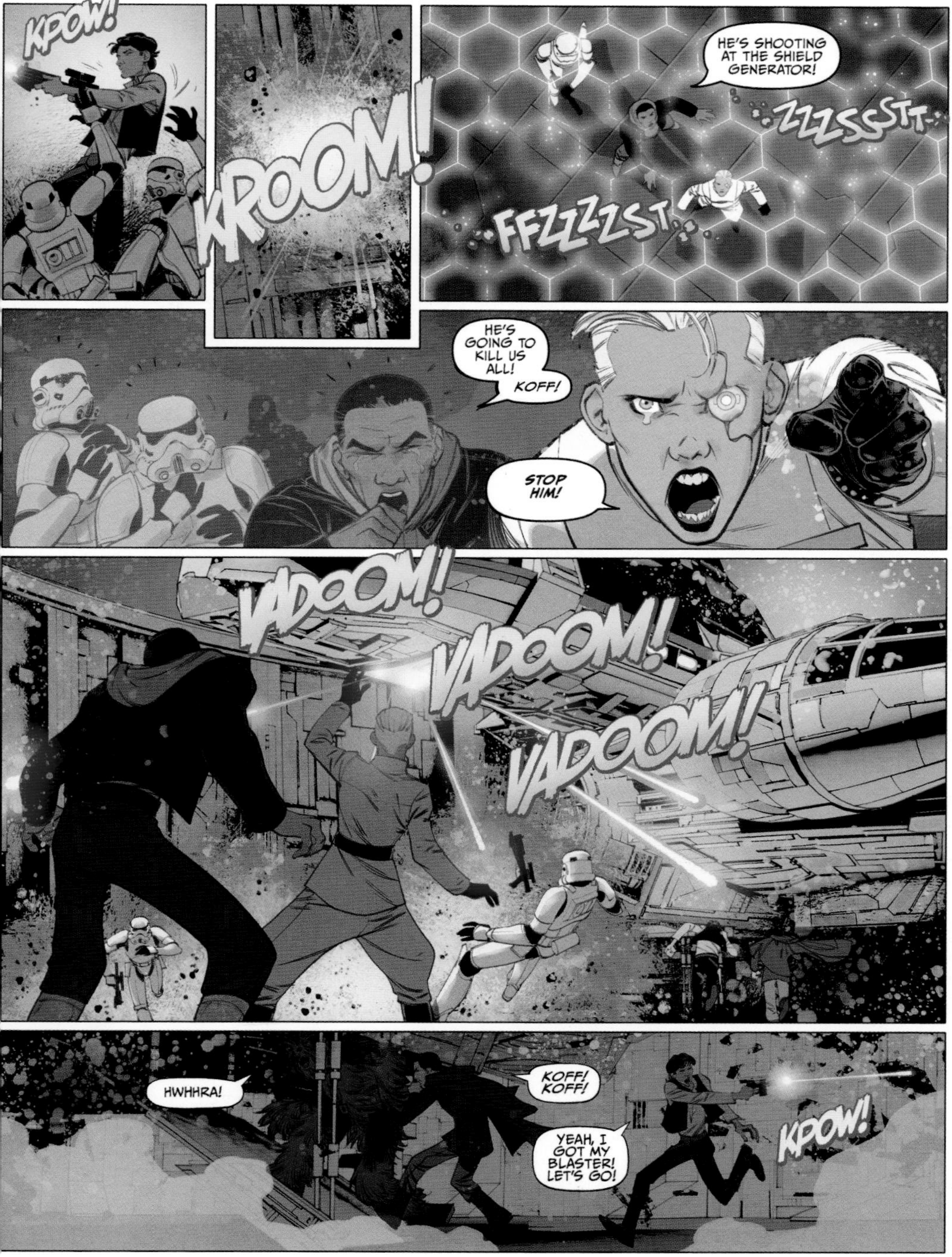
KPOW!
KROOM!
HE'S SHOOTING AT THE SHIELD GENERATOR!
ZZZSSSTT
FFZZZZST
HE'S GOING TO KILL US ALL!
KOFF!
STOP HIM!
VADOOM!
VADOOM!
VADOOM!
HWHHRA!
KOFF! KOFF!
YEAH, I GOT MY BLASTER! LET'S GO!
KPOW!

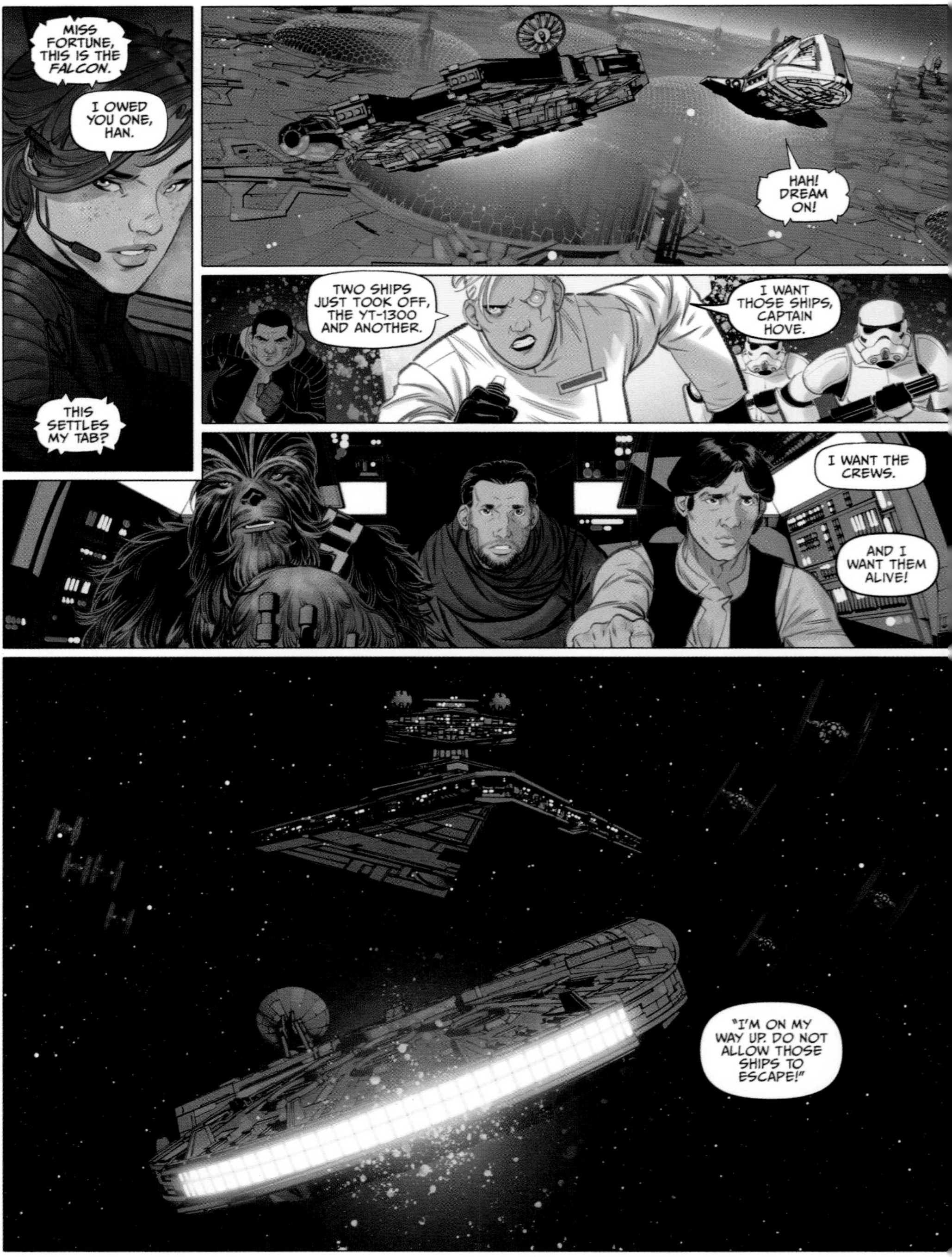

MISS FORTUNE, THIS IS THE *FALCON*.
I OWED YOU ONE, HAN.
HAH! DREAM ON!
THIS SETTLES MY TAB?
TWO SHIPS JUST TOOK OFF, THE YT-1300 AND ANOTHER.
I WANT THOSE SHIPS, CAPTAIN HOVE.
I WANT THE CREWS.
AND I WANT THEM ALIVE!
"I'M ON MY WAY UP. DO NOT ALLOW THOSE SHIPS TO ESCAPE!"

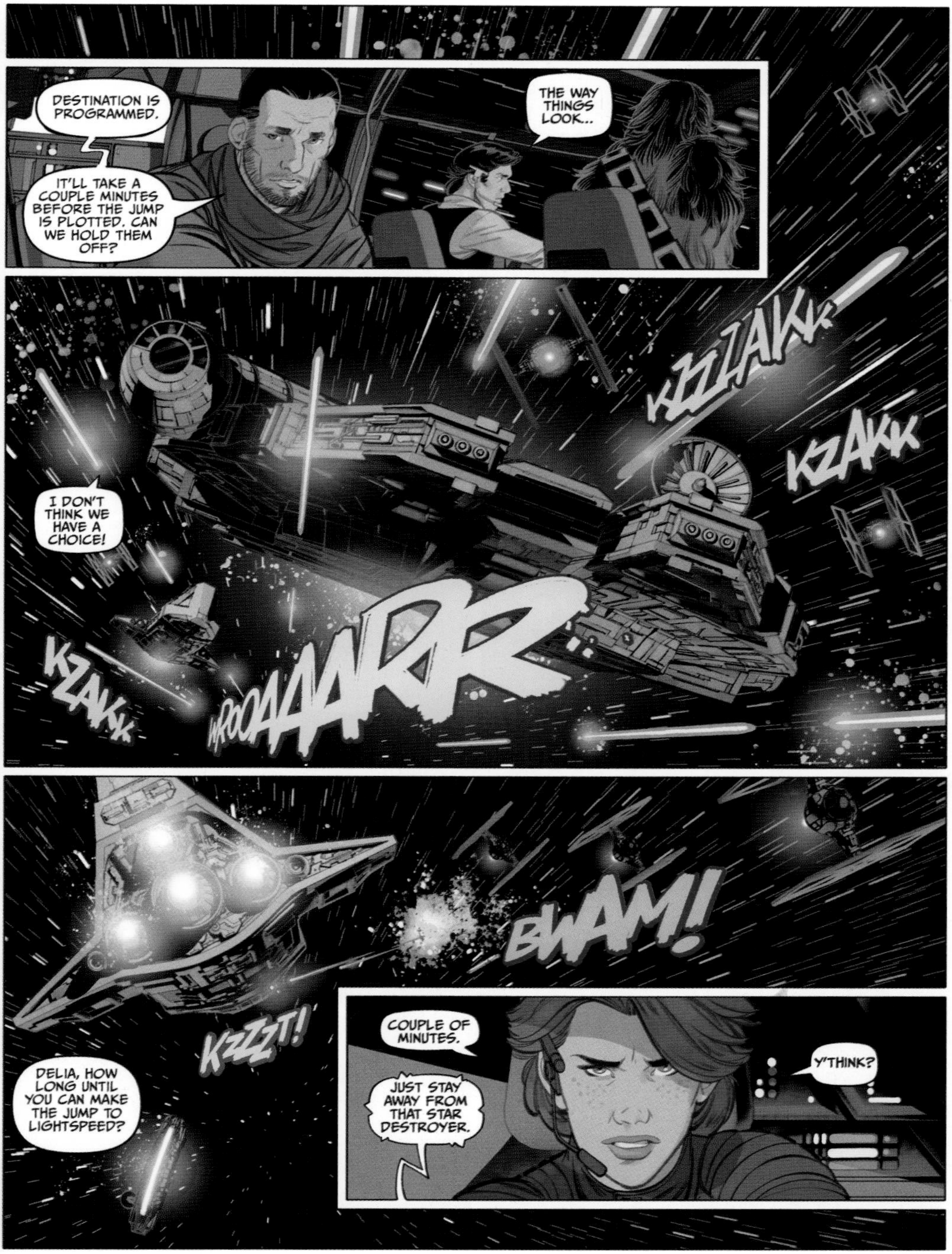
DESTINATION IS PROGRAMMED.
IT'LL TAKE A COUPLE MINUTES BEFORE THE JUMP IS PLOTTED. CAN WE HOLD THEM OFF?
THE WAY THINGS LOOK...
KZZZAKK
KZAKK
I DON'T THINK WE HAVE A CHOICE!
KZAKK
WROOAAAARR
BWAM!
KZZZT!
DELIA, HOW LONG UNTIL YOU CAN MAKE THE JUMP TO LIGHTSPEED?
COUPLE OF MINUTES.
JUST STAY AWAY FROM THAT STAR DESTROYER.
Y'THINK?

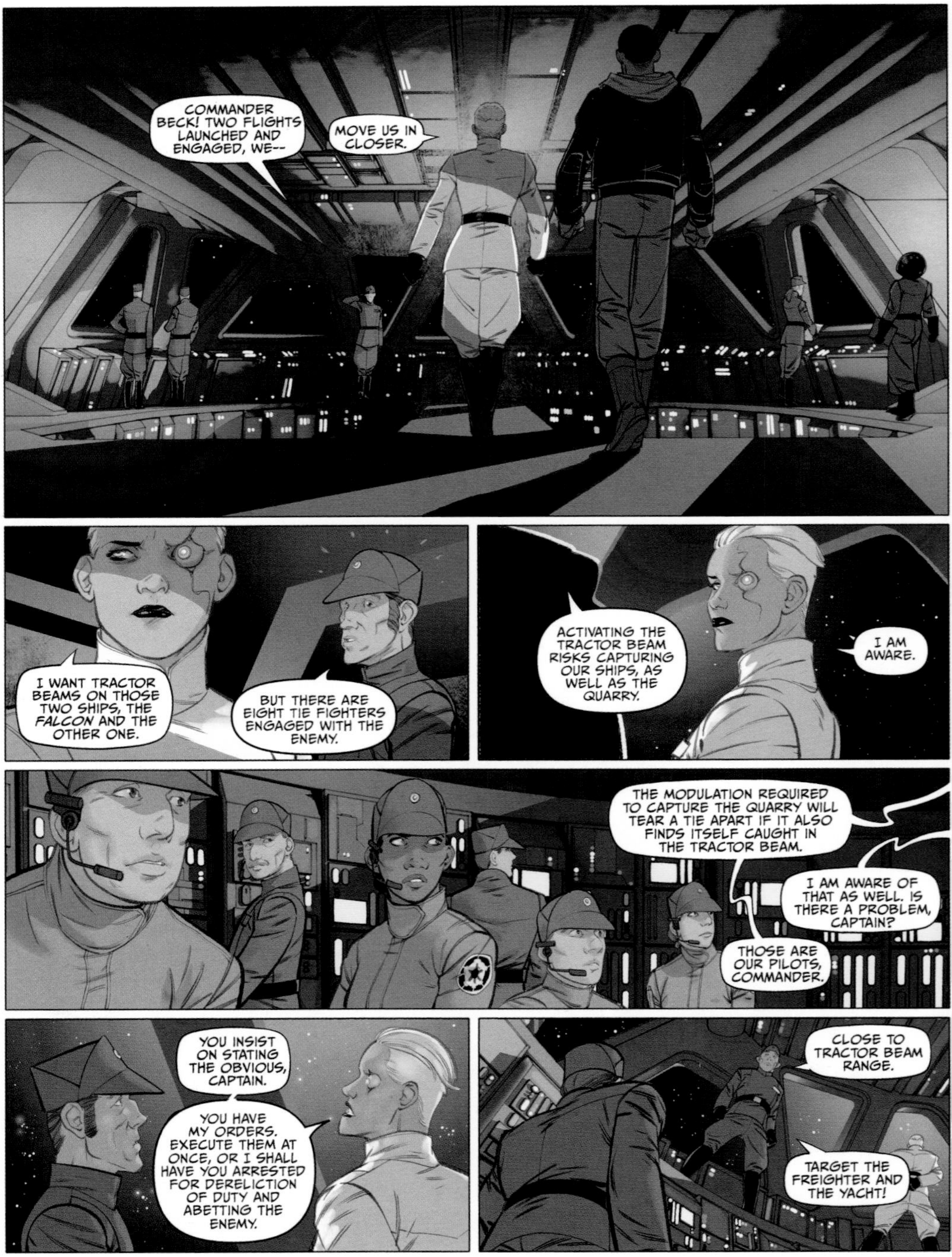
COMMANDER BECK! TWO FLIGHTS LAUNCHED AND ENGAGED, WE--
MOVE US IN CLOSER.
I WANT TRACTOR BEAMS ON THOSE TWO SHIPS, THE *FALCON* AND THE OTHER ONE.
BUT THERE ARE EIGHT TIE FIGHTERS ENGAGED WITH THE ENEMY.
ACTIVATING THE TRACTOR BEAM RISKS CAPTURING OUR SHIPS, AS WELL AS THE QUARRY.
I AM AWARE.
THE MODULATION REQUIRED TO CAPTURE THE QUARRY WILL TEAR A TIE APART IF IT ALSO FINDS ITSELF CAUGHT IN THE TRACTOR BEAM.
I AM AWARE OF THAT AS WELL. IS THERE A PROBLEM, CAPTAIN?
THOSE ARE OUR PILOTS, COMMANDER.
YOU INSIST ON STATING THE OBVIOUS, CAPTAIN.
YOU HAVE MY ORDERS. EXECUTE THEM AT ONCE, OR I SHALL HAVE YOU ARRESTED FOR DERELICTION OF DUTY AND ABETTING THE ENEMY.
CLOSE TO TRACTOR BEAM RANGE.
TARGET THE FREIGHTER AND THE YACHT!

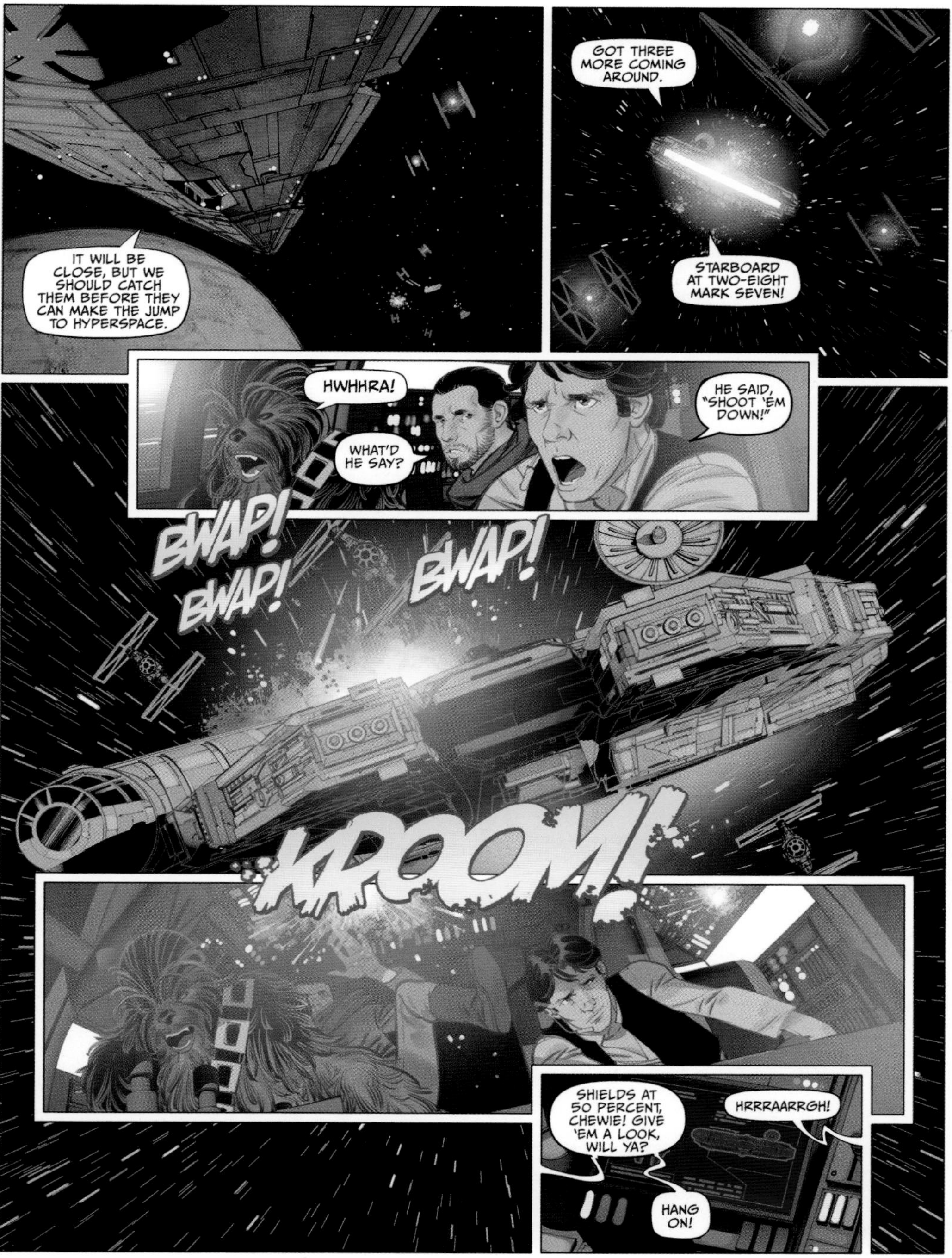
IT WILL BE CLOSE, BUT WE SHOULD CATCH THEM BEFORE THEY CAN MAKE THE JUMP TO HYPERSPACE.
GOT THREE MORE COMING AROUND.
STARBOARD AT TWO-EIGHT MARK SEVEN!
HWHHRA!
WHAT'D HE SAY?
HE SAID, "SHOOT 'EM DOWN!"
BWAP!
BWAP!
BWAP!
KROOM!
SHIELDS AT 50 PERCENT, CHEWIE! GIVE 'EM A LOOK, WILL YA?
HRRRAARRGH!
HANG ON!

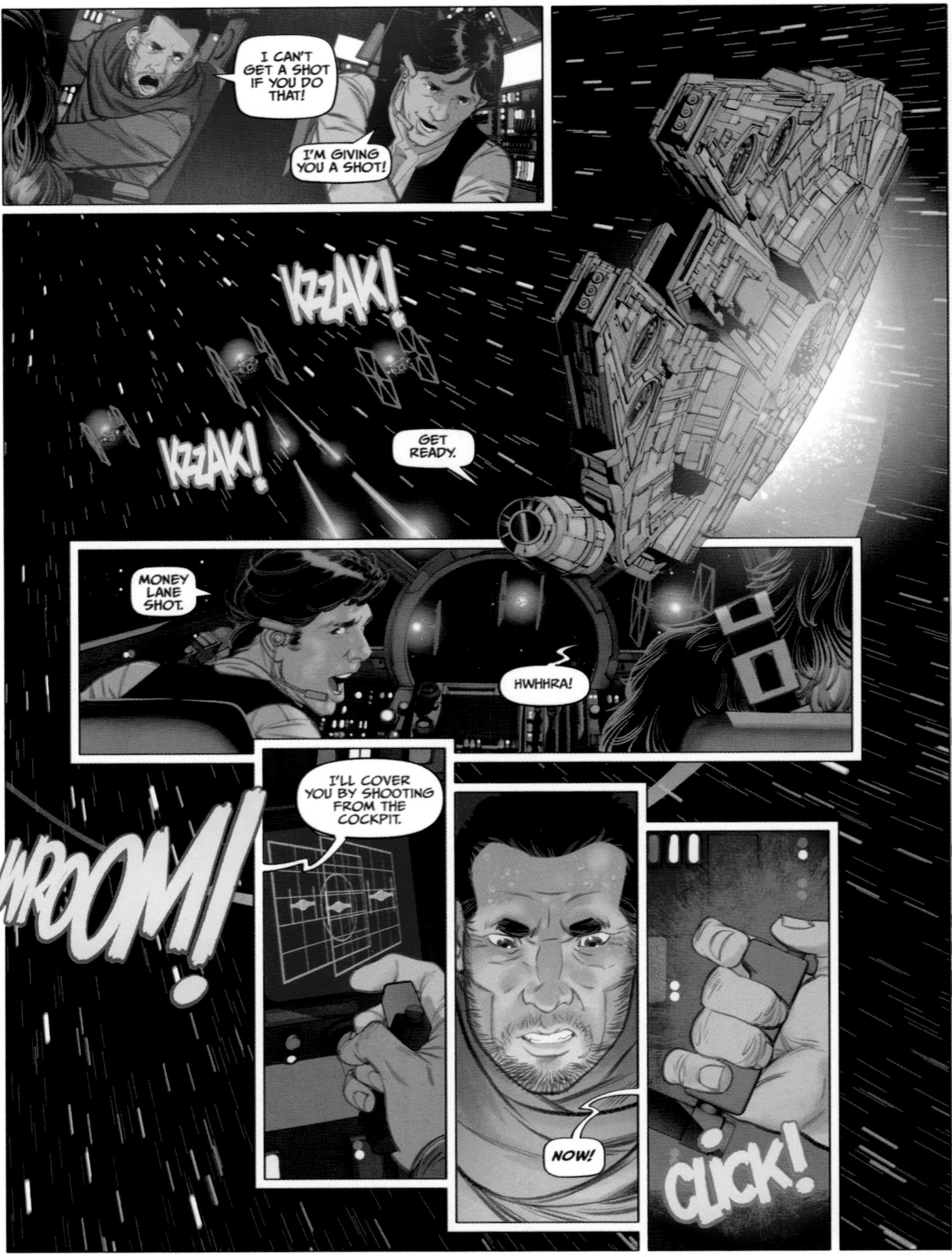
I CAN'T GET A SHOT IF YOU DO THAT!
I'M GIVING YOU A SHOT!
KZZAK!
KZZAK!
GET READY.
MONEY LANE SHOT.
HWHHRA!
WROOM!
I'LL COVER YOU BY SHOOTING FROM THE COCKPIT.
NOW!
CLICK!

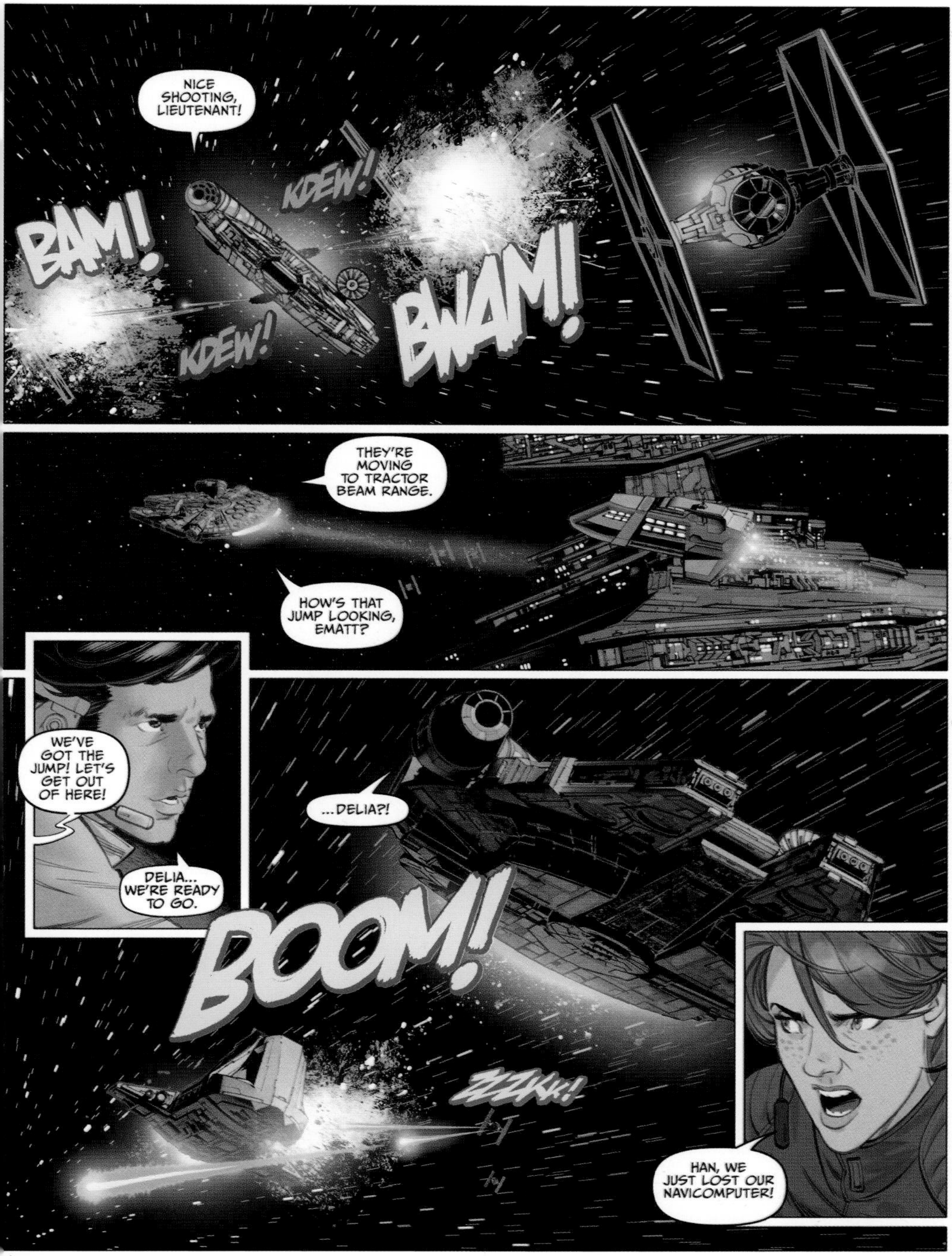
NICE SHOOTING, LIEUTENANT!
BAM!
KDEW!
KDEW!
BWAM!
THEY'RE MOVING TO TRACTOR BEAM RANGE.
HOW'S THAT JUMP LOOKING, EMATT?
WE'VE GOT THE JUMP! LET'S GET OUT OF HERE!
DELIA... WE'RE READY TO GO.
...DELIA?!
BOOM!
ZZZKK!
HAN, WE JUST LOST OUR NAVICOMPUTER!

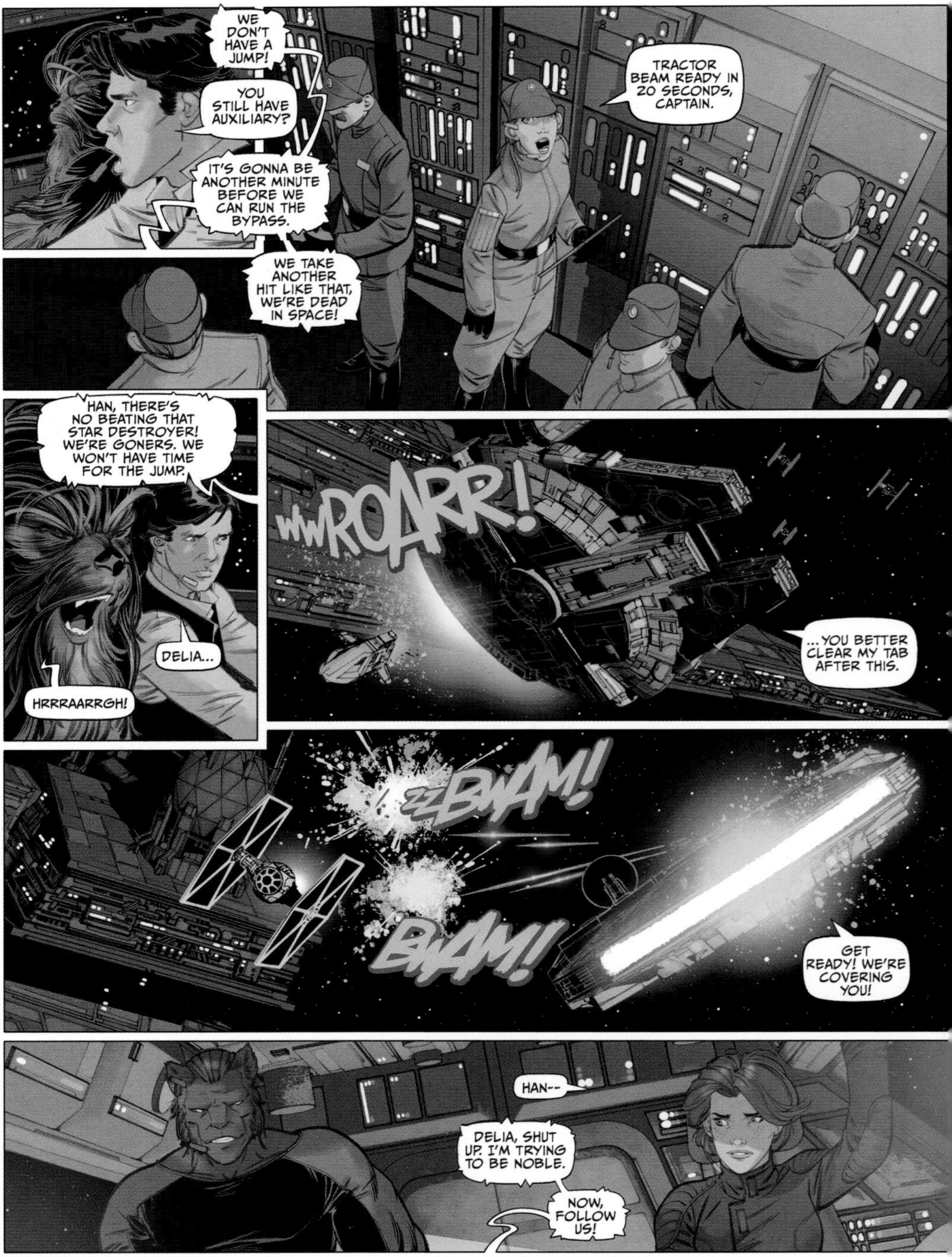
WE DON'T HAVE A JUMP!
YOU STILL HAVE AUXILIARY?
IT'S GONNA BE ANOTHER MINUTE BEFORE WE CAN RUN THE BYPASS.
WE TAKE ANOTHER HIT LIKE THAT, WE'RE DEAD IN SPACE!
TRACTOR BEAM READY IN 20 SECONDS, CAPTAIN.
HAN, THERE'S NO BEATING THAT STAR DESTROYER! WE'RE GONERS. WE WON'T HAVE TIME FOR THE JUMP.
DELIA...
HRRRAARRGH!
WWWROARR!
...YOU BETTER CLEAR MY TAB AFTER THIS.
ZZBWAM!
BWAM!
GET READY! WE'RE COVERING YOU!
HAN--
DELIA, SHUT UP. I'M TRYING TO BE NOBLE.
NOW, FOLLOW US!

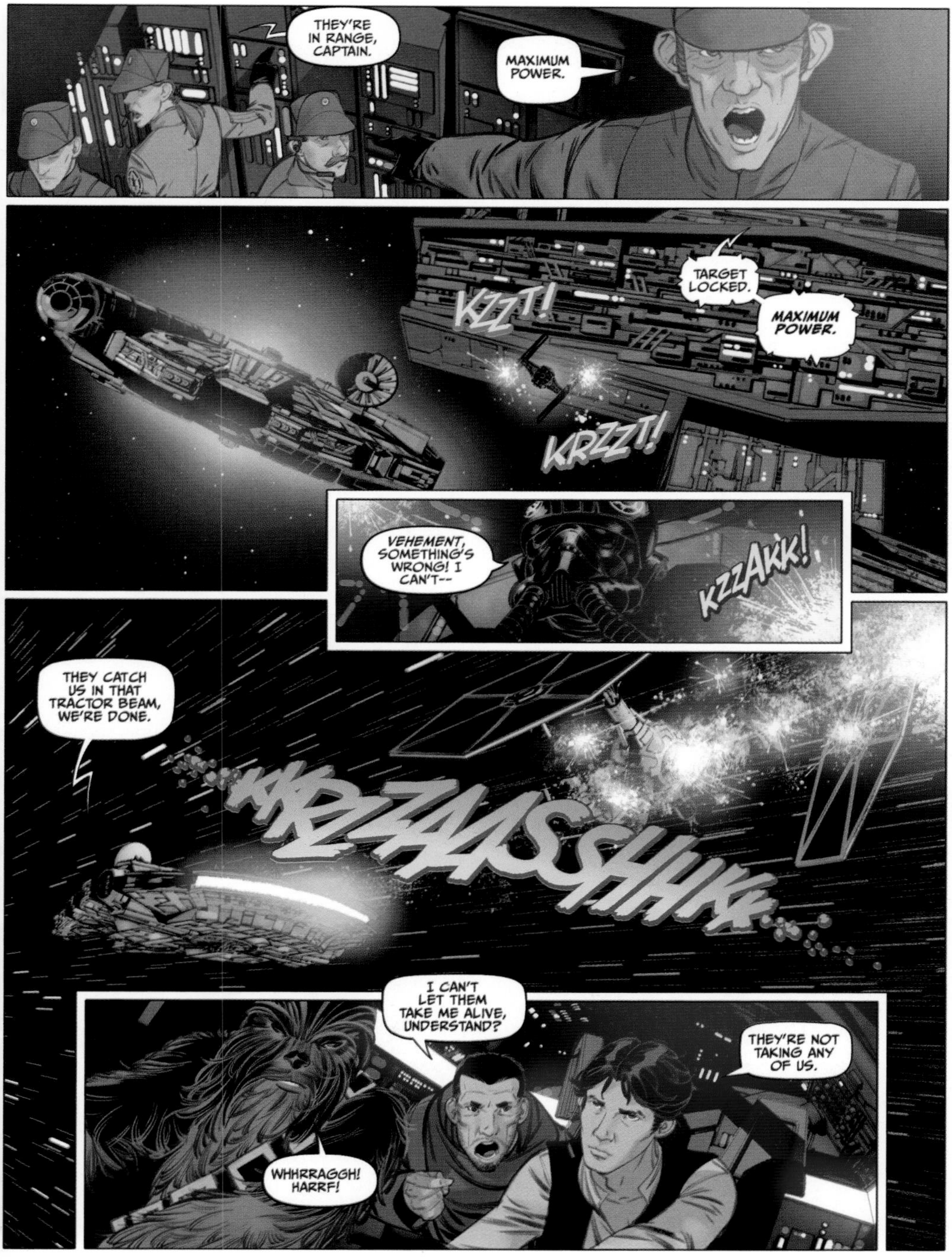
THEY'RE IN RANGE, CAPTAIN.
MAXIMUM POWER.
TARGET LOCKED.
KZZT!
MAXIMUM POWER.
KRZZT!
VEHEMENT, SOMETHING'S WRONG! I CAN'T--
KZZAKK!
THEY CATCH US IN THAT TRACTOR BEAM, WE'RE DONE.
KRZZAASSHHKK
I CAN'T LET THEM TAKE ME ALIVE, UNDERSTAND?
THEY'RE NOT TAKING ANY OF US.
WHHRRAGGH! HARRF!

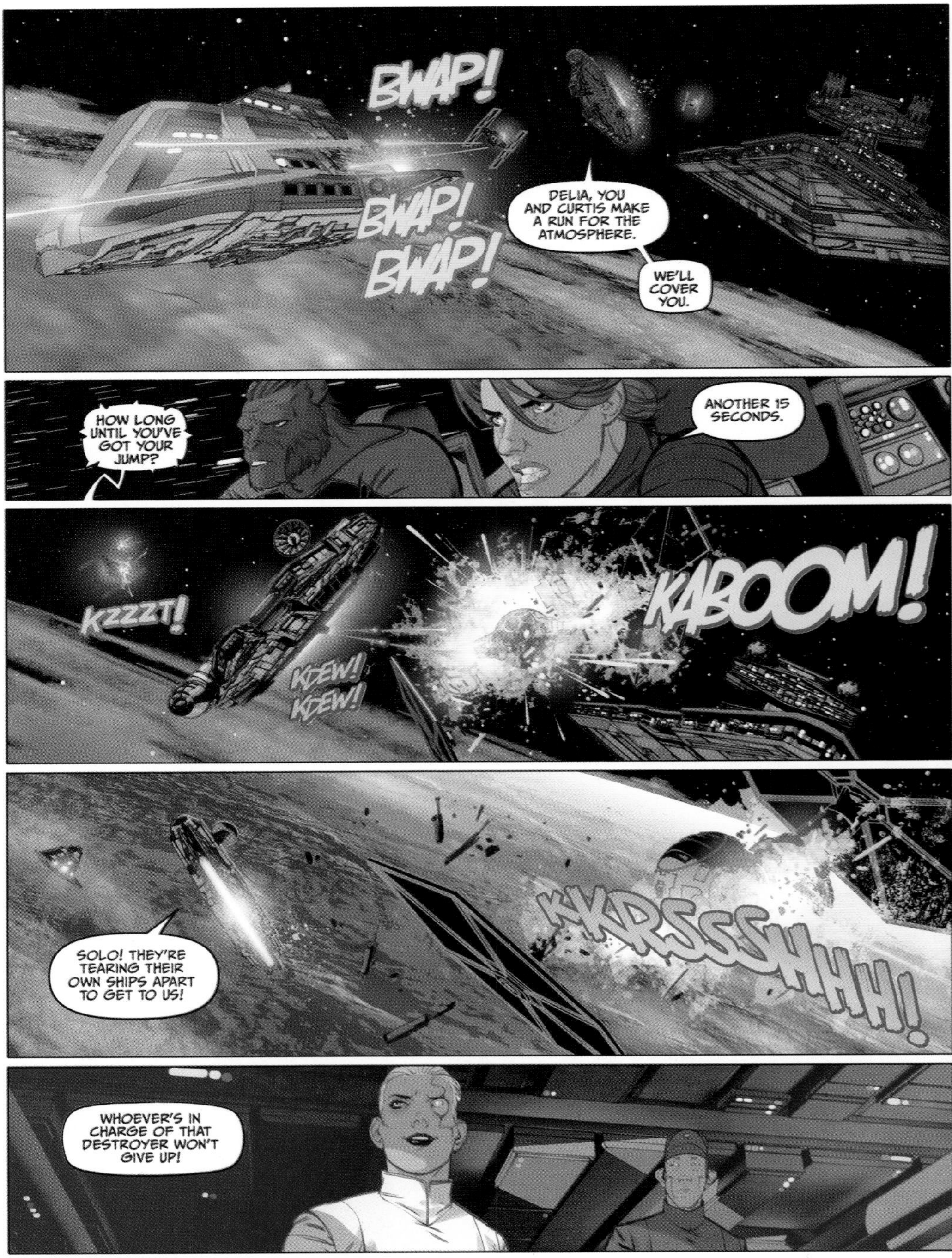
BWAP!
BWAP!
BWAP!
DELIA, YOU AND CURTIS MAKE A RUN FOR THE ATMOSPHERE.
WE'LL COVER YOU.
HOW LONG UNTIL YOU'VE GOT YOUR JUMP?
ANOTHER 15 SECONDS.
KZZZT!
KDEW! KDEW!
KABOOM!
KKRSSSHHHH!
SOLO! THEY'RE TEARING THEIR OWN SHIPS APART TO GET TO US!
WHOEVER'S IN CHARGE OF THAT DESTROYER WON'T GIVE UP!

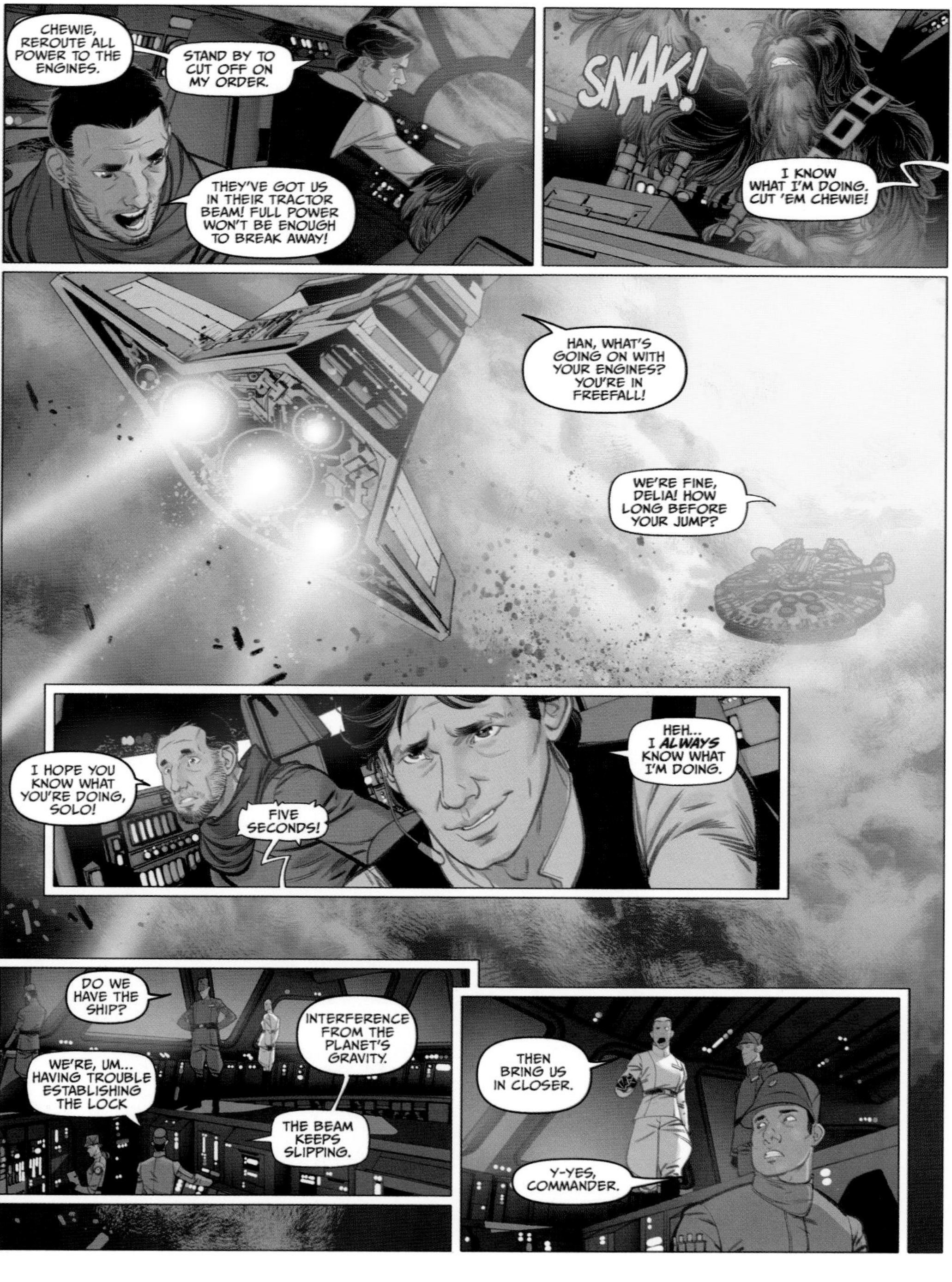
CHEWIE, REROUTE ALL POWER TO THE ENGINES.
STAND BY TO CUT OFF ON MY ORDER.
THEY'VE GOT US IN THEIR TRACTOR BEAM! FULL POWER WON'T BE ENOUGH TO BREAK AWAY!
SNAK!
I KNOW WHAT I'M DOING. CUT 'EM CHEWIE!
HAN, WHAT'S GOING ON WITH YOUR ENGINES? YOU'RE IN FREEFALL!
WE'RE FINE, DELIA! HOW LONG BEFORE YOUR JUMP?
I HOPE YOU KNOW WHAT YOU'RE DOING, SOLO!
FIVE SECONDS!
HEH... I *ALWAYS* KNOW WHAT I'M DOING.
DO WE HAVE THE SHIP?
WE'RE, UM... HAVING TROUBLE ESTABLISHING THE LOCK
INTERFERENCE FROM THE PLANET'S GRAVITY.
THE BEAM KEEPS SLIPPING.
THEN BRING US IN CLOSER.
Y-YES, COMMANDER.

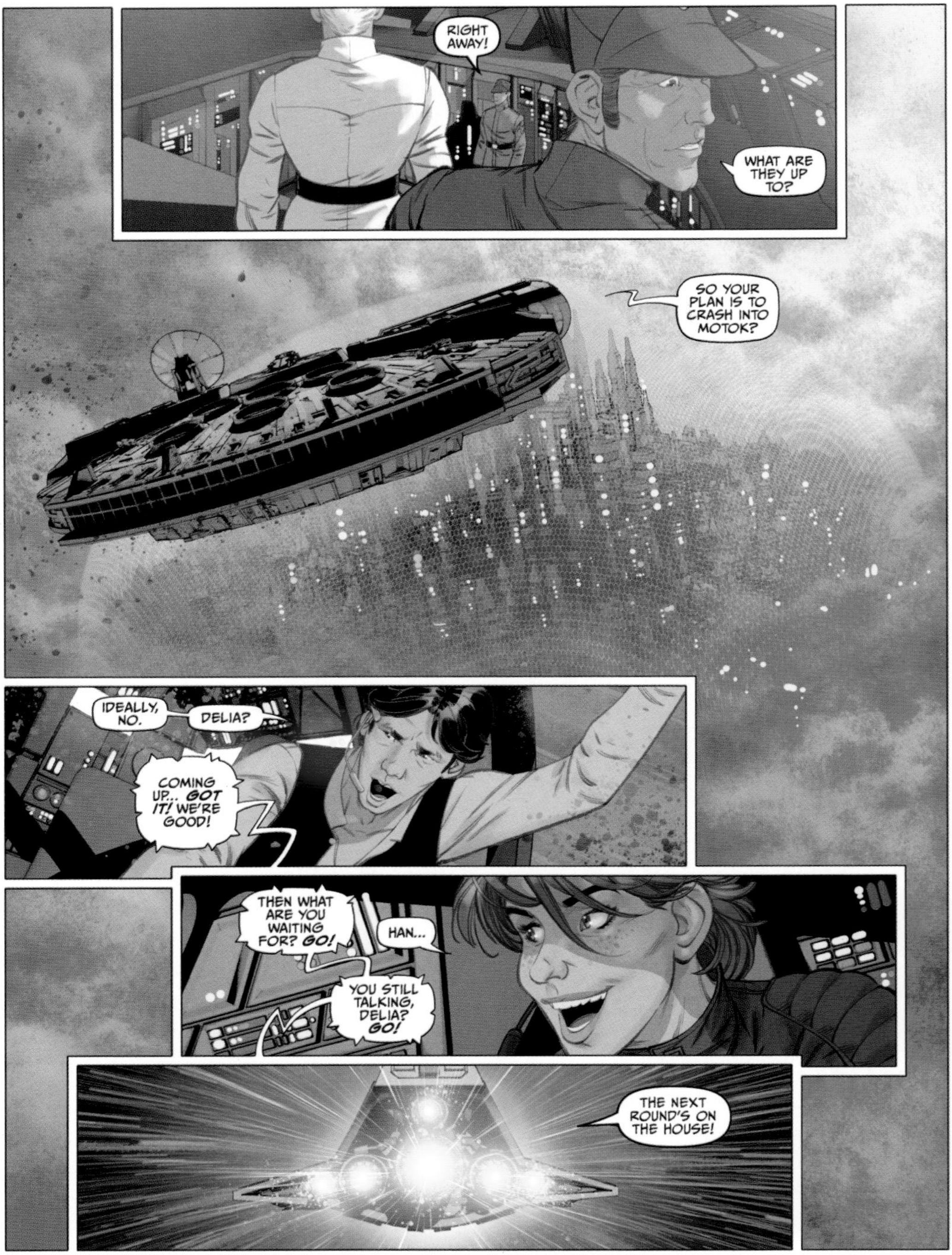
RIGHT AWAY!
WHAT ARE THEY UP TO?
SO YOUR PLAN IS TO CRASH INTO MOTOK?
IDEALLY, NO.
DELIA?
COMING UP... GOT IT! WE'RE GOOD!
THEN WHAT ARE YOU WAITING FOR? GO!
HAN...
YOU STILL TALKING, DELIA? GO!
THE NEXT ROUND'S ON THE HOUSE!

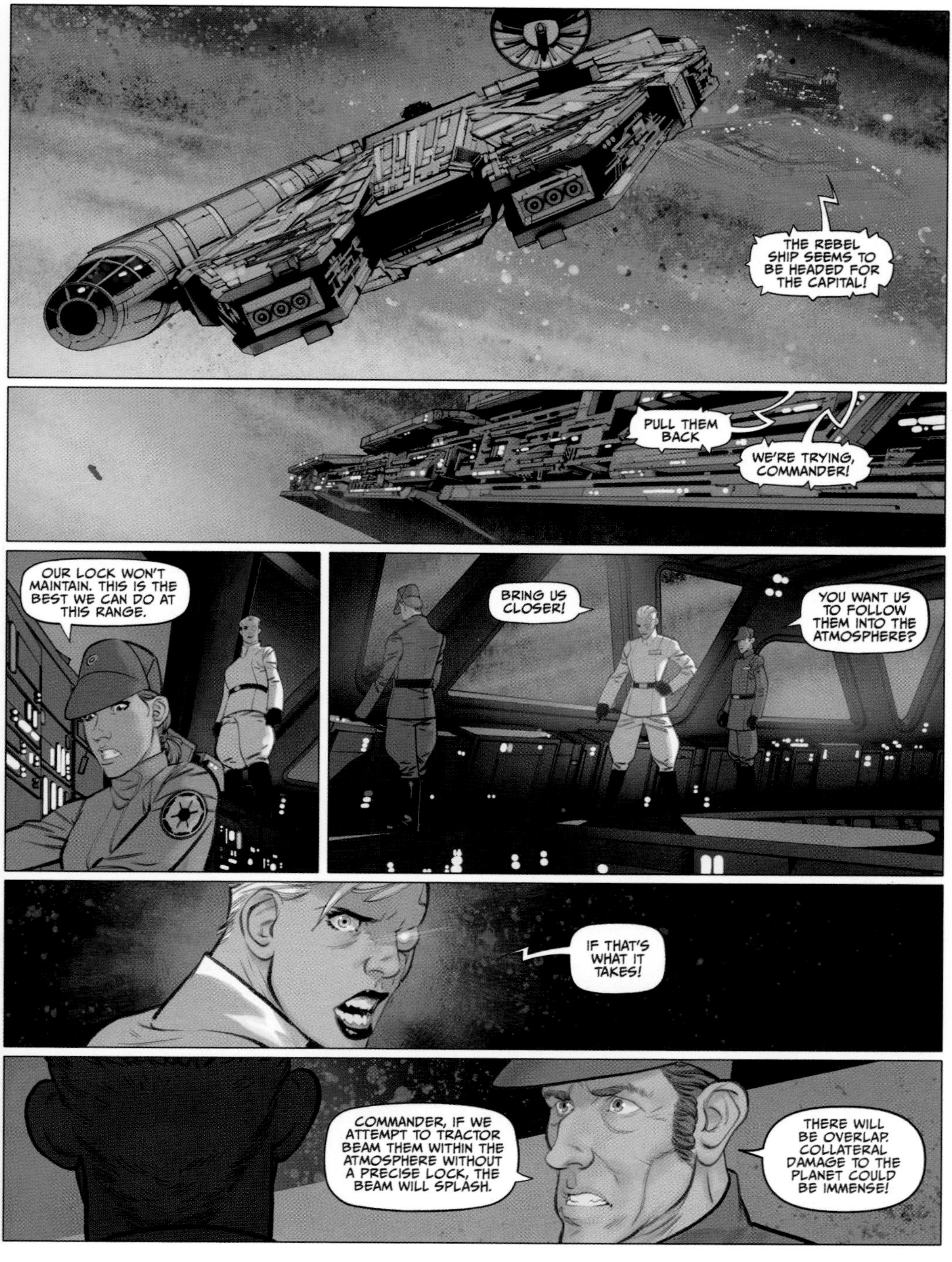
THE REBEL SHIP SEEMS TO BE HEADED FOR THE CAPITAL!
PULL THEM BACK
WE'RE TRYING, COMMANDER!
OUR LOCK WON'T MAINTAIN. THIS IS THE BEST WE CAN DO AT THIS RANGE.
BRING US CLOSER!
YOU WANT US TO FOLLOW THEM INTO THE ATMOSPHERE?
IF THAT'S WHAT IT TAKES!
COMMANDER, IF WE ATTEMPT TO TRACTOR BEAM THEM WITHIN THE ATMOSPHERE WITHOUT A PRECISE LOCK, THE BEAM WILL SPLASH.
THERE WILL BE OVERLAP. COLLATERAL DAMAGE TO THE PLANET COULD BE IMMENSE!

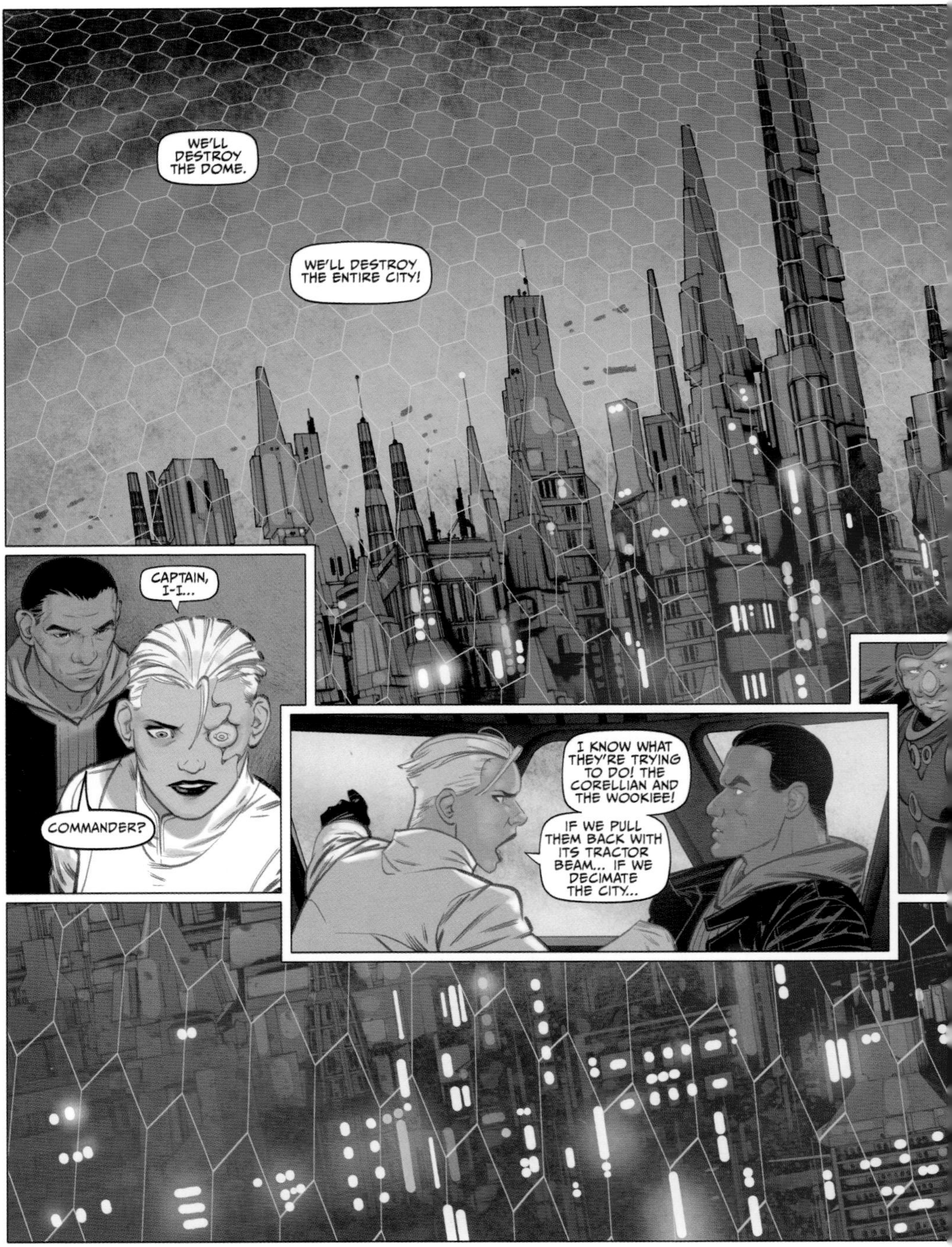

WE'LL DESTROY THE DOME.
WE'LL DESTROY THE ENTIRE CITY!
CAPTAIN, I-I...
COMMANDER?
I KNOW WHAT THEY'RE TRYING TO DO! THE CORELLIAN AND THE WOOKIEE!
IF WE PULL THEM BACK WITH ITS TRACTOR BEAM... IF WE DECIMATE THE CITY...

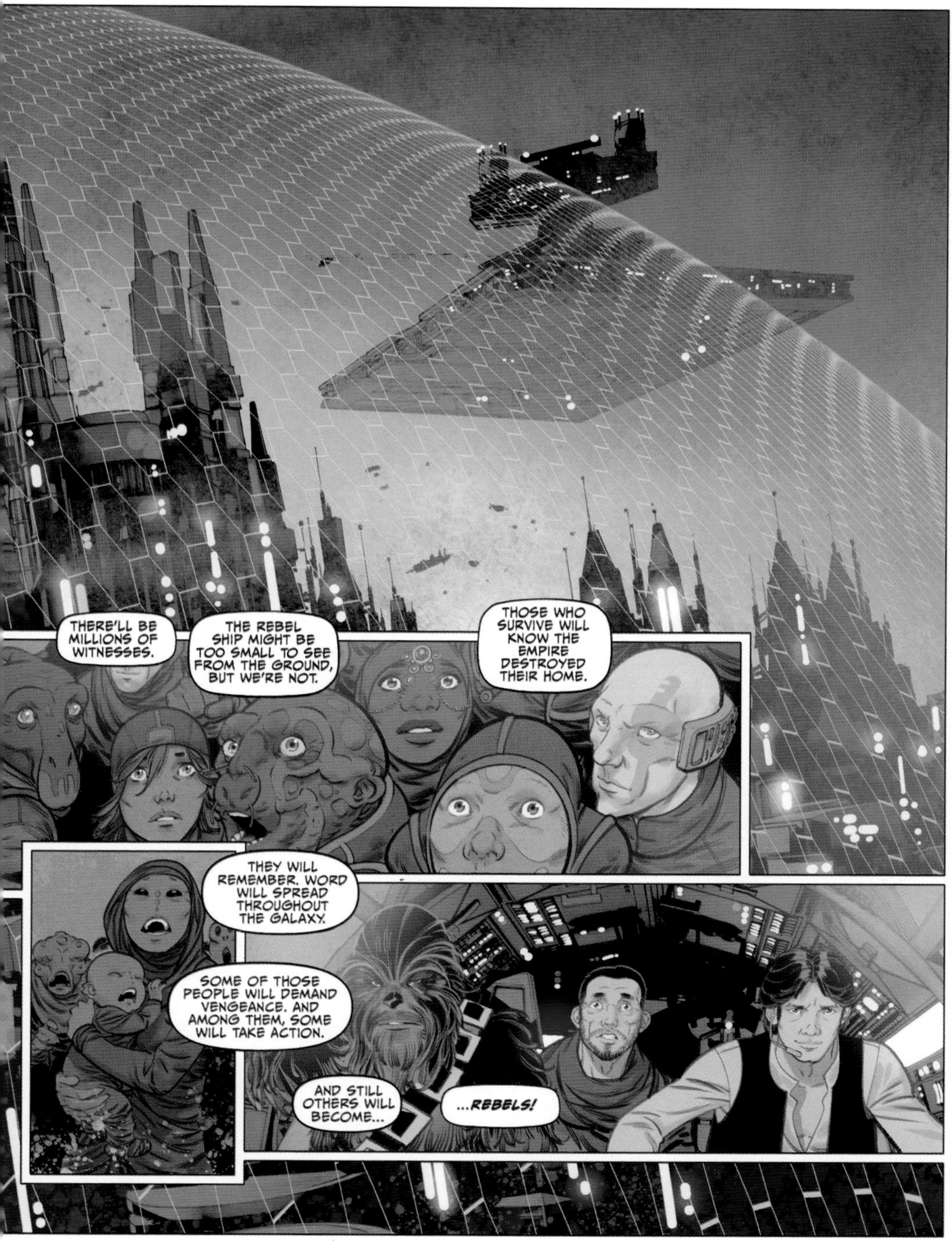

THERE'LL BE MILLIONS OF WITNESSES.
THE REBEL SHIP MIGHT BE TOO SMALL TO SEE FROM THE GROUND, BUT WE'RE NOT.
THOSE WHO SURVIVE WILL KNOW THE EMPIRE DESTROYED THEIR HOME.
THEY WILL REMEMBER. WORD WILL SPREAD THROUGHOUT THE GALAXY.
SOME OF THOSE PEOPLE WILL DEMAND VENGEANCE. AND AMONG THEM, SOME WILL TAKE ACTION.
AND STILL OTHERS WILL BECOME...
...REBELS!

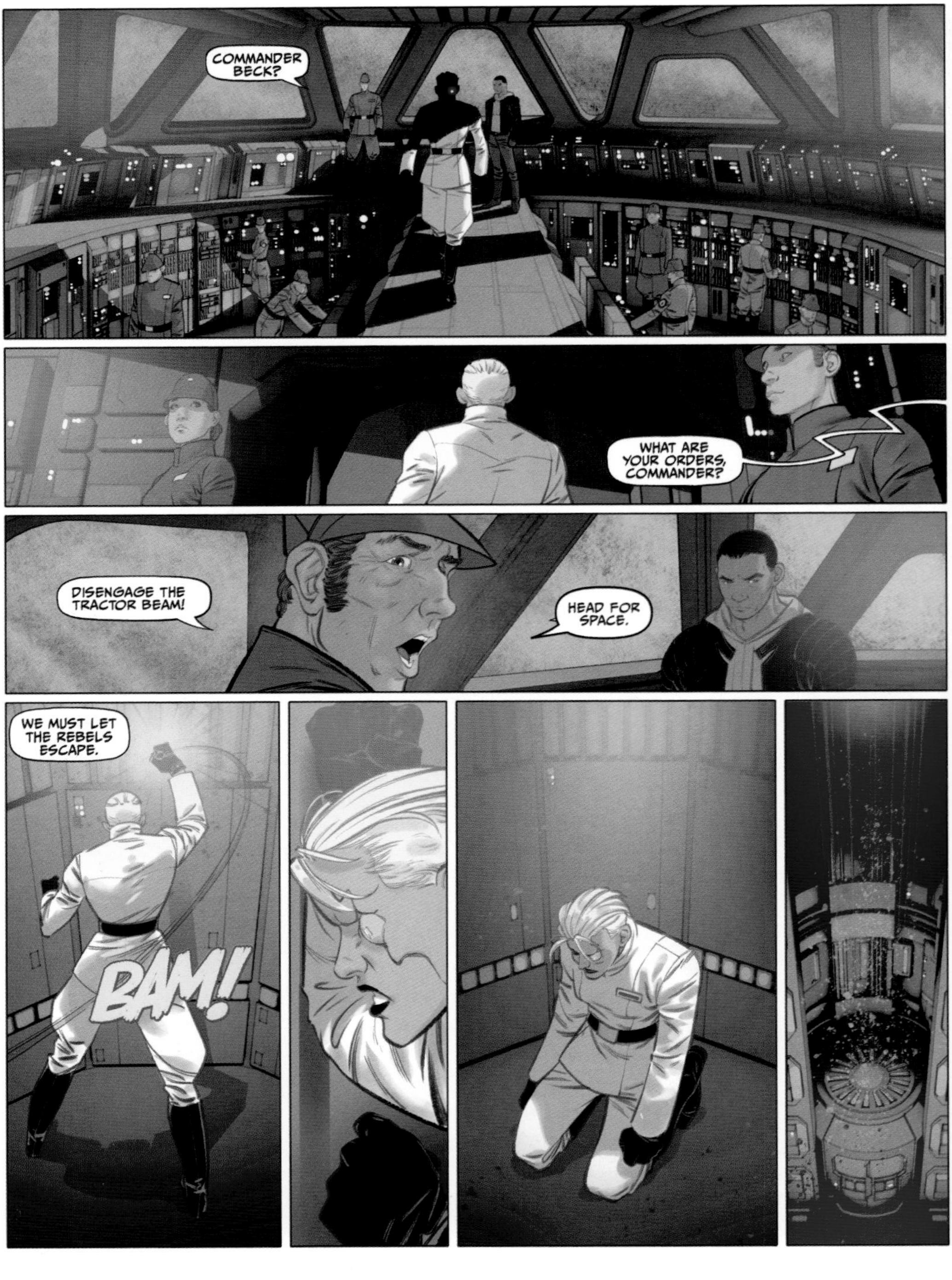
COMMANDER BECK?
WHAT ARE YOUR ORDERS, COMMANDER?
DISENGAGE THE TRACTOR BEAM!
HEAD FOR SPACE.
WE MUST LET THE REBELS ESCAPE.
BAM!

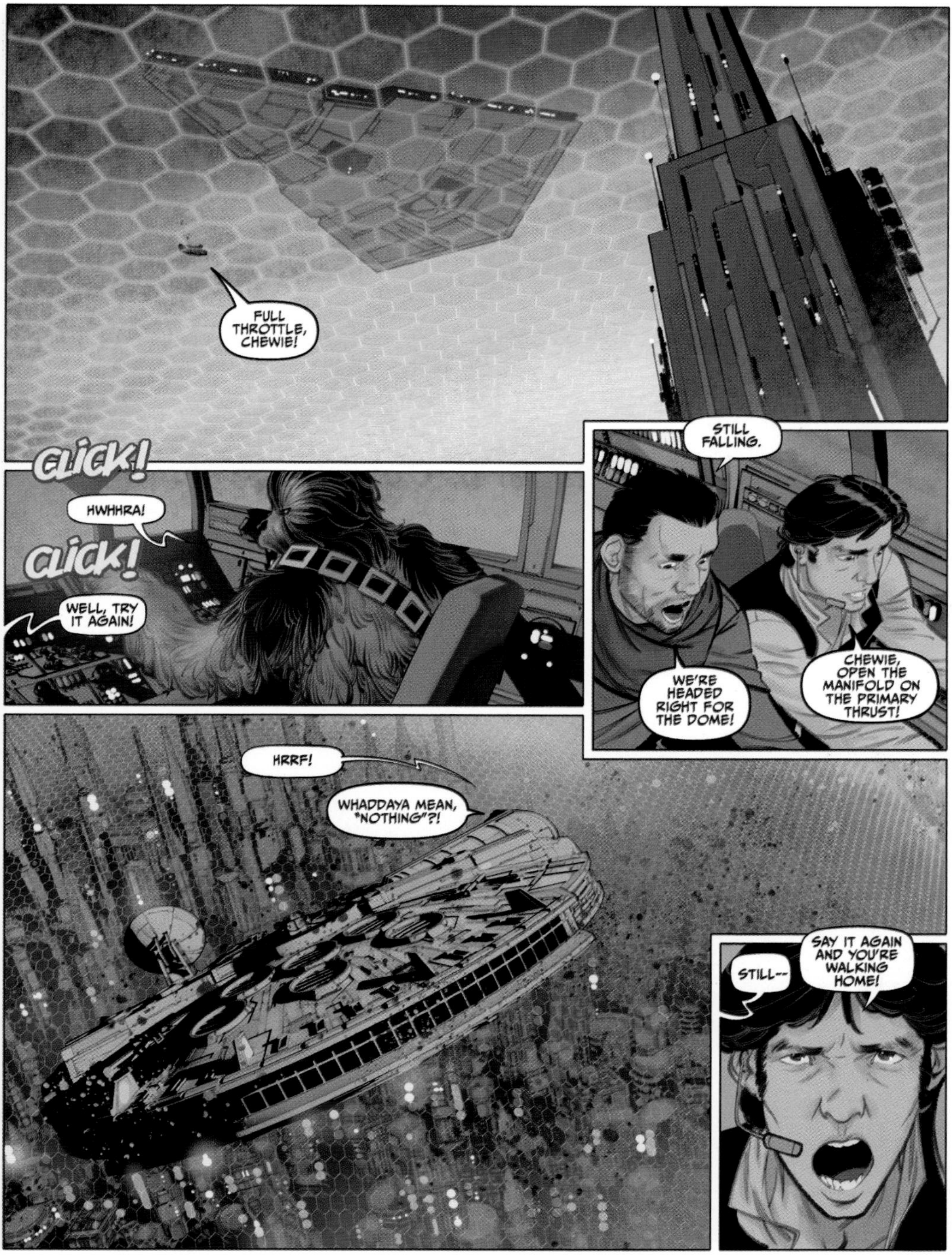
FULL THROTTLE, CHEWIE!
CLICK!
HWHHRA!
CLICK!
WELL, TRY IT AGAIN!
STILL FALLING.
WE'RE HEADED RIGHT FOR THE DOME!
CHEWIE, OPEN THE MANIFOLD ON THE PRIMARY THRUST!
HRRF!
WHADDAYA MEAN, "NOTHING"?!
STILL--
SAY IT AGAIN AND YOU'RE WALKING HOME!

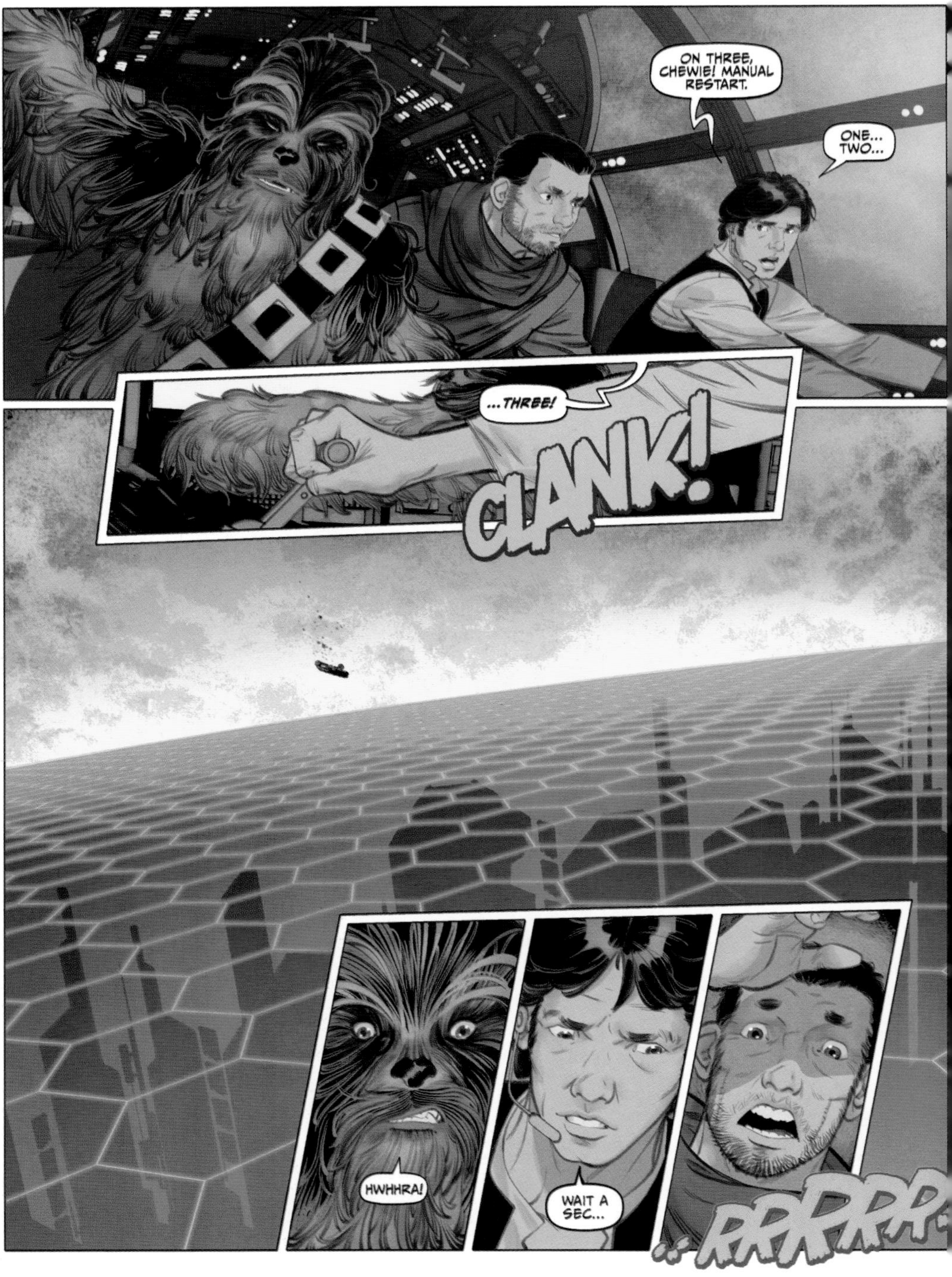
ON THREE, CHEWIE! MANUAL RESTART.
ONE... TWO...
...THREE!
CLANK!
HWHHRA!
WAIT A SEC...

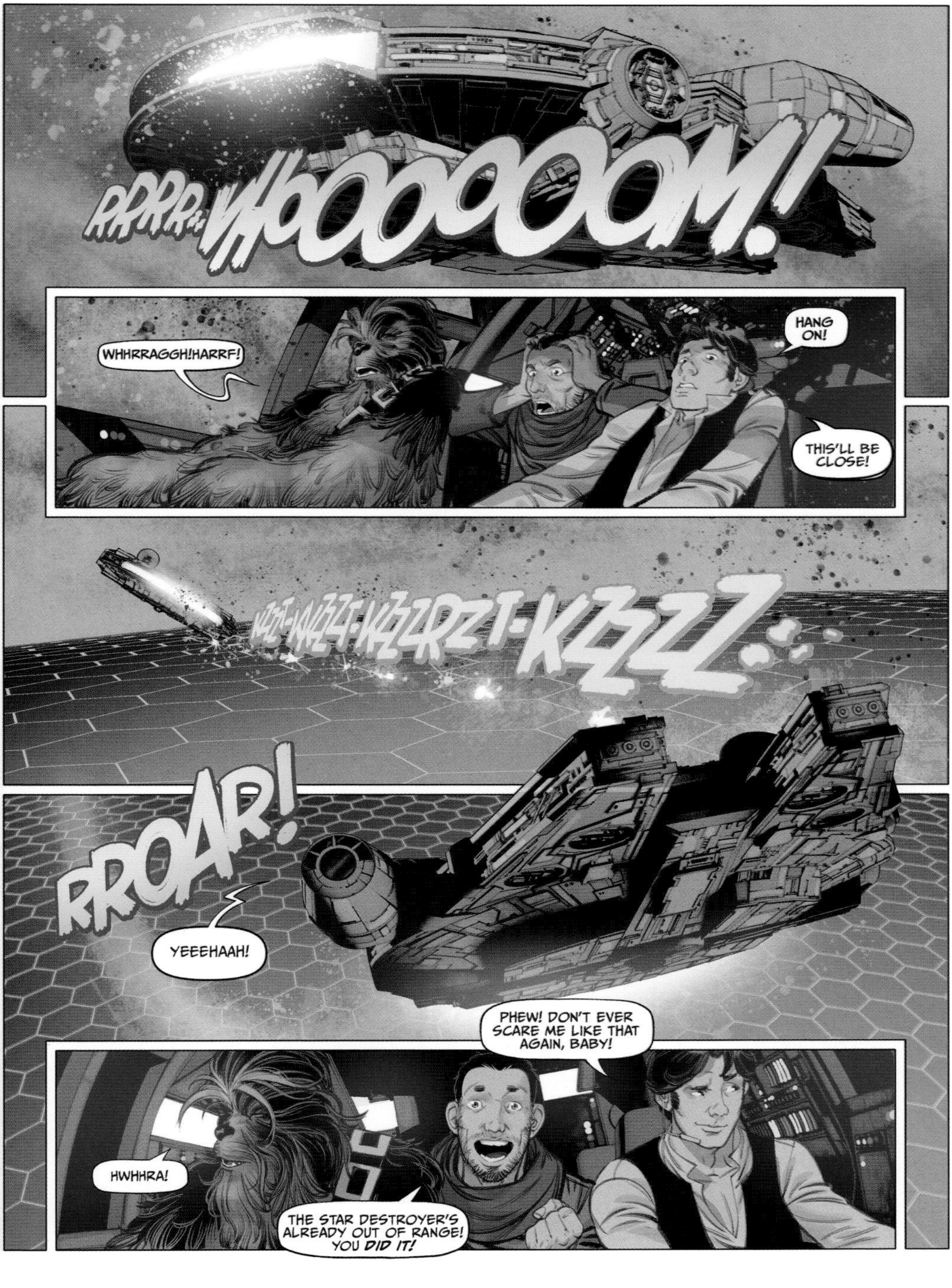
WHHRRAGGH!HARRF!
HANG ON!
THIS'LL BE CLOSE!
RROAR!
YEEEHAAH!
PHEW! DON'T EVER SCARE ME LIKE THAT AGAIN, BABY!
HWHHRA!
THE STAR DESTROYER'S ALREADY OUT OF RANGE! YOU ***DID IT!***

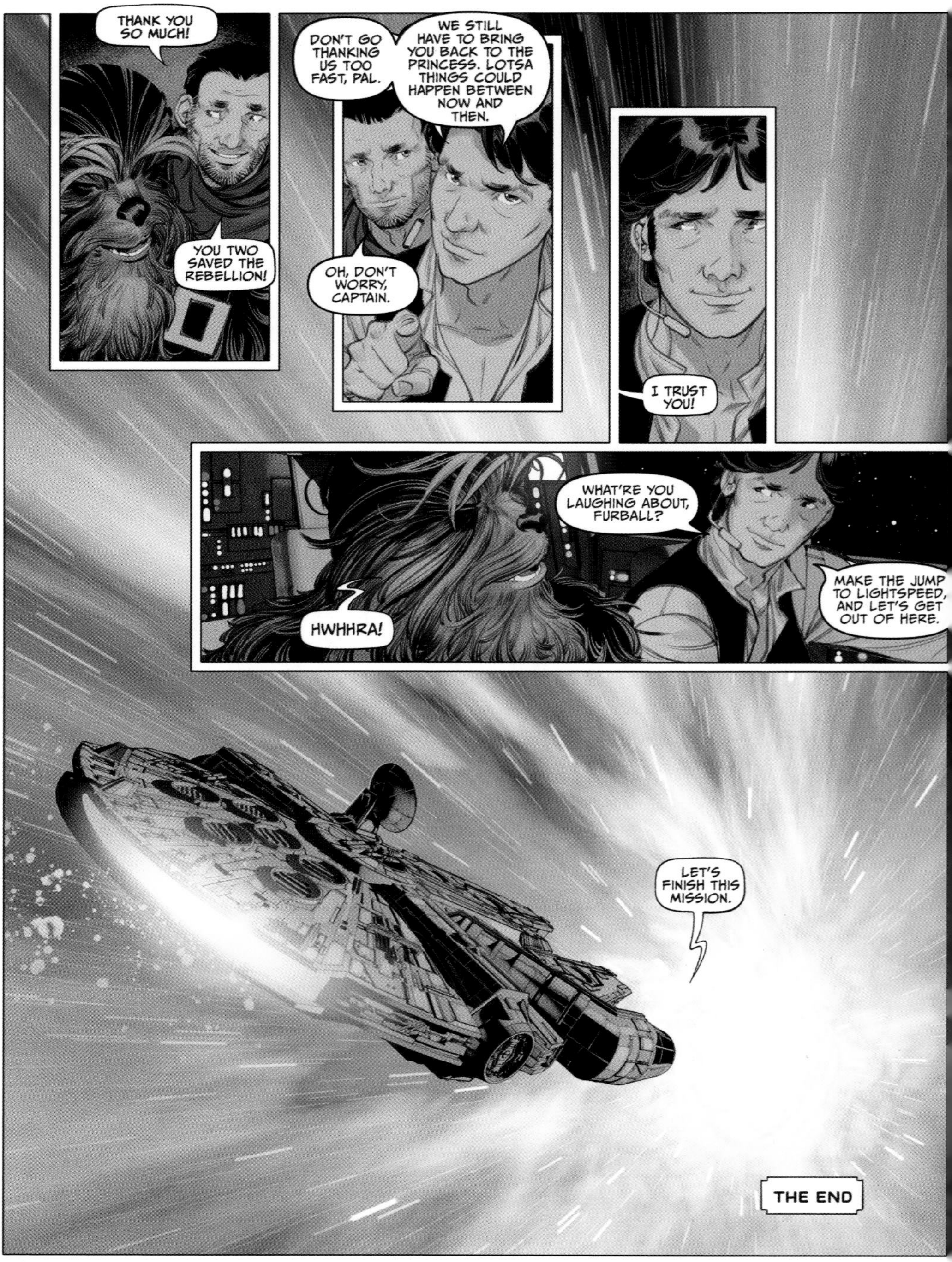
THANK YOU SO MUCH!
YOU TWO SAVED THE REBELLION!
DON'T GO THANKING US TOO FAST, PAL.
WE STILL HAVE TO BRING YOU BACK TO THE PRINCESS. LOTSA THINGS COULD HAPPEN BETWEEN NOW AND THEN.
OH, DON'T WORRY, CAPTAIN.
I TRUST YOU!
WHAT'RE YOU LAUGHING ABOUT, FURBALL?
HWHHRA!
MAKE THE JUMP TO LIGHTSPEED, AND LET'S GET OUT OF HERE.
LET'S FINISH THIS MISSION.
THE END

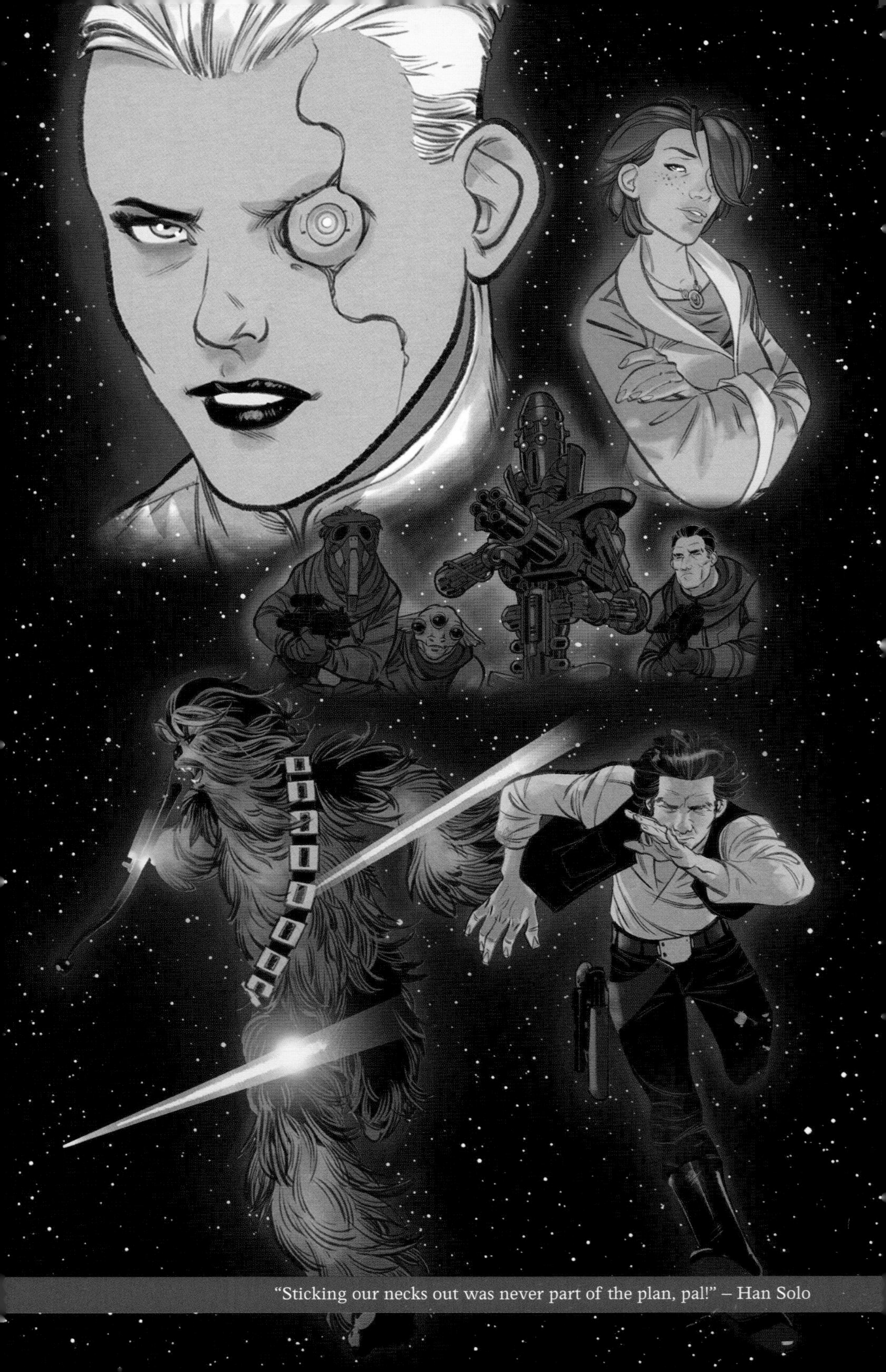

"Sticking our necks out was never part of the plan, pal!" – Han Solo

ART BY INGO RÖMLING

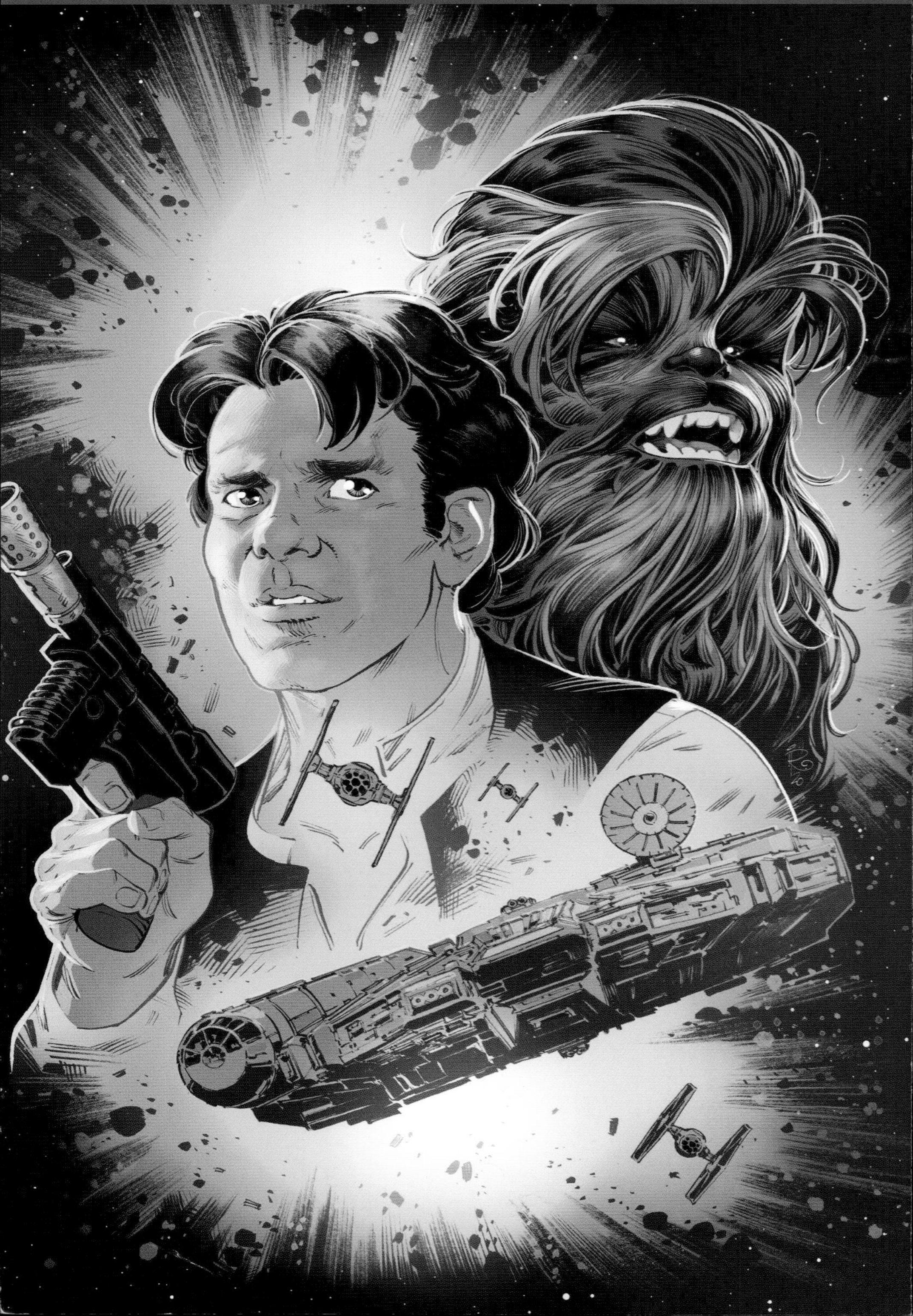

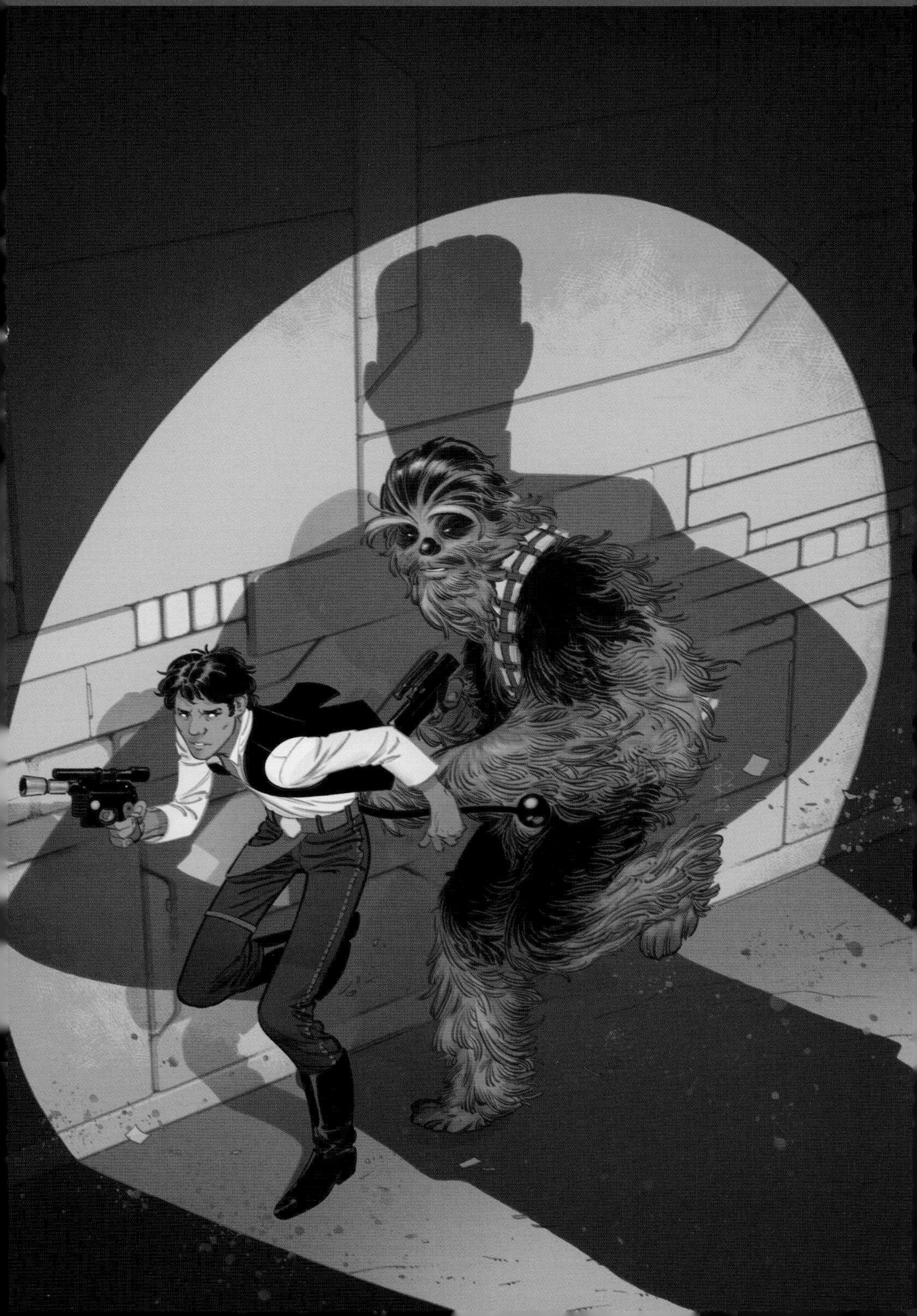

Facebook: **facebook.com/idwpublishing**
Twitter: **@idwpublishing**
YouTube: **youtube.com/idwpublishing**
Instagram: **@idwpublishing**

ISBN: 978-1-68405-811-2   24 23 22 21   1 2 3 4

Nachie Marsham, Publisher
Blake Kobashigawa, VP of Sales
Tara McCrillis, VP Publishing Operations
John Barber, Editor-in-Chief
Mark Doyle, Editorial Director, Originals
Erika Turner, Executive Editor
Scott Dunbier, Director, Special Projects
Mark Irwin, Editorial Director, Consumer Products Manager
Joe Hughes, Director, Talent Relations
Anna Morrow, Sr. Marketing Director
Alexandra Hargett, Book & Mass Market Sales Director
Keith Davidsen, Senior Manager, PR
Topher Alford, Sr Digital Marketing Manager
Shauna Monteforte, Sr. Director of Manufacturing Operations
Jamie Miller, Sr. Operations Manager
Nathan Widick, Sr. Art Director, Head of Design
Neil Uyetake, Sr. Art Director Design & Production
Shawn Lee, Art Director Design & Production
Jack Rivera, Art Director, Marketing

Ted Adams and Robbie Robbins, IDW Founders

Lucasfilm Credits:
Robert Simpson, Senior Editor
Michael Siglain, Creative Director
Troy Alders, Art Director
Phil Szostak, Lucasfilm Art Department
Pablo Hidalgo, Matt Martin, and Emily Shkoukani, Story Group